O9-ABI-845

DISCARD

Also by Anne Lamott

HARD LAUGHTER

ROSIE

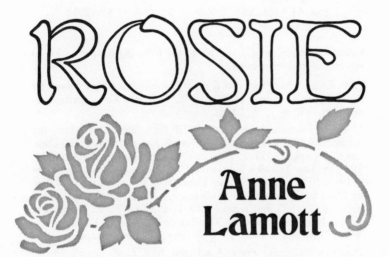

Anne Lamott

THE VIKING PRESS NEW YORK

First published in 1983 by The Viking Press
40 West 23rd Street, New York, N.Y. 10010

Published simultaneously in Canada by
Penguin Books Canada Limited

LIBRARY OF CONGRESS CATALOGING IN PUBLICATION DATA
Lamott, Anne.
Rosie.
I. Title.
PS3562.A4645R67   1983   813'.54   82-42733
ISBN 0-670-60828-9

Grateful acknowledgment is made to the following for permission to reprint copyrighted material:

E. P. Dutton, Inc.: Excerpts from *When We Were Very Young*, by A. A. Milne. Copyright © 1924 by E. P. Dutton Co. Copyright renewed © 1952 by A. A. Milne.

Liveright Publishing Corporation: "if there are any heavens my mother will (all by herself) have" from *ViVa*, poems by E. E. Cummings. Copyright 1931, 1959 by E. E. Cummings. Copyright © 1973, 1979 by The Trustees for the E. E. Cummings Trust. Copyright © 1973, 1979 by George James Firmage. A selection from "Humanity i love you" from *Tulips & Chimneys*, by E. E. Cummings. Copyright 1923, 1925 and renewed 1951, 1953 by E. E. Cummings. Copyright © 1973, 1976 by The Trustees for the E. E. Cummings Trust. Copyright © 1973, 1976 by George James Firmage.

Princeton University Press: A selection from *C. P. Cavafy Selected Poems*, by Edmund Keeley and Philip Sherrard. Copyright © 1972 by Edmund Keeley and Philip Sherrard.

Random House, Inc.: A selection from *W. H. Auden: Collected Poems*, by W. H. Auden, edited by Edward Mendelson. Copyright © 1976 by Edward Mendelson, William Meredith and Monroe K. Spears, Executors of the Estate of W. H. Auden. A selection from *Rabbit, Run*, by John Updike. Copyright © 1960 by John Updike. A selection from *Green Eggs and Ham*, by Dr. Seuss. Copyright © 1960 by Dr. Seuss.

Printed in the United States of America
Set in CRT Caslon
Second printing October 1983

This one is for Abby Luttinger, Warren Wallace, Mary Lowry, Pam Murray, and Leroy Lounibos, whose love and input were central to the writing of this book.

And for my brothers John and Steve, and my mother, and her family, and my father, and his family, and the Schleigers.

And for the people who let me live with them while I was writing this: Carol Adrienne in Petaluma, and her family, Gunther, Sigrid, and Charles. Pat Gomez, and her family, John, Margaret, Grammy Perrett, and Stephanie. Doris, Amelia, and Lucy Wallace in New York. Sharon Weld and Sally Wood in Cambridge. Someday I'm going to make it all up to them.

And for Lynn Atkison, Jack Erdmann, Don Sherwood, and Joanne Greenbaum, kind and gorgeous people.

And for Michael Fessier and Sylvie Pasche, my writer friends.

And for Cork Smith, Elizabeth McKee, and Ann Brebner.

And for Robert Filipini and Gordon Wallace and Larry Barnett, and Allan Ruder.

And for Norma Campbell, Dierdre Campbell, Zoe Barnett, and the Wetzells, who have made me smarter.

And for the gang at the Lakeville Marina—Phyllis, Leon, Linda, and Grace; and for Rosalie Wright, B. K. Moran, and Jon Carroll.

And for Megan and Betty and Lowell and Adele and Susan . . .

This one is for my friends, again.

if there are any heavens my mother will(all by herself)have
one. It will not be a pansy heaven nor
a fragile heaven of lilies-of-the-valley but
it will be a heaven of blackred roses

my father will be(deep like a rose
tall like a rose)

standing near my

swaying over her
(silent)
with eyes which are really petals and see

nothing with the face of a poet really which
is a flower and not a face with
hands
which whisper
This is my beloved my
                    (suddenly in sunlight

he will bow,

& the whole garden will bow)

—e.e. cummings

PART ONE

Chapter

🌿1

There were many things about Elizabeth Ferguson that the people of Bayview disliked. They thought her tall, too thin, too aloof. Her neck was too long and her breasts were too big. The men, who could have lived with the size of her breasts, found her unwilling to flirt and labeled her cold. The women were jealous of how well her clothes hung on her, and that she managed to look elegant in outfits that would have made them look like the bag ladies of late autumn. She said little in town unless spoken to, in which case she had the gall to be civil and clever. They distrusted her because her husband and parents were dead and because she called herself Elizabeth instead of Lisa or Betsy or Liz. In a town where the sole taxi driver delivered pints at breakfast to a dozen people, a town where alcohol was the cornerstone of all civic and social endeavor, they did not like that she could drink so much at the bar without becoming sloppy or degenerate. They found it alarming when, in the market or the bookstore and for no apparent reason, she burst out laughing; she might have just remembered the eccentric horse in the Saki story who has what its owner called "the swerving sickness," but the people the Bayview could not guess this and took these abrupt outbursts to indicate that she was slowly going mad. They resented that Andrew Ferguson had left her a comfortable trust, and they blamed her for his death; however she had managed to cause him to crash, while drunk, 3,000 miles away, they knew she had done so for the money. And what they especially didn't like was that, a week after he died, a man had left the Ferguson house at seven in the morning. Old Mrs. Haas, in the breakfast nook of her Victorian across the street, had watched through binoculars as the man left and had had to suppress her gleeful outrage until nine, when she began making phone calls.

Rosie Ferguson was four when her father died. As she sat on her mother's lap at the crowded Episcopal service, she knew that her father was dead but kept waiting for him to join them in the first pew, wondering what he would bring her: a book maybe, or taffy. She hoped for the cinnamon kind, the prettiest, pink with a glassy red stripe. Several days before he had left for the East Coast, she had cut off the legs of all his suit pants at the knees, but she had forgotten this by the day of the service. She stared at the stained glass, the crucifix, the candles, the flowers, the man on stage in a black dress; spellbound, she bit her bottom lip and appeared to be getting a feel for it all before doing some interior decorating.

Elizabeth held Rosie on her lap, dimly aware that her daughter was trying to take care of her—Rosie kept patting her and smiling bravely—but Elizabeth couldn't concentrate on what was happening. It was too surreal: Andrew's now permanent absence, her presence in church for the first time in years, "The Lord is my shepherd, I shall not want"; over the minister's voice she heard Andrew reading to Rosie the night before he left, *"James James Morrison Morrison Weatherby George Dupree,"* saw Rosie in the closet with the scissors, black curls flattened on one side after a nap, Siamese blue eyes squinted in concentration, cutting up the pants. "For Thou art with me," the minister said, as an abrupt, hard laugh escaped from behind Elizabeth's nose.

Rosie whipped her head around and gave her mother a stern look. Elizabeth bowed her head. ". . . Lord for ever." Elizabeth was racked with waves of silent laughter, until another cramped laugh burst out of her nose and she pretended to sob, but Rosie, not fooled, crossed her arms and glared. Behind them, skeptical looks were exchanged. The choir began singing "Just a Closer Walk with Thee," and Elizabeth, hugging her child tightly, shook with suppressed giggles and emitted staccato nasal scraping noises into her daughter's black hair, until tears for the man who had given her Rosie ran down her face.

The people of Bayview, a small town in the San Francisco Bay area, thought that she was too handsome to have suffered sufficiently in her life, to have suffered as much as they had. They knew almost nothing of her past and resented how easy it had always seemed for her.

But Elizabeth had few happy memories of childhood. Both her parents had been alcoholics. Her father, who was dashing and funny, left her mother when Elizabeth was ten, after which Elizabeth stopped bringing friends home from school because her mother was apt to have passed out on the couch.

In seventh grade Elizabeth was taller and more buxom than her teacher and had inherited her father's eyebrow, one long black line of hair that spanned both eyes like a mustache, and her mother was too undone to help Elizabeth pluck a clearing in the brow. Elizabeth was the shyest and most frequently teased girl in school. She often read alone, at lunchtime and stayed up half the night reading, because on top of—or because of—it all, she was an insomniac.

At sixteen she was five-foot-ten and striking in the way of the young Charlie Chaplin. Her thick black eyebrows, plucked by now, were awesome, and her breasts were magnificent. She had her first affair, with a man in his mid-twenties. It lasted two years. He was wildly funny, and she thought they would marry but he fell in love with someone else, "Somebody less moody," he said.

She went east for college, majored in literature, minored in math, dabbled in philosophy, marched for peace and human rights, wondered what on earth she would do with her life after college, and had a series of affairs with witty bookworms, each more passionate and disastrous than the last, each having begun so happily. What is wrong with you, Elizabeth?

It seemed to her that in essential ways she had not changed much since seventh grade. Her moods were as volatile as the weather. She was riddled with anxiety, prone to depression, constantly terrified of losing her mind or life, sometimes so much so that she couldn't leave her bedroom.

She got almost all A's in college, could hardly have cared less. In the audience at a concert, her mind sometimes wandered so far away that when it finally returned to where her body sat, she wasn't absolutely sure that she hadn't just screamed at the top of her lungs, wasn't sure that the stunned observers were only pretending that nothing had happened. There was something uniquely wrong with her; she was the stranger in the strange land; her skin didn't fit correctly.

The most popular professors fell in love with her—one of them described her as *diabolically* brilliant and witty—but she came to doubt that she was the sort of woman who could have a long-term relationship with a man. She grew more aloof after each affair ended, came to think that being in love was like having an infection, swore that never again would she wait by the phone for a man to call, swore that she would be more selective about the men to whom she gave her heart and soul because each time the love died it nearly killed her, swore all sorts of things and then went on to repeat the same mistakes. She grew bored with hearing the same old tapes playing in her mind, grew bored by how easy it was to get men and A's, grew bored with her friends' melodramatic, obsessed love affairs, grew bored with the smartest people's stupidity when it came to love, and came to believe that people sought to recapture those senses of failure and rejection which had so dazzled them. She grew bored with demonstrations for peace and human rights, grew *insanely* bored with her boredom, and with her anxieties of winding up an insane alcoholic like her mother. Boredom is the root of all evil, she read in *Either-Or:* evil, the source of sorrow and distress; evil thoughts of men and her mother had been lurking in her mind almost all her life; what was she going to do with it all, what would she do with her life?

❦ ROSIE

She read, studied, went to movies, discarded lovers when they became too clingy, smoked, had long talks with other women about men and mothers, drank on occasion, and graduated with honors in both English and math. Neither of her parents came east for graduation. Elizabeth did not seem to care.

The day after graduation, lanky and self-righteous, she participated in a March of Dimes Walk-a-Thon: walked fifteen miles of the twenty-mile course and then developed fierce shin splints. She sat down by the side of the road waiting for one of the trucks which periodically drove by collecting exhausted walkers. She was massaging her legs, daydreaming of a hot bath, when a young legless man on a wooden dolly passed by where she sat, pulling himself along with his gloved hands. And, by God, Elizabeth got up and walked the last five miles. Three days later, when she was able to walk again, she flew back to San Francisco.

Five years, six jobs, and three affairs later, she met and fell in love with Andrew Ferguson. He had three things Elizabeth wanted—playfulness, money, and a kind of faith. He was a truly kind man, who loved to read. By now, they had between them one living parent, his mother, who flew to San Francisco for their wedding.

Being married to Andrew did not feel real to Elizabeth, but— or so—it felt wonderful, so wonderful that Elizabeth expected him to die or kick her out of the house he had bought in Bayview with part of his considerable inheritance; the closer and more comfortable they became, the more apprehensive Elizabeth grew, feeling that it would all be snatched away.

Neither of them worked for the first months of their marriage: side by side they lay in bed reading, side by side they created a magnificent garden of flowers and rosebushes; made dinner, plans, love; went to movies, operas, the San Francisco Symphony, museums, libraries, bookstores, an occasional party: needing only each other, they did it all up royally in their elegant, well-worn clothes.

Then Andrew decided to become a carpenter for the exercise

and camaraderie, and Elizabeth was left alone. Boredom and panic set in the day he began his first job. She spent the next six months tending the garden and the house, reading, killing time, waiting for him to come home to play with her again, and slowly going mad.

"Well, what kind of work do you want to do?"

She shrugged.

"Wouldn't you like to do something in the book world?"

"I worked for that publisher, remember? All I did was type."

"You know that publicist you worked for? Could you do promotion again?"

"No."

"Why?"

She shrugged.

"Now don't go into a brood on my account. I'm trying to help."

"See, with the publicist, I thought I'd be—I don't know, promoting good books that the world wouldn't know about otherwise, strengthening the literary gene pool—but all I did was type, for a pimp."

"How about teaching? English? At a private school? I don't think you'd need a teaching certificate."

"I don't like kids."

"But we'll have kids someday, won't we?"

"I don't know. Yes, sure we'll have a kid someday. But I don't want to teach."

"What *do* you want to do? You're a great cook and love it—"

"I don't know!" she yelled at him. "If I knew, I'd go look for a job."

"What's it going to be that helps you figure out what you want to be?"

"I *don't know!*"

"I think you're going to go crazy if you don't find *some*thing to do; you're so goddamn smart, and funny, and literate—do you want to write? Do you have any compulsions to write a book? Or a screenplay? Book reviews?"

"I don't know. I don't know."

🌿

She still didn't know a year later, or a year after that. She panicked frequently at how quickly the time flew and yet how every
day loomed before her like a dragon, waiting to be slain. Looking
in the mirror she saw how quickly she was aging, saw herself as
Dave the Spaceman at the end of *2001;* laugh lines had turned to
crow's-feet. She slept late, spent an hour at the breakfast table
mechanically reading the *Chronicle,* cleaned up the kitchen, went
around the house picking up Andrew's carpenter's stuff, clothes,
shoes, apple cores, and books. Then it was time for lunch. She
read while eating, often ending up in the living room reading just
one more chapter, and then just one more chapter. Then she
might pore over the Help Wanted listings in the paper, maybe
reread the entire front section. An hour or two in the garden,
and then a mile walk into town for the exercise and to shop . . .
and eventually Andrew would return from his happy work, and
they would have cocktails and dinner and funny talks and read or
go to a show, and then it would be time for bed, for sex and
sleep. Unless she had insomnia. And most of this was done
swathed in the gauze of loneliness and boredom and anxiety.

One day she would get around to writing a book, a comic
treatment of a good marriage to an easygoing and interesting
man. About insomnia, and depression, and idiosyncrasies. About
her mood swings; about how infuriating an easygoing person can
be. About the things that drove her crazy with impatience or irritation: no "Briefly Noted" fiction in *The New Yorker,* or Herb
Caen's vacations from the *Chronicle*; Andrew's exuberant dental
flossing which left flecks of food on the bathroom mirror; how
the sound of him crunching away on an apple or celery could
send her into an inarticulated rage, how it would remind her of
how much she'd hated—*hated*—the sound of her mother eating
bacon, how she would begin to think it would make her lose her
mind. One day she would write a book about the love and pa-
tience that bind one person to another after all the glinty romantic stuff has worn off.

And, in the meantime, waiting—waiting to figure out what it

was that she was waiting for, waiting for the revelation of her professional destiny, waiting to find labor that was its own reward, something that would benefit others at the same time—she remained somewhat surprised that fame was evading her.

She became pregnant at thirty—an accident of laziness—and planned to have an abortion. A child would postpone her finding her true calling. Other people's babies made her, at best, nervous, made her fingers twitch. She slept poorly enough as it was, a baby screaming at dawn to be fed or changed would. . . .

"*What?* You're thinking of killing our baby?"

"Andrew. It's not a baby. It's an inadvertently fertilized egg, a blob of embryonic tissue with a yolk sac."

Andrew went to the library and checked out a book on human fetuses. Seven weeks pregnant, she was carrying an embryo whose arms and legs were budding, whose mouth and eyes were appearing. It had ridges on its kidneys that would become sex organs; it had fingers and a vestigial tail.

"I rest my case."

"Andrew, I don't want a baby yet. I think I'd *abuse* it."

"No, you wouldn't. A baby would be lucky to have you for a mother and me for a father."

"I'm too selfish. I'm antisocial. I need too much privacy."

"You piss and moan about how bored you are. . . ."

"*Not* very often. And the news is so awful. What sort of world is this to bring a baby into?"

"Same old world it's always been, beautiful and cruel."

"No, it's much worse; it hovers on the brink of destruction."

"Elizabeth. Living on earth has always been a dangerous way to spend your time. Before the Bomb there were Huns, plagues, beasts. There has always been war; mothers have always worried. Mothers used to have to worry about polio, and before that, chariot accidents, and before that : . . you've just got to have faith."

"But I don't."

"But I have a *lot.*"

"What if it's retarded? What if it grows up and kills people? What if—what if it's as neurotic as I am?"

"You're my favorite person in the world."

"I'm an insomniac. I'm prone to depression. I probably drink too much. I'm too scared to have a baby right now."

But she reconsidered. She had nothing to show for thirty years except an increasing amount of knowledge not yet applied to anything and a great garden. A child would give her something to do with her time; she was watching the clock too much. It would give her a sense of purpose, relatedness, an excuse not to have to come up with something to do with her life; maybe it would give her that elusive and craved carrot, peace of mind.

Oh, what the hell.

"What shall we name it?" Andrew asked, holding her.

"Demo," she said.

They named their baby girl Rosie and watched her grow. Elizabeth loved the first two years: her days were full, her nights were full, and nursing was the purest, simplest communication she had ever known. Rosie was quiet, content, funny, and responsive, a bright little animal who considered Elizabeth to be the most wonderful thing in the universe. Elizabeth marveled that she had given birth to such a creature, and Andrew, changing diapers or rocking her to sleep at dawn, had never been so happy. Elizabeth smoked less, drank less, smiled more often, and only rarely felt like throwing the tiny body at a wall.

Rosie cried very little and had eyes as blue as Andrew's, eyes as blue as a Siamese cat's, and soft black curls. She was tiny, too thin perhaps, but had an already beautiful triangular face.

One sunny day Elizabeth was planting sweet williams, with Rosie beside her in a red sunsuit, playing with a trowel, both of them peaceful and in their own worlds, when Rosie suddenly flung a handful of dirt into her mother's face. Elizabeth yelped, eyes stinging and wet, grabbed her daughter's hand, and slapped it, hard. Rosie lost her balance and fell face down into the dirt, bawling until her terrified mother picked her up, wiped away the muddy drool, and carried her inside. In the rocking chair she nursed her baby, whose eyes never left Elizabeth's face, and they sat sadly for a long time, rocking, nursing.

At two, Rosie had become a proud, willful, irrational, demanding, and fast little person, who had yet to say her first word of English but made it clear that she now considered her mother to be the only fly in her ointment. Andrew and Rosie were in love, while Elizabeth was a jealous, moody stranger to them both. Andrew began to do carpentry again, this time sheerly for the fun of it and—thought Elizabeth—to get away from her.

The house felt like a cage, and Elizabeth had occasional fantasies of running away forever, but by then Rosie was so much a part of herself that she could never have done it. She kept remembering the old cartoon in which two men are manacled to the wall of a windowless prison cell, two feet above the ground, with snakes crawling on the floor, one man saying to the other, "Okay. Here's my plan." But this stage of the relationship passed, and mother and child were close again, mutually needed and amused.

At two and a half, Rosie finally spoke. Andrew said that she'd been taking notes until then. She was on his lap, watching television, when Elizabeth, in the kitchen, turned on an electric mixer which shattered the picture on the tube into undulating lines of static with a steady white blip swimming back and forth across the screen. Rosie studied it for a moment, turned to look up into her father's face, and said, "Fush."

After that she wouldn't shut up. "Me do it!" was her battle cry. She was incompetent at practically everything but insisted on trying, threw tantrums unless she got a shot at tying her shoes or washing her mud-caked face or pouring juice into a glass, even though she knew that her mother knew that she knew she couldn't do it. She was developing dignity, and once again Elizabeth began to worry about going crazy, began to understand how her own mother had grown into a dipso. Eager once again to please Elizabeth, Rosie took everything so seriously—stepping into her tiny underpants, brushing her teeth, pasting twenty dollars' worth of postage stamps to a wall—that Elizabeth heard *Thus Spake Zarathustra* playing constantly as the soundtrack of Rosie's life.

They took her to the zoo, the planetarium, the park, the library. They got rid of the television and Andrew read her fairy tales, Bible stories, and poetry, and Elizabeth patiently helped her learn to read before she was four. She'd filled out a first-grade workbook soon after: 1 cat, 2 dogs, 3 piggies. She understood the difference between "up" and "north"; Heaven was up, Mendocino was north. She asked endless questions: Why was water wet? And the sun so hot, and the night so dark?

"Because that is their nature; that is the nature of water, sun, night."

"Why does the moon follow us when we walk at night?"

"It just seems to. It just looks that way."

The three Fergusons flew back east to visit Andrew's mother when Rosie was three. And Nana flew out for Rosie's fourth Christmas. Elizabeth had bought her a tea set, a pot and cups of white enamel with tiny violets, but didn't tell Rosie about it. Rosie found the parcel under the tree, begged, cried, and was obviously going to die unless she knew what the present to Nana was.

"You'll find out on Christmas. It's a secret."

"Pleeeeeeze."

"I don't want you to tell her. It's a secret."

"I won't tell her, I promise. Pleeeeeeze," and so on until finally Elizabeth said that it was a tea set.

"You *promise* not to tell?"

Rosie nodded, determined.

When Andrew returned from the airport with Nana, Elizabeth and Rosie went down the stairs of the porch to greet her, Rosie wearing a blue velvet jumper the same color as her eyes, tiny white blouse and socks, crying at the top of her lungs, "Naaaaaana, we got you a teeeeee set."

❧

When she was four and a half, she asked vague questions about what Elizabeth and Andrew did in bed, which she sometimes overheard.

Elizabeth explained the mechanics of lovemaking, and that it was also called "fucking" or "screwing," words Rosie had by then heard countless times, and that two people did it if they wanted to have a baby, and because it felt so good.

One day she told Elizabeth, "I'll never get married."

"Why?"

"Oh, you know," she said, and then whispered. "All that fucking."

Her first best friend, Mukie Conga, rarely left her side until he was killed by pirates and went to Heaven. His successor was the little boy next door. She learned to feel jealousy, learned to feel greed, and learned to feel the pleasures of giving. They gave Elizabeth and Andrew jars and jars filled with sow bugs, or tadpoles, or ladybugs, and presents wrapped in miles of Scotch tape—a leaf or a bluebellied lizard's tail.

He let her touch his penis.

She told Elizabeth.

"Did you like it?"

"No. It was all squiggly."

Pain, fear. Rosie was attacked and badly bitten by hornets after dropping a rock onto their nest; fell from the branches of trees and bounced; went through early childhood with scabs on her knees and elbows; experienced—again and again—the cruel, chilling pain of stubbed toes; burned her bottom and thighs on blazing slides in the park; fell off a ten-foot wall and bounced, bloody and stunned.

Life was perfect on top of her father's shoulders, with his hands around her ankles and her mother beside them. Life was worst alone in bed, in the dark, when a pile of snakes began to writhe, or she awoke from a dream and saw the amber eyes of a tiger looking into her window. If she screamed, her father would come in, hold her, show her in the light that the pile of snakes was really a pile of clothes.

She ran out into the street once and was barely missed by a car; swallowed a bottle of baby aspirin and threw them all up on the way to the hospital; nearly drowned in the Russian River, blue by the time Andrew brought her up to the surface. Still, the inadvertently fertilized blob of embryonic tissue had survived to grow into a brilliant and consumed little person with dignity, humor, and frequently poor judgment.

Meanwhile, Elizabeth tried to figure out what she would do with herself once kindergarten started, swore that she wouldn't lapse back into the wasteful, gauzy days she had lived out—killed, rather—before Rosie was born. Was there a niche for her out there? If only she had . . . *more* time, *more* pressure, *more* inclination, *more* contacts. It was her if-only-I-had-more-this-or-more-that carrots that kept her from giving up the future completely. She thought of all the things she could have been, thought of all the unsatisfying things she *had* been, and pretended with a grudge that she would have had the discipline and talent to become a success *somewhere,* if only it hadn't been for her mother, or for the curse of Andrew's money, which allowed her not to *have* to try very hard. Frustration, born of ennui, fueled by inertia and the escalating speed of time's passage, welled up inside her and made her palpitate. She came to think of herself as a thwarted workaholic while she spent each day waiting for it to be over.

Andrew was her ally and only close friend. They had grown closer, more familiar, because of Rosie and—for the same reason—less needy, so that he became for Elizabeth everything she had wanted in a man, someone she could keep at arm's length and still keep around. In bed, pressing up against and into him, with his arms around her, she was peaceful.

She had several casual women friends, no one special. She kept in touch, by mail, with two roommates from college. There were people in town she liked to bump into at the library or nursery: clever, crazy people who read a lot and were therefore good for a short conversation, but she found that, following such a conversation, they would try to crowd her and make unreasonable demands on her time, like wanting to get together for a meal every few months, and she would feel the walls close in and shun their advances tactfully—usually lying—until they gave up. And then this private and lonely woman could look forward to bumping into them again at the bookstore or the market.

She longed for and feared the day that Rosie, her pride and joy, would start school. With a polished gift now of blocking out almost anything she couldn't stand—which was to say anything even remotely unpleasant, especially the pangs of bad conscience that plagued her—she waited for her destiny to reveal itself.

Andrew answered Rosie's questions about death, usually when they came upon wrecks or flattened animals on the highway. When something's body got too old or sick or banged up, it stopped working, like when a flashlight's batteries ran out, or if you smashed the flashlight with a hammer; but the soul, which was the light that lived within your heart, flew up to Heaven to live with God and the Angels. The Angels were spirits with wings, friendly ghosts, who took care of everyone. Rosie imagined them as stewardesses: beautiful, smiling blondes with haloes and trays of soft drinks.

Neither Rosie nor her mother cried much immediately after Andrew died; there was too much taking care of the other to do. Rosie, on the one hand, clung to her imperious religious faith: Daddy was in Heaven now with God and the Angels and smiling down on her; on the other, she kept expecting him to show up, as if his death had been a game of hide-and-seek.

Elizabeth remembered the earth-shattering fear of having seen her own mother cry when she had been a small girl, and so held back most of her tears. At first she thought of him constantly, every other second, but then only several times a minute, and eventually only several dozens an hour, like when, not long after, she quit smoking. Each new stage, each decreased level of obsession, felt like the best she could hope for—the new me, and a relief at that—but then a week later the preoccupation would have grown even dimmer.

They missed his kindness and teasing and hugs and smell and his reading out loud to them, but of course life went on.

James James said to his mother, "Mother," he said, said he: "You must never go down to the end of the town without consulting me."

Rosie took care of her mother by teasing her and hugging her. She insisted on being read to, insisted that they walk together on the beach, learned how to make Elizabeth laugh when she was in the doldrums, chastised her when she drank too much whiskey. Andrew lived on in Rosie.

Rosie's first comedy routines were impersonations. She could do old Mrs. Haas, she could do actors in television commercials she had seen at a friend's house—Mr. Big Fig, the Raisin Bran raisins, an uncanny Ricardo Montalban—she could do the Munchkins, Louis Armstrong, and the freakishly buxom woman who lived next door, who eased her breasts onto her dining room table as if she'd been holding two big bags of groceries. And she learned to love to make her mother laugh.

By the time she started kindergarten, she'd been published in the *Chronicle,* in a letter to the pet doctor.

"Dear Mr. Miller," she dictated to Elizabeth. "These friends of ours, names Grace and Charles, had two cats. This one named Bert who is orange ran away. Mama says it found a new home. Do you think its new owner is nice?" (signed, in her own hand) "Rosie Ferguson."

"Dear Rosie," he answered in his column. "Yes."

Rosie was the star of kindergarten, loved every minute of it, was the only child who could read, had attention lavished upon her by the teacher and the children. She was the only child with a dead father and seemed rather proud of it. There was only one bad day in those nine months of finger painting, stories, naps, snacks, and playing with her friends. When she was proudly reading *Little Black Sambo* to the class, bile came up into her throat. She fought it back, kept reading, but soon she was on the verge of throwing up and began to cry—with her mouth closed. While being held and comforted by her adored teacher, Rosie threw up all over her, an event she would never forget.

Elizabeth reasoned that she couldn't very well find a job, since she had to be—wanted to be—home at noon, when an ecstatic Rosie returned. She was worried that Rosie was so sensitive, cried at the drop of a hat, cried upon hearing "The Streets of Laredo," cried upon hearing "The Titanic" (although she was momentarily cheered upon learning that it was little kiddies, not kitties, who had wept and cried as the water poured over the side), cried when her mother was noticeably drunk. She cried when she thought about orphans, and blind people, and dead puppies, and old dogs at the pound. She cried when she thought of poor little lambs who had lost their way, she cried about the Little Match Girl, she cried on those rare occasions when Elizabeth cried, and she cried about war. She cried because Abraham Lincoln had been shot, mostly cried for little Tad, and cried with terror late at night when she thought she heard the mice gnawing through the electrical wires—sure to set the house on fire. And she cried with an unquenchable homesickness for her father.

A year had passed since his death. One Saturday, Elizabeth sat reading on the porch while her skinny child sat in the lowest branches of the plum tree, chucking the hard green plums at various targets—cars, for instance, which drove down the narrow, rustic street on which they lived.

"Be *care*ful, sweetheart. Those branches are thin." *Get down out of that tree before you fall and break your neck,* says her mother's voice, inside.

"I'm being careful, Mama."

Elizabeth returned to the book, *Rabbit, Run,* which she was reading for the second time: "Sun and moon, sun and moon, time goes." In the tree, Rosie stopped throwing plums when Mrs. Haas emerged from her house and crossed the street to the picket gate outside the Ferguson house.

"Your roses look lovely," she called to Elizabeth.

"Thanks."

"Rosie, darling, you're not eating those nasty green plums, are you?" Even from the porch, Elizabeth could see her blinking her nose like a rabbit, had to bear down on a laugh as she remembered Rosie's impersonation: Rosie could do a better Mrs. Haas than Mrs. Haas.

Rosie shook her head—the heavy black curls.

"Because if you do, you'll get the trotties."

Rosie looked back at her mother, checking in.

"And another thing," said Mrs. Haas, puckering her mouth and brow like young Shirley Temple at her most nobly indignant. "If you eat the little plummies *now,* they won't have a chance to grow up and *ripen.*"

Rosie, with a roll of her eyes, a horrified mouth, and a sarcasm impressive in one so small, said, "Ohhhh, pooooor plummies!"

Elizabeth smiled.

Chapter
🌺2

On the night before first grade began, Rosie climbed into bed dressed in brand-new jeans, T-shirt, and running shoes. Hearing footsteps in the hallway, she pulled the covers up to her neck, closed her eyes, and breathed in a sleeping, almost snoring way. Her mother sat down beside her, stroked her bottom, and then leaned forward to kiss the side of her face several times, with a thick vinegary breath. Rosie's lids flickered, and she turned her head to bury it face down in the pillow, now smelling clean, soapy cotton: Go away, Mama.

Her mother whispered, "God, I love you, Rosie." Rosie didn't move a muscle, and finally her mother got up and left, turning off the light at the door, which she left open.

Rosie tossed and turned for the next few hours, while her mind spun with picture shows of first grade. She imagined herself reading to an impressed Mrs. Gravinski, cheered on by the kids in her class. She saw herself telling jokes, everybody laughing, especially the beautiful Mrs. Gravinski. She had a moment of terror in the dark when she watched herself, sitting in the first row, fart a stream of little green bubbles which would hang tell-tale above her head, and another bad moment when she remembered throwing up on her kindergarten teacher.

The pillow grew hot and scratchy and she kept turning it over; the sheets felt sandy, and she couldn't keep her eyes closed. She put one leg on top of the covers to cool off, dozed fitfully, dreamed that when she got up to write on the blackboard she was naked, and the kids were laughing, and even beautiful Mrs. Gravinski was doubled over with laughter, and Rosie was trying to cover herself up with paper towels . . . She awoke with a start and looked around the room, breathing rapidly. It seemed like hours until she fell asleep, and it seemed, when she woke up to sunlight and her mother shaking her shoulder, that she had been asleep for ten minutes.

"Rosie," her mother said, laughing. Rosie propped herself up, surveyed her leg in the new blue jeans and shoe on top of the cover, made a whining moan, and rubbed her eyes. Teary, sleepy, and mad, she got brusquely out of bed, stomped out to the hallway, clomped down the hall to the bathroom, and slammed the door.

Elizabeth followed after her but stopped outside the closed door.

"What's with the angry clubfoot routine?"

"Chh."

"Are you mad at me?"

"No. Derrr."

Elizabeth heard water running. "I'll go make you some breakfast, okay? Come on down when you finish shaving."

"Tss."

"Don't be nervous, Rosie. You'll love first grade."

"I *know* I will. Just leave me alone."

Rosie threw a small, troubled fit at breakfast because the fried eggs were all snotty, another fit when she saw that her mother had cut the tuna sandwich in her Wonder Woman lunch box the wrong way, another when her mother tried to run a brush through her thick, soft, shoulder-length black curls, and yet another when the toothpaste squirted all over the sink. But when the yellow school bus pulled up across the street, she rushed downstairs ecstatic, blue eyes shining, cheeks flushed. She grabbed her lunch box, kissed her mother, and ran for the bus.

Elizabeth read the paper and drank coffee in the kitchen, wishing the morning had already passed. After cleaning up the dishes, vacuuming the downstairs, and reading the paper again, she made herself some breakfast—Irish oatmeal, with raisins and brown sugar—and read the want ads. In three pages of Help Wanted listings, one job caught her eye: a cook, with baking experience, was needed at San Quentin. She smiled; she would probably meet more interesting men there than the ones she knew. She closed the paper, sat staring at the kitchen wall for a long time.

Her life—or her days, at any rate—was a drought, too much time on her hands,. nothing that *had* to be done. She started to think about lunch. It was ten o'clock. Rosie kept flashing through her mind: Rosie in school, in class, on the blacktop, four-square, the rings, hopscotch; Rosie, the angry clubfoot, stomping down the stairs; Rosie sprawled in unlikely positions on furniture and floors throughout the house, reading, with a baby finger hooked absently over her bottom lip, completely absorbed. Elizabeth sighed deeply at the kitchen table, sighed again a moment later under the strain of boredom. She drummed her long fingers against the table, hit it lightly with a fist, got up and went to the study.

She sat down in front of the typewriter. Maybe she had it in her to write. One way to find out. She inserted a piece of paper, drummed all eight fingers against the keys, scratched her tilted head, rubbed her eyes, sighed, stared at the paper, was distracted by the plastic Disneyland paperweight out of which Rosie had sucked the water and the apparently nontoxic snow particles so that Tinker Bell lay on the floor, face down on top of her wand . . . *concentrate.* Okay. Here we go. Fingers on the keys, she rocked slightly with a look that said that once she got the first word down on paper she wouldn't be able to keep pace with her thoughts. "Once" she wrote—no, wait. She xxed it out. "Many years ago"—no wait. "I rememb"—no, xxxxxxx. Poised again, hands on the keys, she stared at Tinker Bell for a long time, hardly blinking—leaped up, walked quickly to the mirror in the hall, and checked herself out. Great straight nose, the long full lips Rosie had inherited, hazel eyes flecked with gold, thick black lashes: handsome, interesting, not pretty, goddamn it, not pretty. But regal. She imagined Johnny Carson asking her what had gotten her going as a writer in her mid-thirties.

Well, Johnny, when my daughter, Rosie, started first grade, I thought I'd give myself some time to see if I had the talent and drive to write; I'd always thought I'd be good at it, but of course the success of the book surprises me as much as . . .

Back to the typewriter. She sat down, got up, walked to the rear of the house, put some laundry and detergent in the washing machine, turned it on, and went back to the study, but before sitting down, went to the kitchen for more coffee, then back to the study after stopping off again briefly at the mirror. "Lately it occurs"—no, wait. "Sometimes when"—no, wait, fuckin' *A,* man, come on. *Con*centrate. Think of a story to tell. Okay. "After leaving Mr. Braithewaite"—the phone rang; goddammit! Just when she was starting to really cook. She got up, walked to the kitchen, picked up the receiver, expecting, as usual, bad or inconveniencing news—Gordon was canceling for tonight, or . . .

"Hello, Elizabeth," said her aged friend, Grace Adderly.

"Hello, Grace."

"Isn't it a *bad* wind?" she said, in a tone which made Elizabeth feel like she'd done something wrong.

"Yes."

"Am I interrupting you?"

"No, no. How are you? How is Charles? How do you like living in the city?"

"We just *love* it. In fact, I'm calling to invite you to an apartment-warming party next week, you and Rosie both."

Oh, damn, I can't make it, Elizabeth almost said, before realizing she didn't know what day the party was to be.

"Saturday night at six."

"Oh, damn, I can't make it. Unless I can change some plans—can I call you back?"

"Oh, try, will you?" Grace asked. "And of course, you're welcome to bring your nice young man."

Elizabeth smiled to herself. Gordon, the man Grace was thinking of, was not nice, not young, and not hers, but he was the most presentable of her three current candidates: single and not too alcoholic.

"Listen. I'll have to call you back. I'll see if I can get out of what I'm sort of lined up to do."

"Oh, dear. Hang on a moment, please. Kittykittykittykitty-kitty. Kittykittykitty. Oh, you're hot, aren't you—and you want to take off your little jacket! But I can't find the zipper! Now, how about a nice glass of water and some little cookies. . . ."

"Grace!" Elizabeth hollered into the phone. After a moment, Grace hung up. Elizabeth laughed—she had an idea for a story—and called back.

"Hello?" Grace asked.

"Hi, Grace."

"Elizabeth!"

"Hello?" said a drowsy male voice on an extension.

"Charles, darling," said Grace. "I thought you were taking a nap."

"I was, until the phone rang."

"Well, then, come into the kitchen and have a nice toddy with me."

"I'll be there in a moment," he said, and they both hung up.

Elizabeth stood shaking her head, smiling. A story was forming. She went back to the study, sat down, xxed out "After leaving Mr. Braithewaite," and began again:

At one of the first parties Sarah Braithewaite could remember, Emily Nickerson's father had broken his wife's front teeth during a home viewing of *Gidget Goes Hawaiian,* and it seemed retrospectively to her that every party since had boasted a couple who had ended a discussion of divorce moments before stepping into the gathering. Mrs. Braithewaite found it most intolerable when it was the host couple, for the house would reek of bad feeling as if the

walls were moldy with it. She imagined them in the moments before the first guests arrived: "You pig. You
whore." "I want you out." "I wish you would die." "I want
the house; you'll never see the kids again. . . . Phil! Beverly!
Marvelous to see you both, come in, come in, there's a
lovely clam dip by the fire."

But she had dutifully attended parties with Mr. Braithewaite, although the entire time, eating drinking talking, a
voice within was saying, "I have to go home now, thanks
for the lovely time but I have to go home now, wish I could
stay for dessert but the sitter is so-on-and-so-forth and I
have to go home." She'd always had a drink or two before
arriving, could no more attend a party sober than she could
naked, and on several occasions embarrassed Mr. Braithewaite with loud *vino demento* scenes for which she would be
punished by silence on the drive home.

Better go put the clothes in the dryer.

When she sat back at the typewriter, she reread what she'd
written, pleased. *Well, you see, Johnny, it's a funny story: the first
chapter, "Parties," came about on the day my daughter Rosie started
first grade. . . .* The phone rang again. Jesus! The great artist
rose, glaring, and went to the kitchen. It was probably Grace
again, or else it was Gordon, canceling for tonight.

"Norma?"

"No."

"Is she there?"

"No. Wrong number."

Elizabeth returned to the study, sat down, stared, with her
hands on the keys, for a good fifteen minutes at what she'd written, then got up to take the clothes out of the dryer.

Back at the typewriter, she mentally computed the calories she
had consumed at breakfast: about 450, she figured, not bad. So if
for lunch she had two pieces of bread—160, say—a few slices of
chicken—100? 150?—and a tablespoon of mayonnaise—100—
Concentrate!:

So when her aged friend, Gladys, called to invite her to
supper with a small group of "darling" people, Sarah's first
impulse was to lie.

Oh, there was milk in the coffee: maybe another 50 calories. Elizabeth stared for the next half hour at a color photo tacked to the wall, Rosie on the porch at three, naked except for a red plastic fireman's hat on her head. Then it was time to fold the laundry and put it away.

Back to the study; but before sitting down she turned and went to the kitchen, stopping for only the quickest glimpse in the mirror, back to the study to get what she'd written to read over lunch. No wonder she was so hungry. She'd probably put in three miles since breakfast.

It was twelve-thirty, a little too early for a beer. She got chicken, a tomato, mayonnaise, cilantro, and an English muffin out of the refrigerator, popped the muffin in the toaster, and went back to the refrigerator for red onion. Partially hidden behind the milk, an ale winked at her, wet and cold. She stroked her nose, sniffed, reached for it.

Elizabeth lay reading *Bleak House* in the window seat that afternoon, no longer driven to write, waiting for Rosie to come home from school. When the doorbell rang, she started as if she had heard a pistol shot.

Who on earth could it be? Even Gordon wouldn't dare drop in unannounced. Was it a sad policeman? Had Rosie been killed by the man who had murdered those women at the lakes? Was it the man himself? Shit, it was probably the Jehovah's Witnesses again; they had been stalking her lately. Yesterday there'd been a *Watchtower* on the doormat with the headline CAN YOU SMOKE AND LOVE YOUR NEIGHBOR?

She walked to the front door. "Hello?"

"Hello," a woman's voice said.

"Are you a Witness?"

"I swear to God I didn't see a thing."

Elizabeth opened the door and found a fat, long-haired woman standing on the doormat, anxiously looking over her shoulder.

"Can I help you?"

"Are you E. Ferguson?"

"Yeah."

"I'm Rae Meltzer. I just moved into the house at the end of the street."

Elizabeth nodded. "Why don't you come in for a moment?"

"Thank you, E."

"Elizabeth." Five minutes. Then you'll have to be going because I've got any number of things to attend to. The fat woman was pretty, with huge almond-shaped brown eyes, wavy auburn hair, a smallish, distinctly English nose, pinched on both sides.

"So, what can I do for you?"

"Oh, nothing. I was just in the neighborhood." Rae, hands jammed into the pockets of her worn baggy Levi's, shuffled off toward the living room, leaving Elizabeth standing, puzzled, at the door.

"God. Look at all these books."

Elizabeth walked to the living room, leaned against the wall, and watched as Rae darted from bookcase to bookcase, reading titles, ricocheting from wall to wall, stopping for a few seconds at a framed print, then back to a bookcase, expressing admiration in her cheerful, woolly voice: Margaret Rutherford in *Blithe Spirit.*

"We've got most of the same books."

"Yeah?"

"But you've got more. I thought I'd just stop by, you know, say hello and introduce myself."

"Ah." Now gooooooooo away.

"I just moved in last week."

"Oh." Elizabeth nodded.

"I'm renting Hanuman's studio apartment. You know her?"

"The Pride of Cucamonga?"

Rae laughed.

"That's an old Grateful Dead song," said Elizabeth.

Rae nodded, shuffled off toward the pewter mugs and vases on the mantelpiece, now seemingly oblivious to Elizabeth, who watched, bemused.

I've got to get rid of her. Listen, Rae, I'm glad you stopped by, but I was just leaving the house. . . .

"She made a fortune on that odic force book," said Rae. "She's still collecting royalties."

"So I heard."

27

"When I went to see her about renting the place, she stares deep into my eyes for a while—you may not have noticed, but my lower lids are big—and she goes, 'You've got beautiful eyes,' I say—shuffle shuffle—'thanks,' and she says, 'Do you have a thyroid condition?' "

Elizabeth smiled.

"Did you like *Henderson?*"

"Yeah. A lot."

"Me too. Hanuman's boyfriend just left her."

"Yeah?" I really care, I really care enormously.

"So she's holed up, getting into her mind-grief; I swear to God she says, 'I'm getting into my mind-grief.' "

Elizabeth smiled again, leaned against the wall. Rae came shuffling over.

"Am I interrupting something?"

"Yeah, no, I don't know. You want to have a quick drink?"

"Okay, sure."

"I'll get them. Have a seat." You're making me nervous.

Rae was sitting on the blue velvet couch reading Auden when Elizabeth returned with two screwdrivers.

"Here you go."

"Thanks."

"So. Welcome to the neighborhood."

"Thanks."

"What do you do?"

"I'm a weaver. I make these artsy-fartsy little potholders for a boutique in Sausalito to pay the bills, and I make big weavings—pictures, sort of—that I . . . I don't know. As soon as I screw up the courage, I'm going to take them . . . I don't know. What do you do?"

Ah, the question on all of our lips. What *do* I do?

"I—uh, do—uh, I don't know." Elizabeth grinned, shrugged. "I raise my daughter, Rosie, who's six. I'm sort of in between jobs right now." Oh, that's a good one, Elizabeth, the last job was nine years ago.

"But what line of work are you in?"

What line of work. Elizabeth cleared her throat, nodding. "I love books, more than anything except for Rosie. I've been an editor"—well, sort of; I mean I typed for an editor—"and I've been a publicist's assistant, and—I don't know." She shrugged again.

"Are you divorced?"

"Widowed. Two years ago."

"Oh, my *God.* How did he die?"

"Car accident."

"Oh, my God. How *sad.* Jesus."

"Well. These things happen."

Rae looked at her with horror, closed her eyes, shook her head. "Do you mind if I smoke?"

"No, go ahead."

"You want one?"

"No, thanks. I quit last year."

"Oh, my *God.* I would give anything on earth to be able to quit. How'd you do it?"

"It wasn't that big a deal. I just stopped smoking. I didn't smoke much to begin with. Rosie was all flipped about it, told me that if I kept smoking I wouldn't grow old enough to be a grandmother because I'd be dead. You know, the first week's a bitch; after that, the self-righteousness carried me through. I have one every few weeks."

"That's amazing. See, I don't have the merest *shred* of strength of character, I swear to God. Well, yeah, I do, but—like, for instance I can weave all day every day, but say I start eating, there's no stopping me; it's like there's this savage pig animal in my heart that emerges roaring 'more more more,' and I feel if I stop eating I'll die; the only way to stop me once I get going would be to shoot me with a tranquilizer gun like the ones they use on elephants at the zoo."

"Do you drink much?"

"Not particularly. Do you?"

Elizabeth shrugged. "Off and on." Mostly on. She smiled. "Would you like another?"

"Are you going to have one?"

"Yeah."

"Okay."

"Let's take them out to the porch."

It was warm and blue outside; the wind had died down.

"I wouldn't sit in that chair if I were you." Rae stopped in mid-squat above the folding chair. "It's a pain. It looks nice, doesn't it, but it'll turn on you, like a Venus's flytrap. Here, we'll sit on the swing."

"This is a great place you've got."

"Yeah, thanks." They looked out to the yard, at the trees, rosebushes, flower beds, vegetable garden, Rosie's two-wheeler lying on its side by the gate.

"Do you have a man?" Rae asked, lighting another cigarette.

"Well, no one special. I see this man named Gordon a couple of times a week, but I also see other guys. How 'bout you?"

"I've only been here a week. But—I sort of like that guy who bartends at Mickey's—you know him? That guy Brian, tall, reddish beard? Kind of funky genteel?"

"Yeah."

"But I'm trying to take it slow, see, romance is not my strong suit. It brings out my most foolish, self-destructive tendencies. I *always* get in way over my head; I get strung out, totally obsessive. Like, for instance, one of the reasons I left New York was to get away from my last boyfriend, who was a shit of a shit of a shit, a liar, a two-timer, but funny, you see, and cute. And I kept thinking I'd change him, my great love for him would cause God to restore his glorious gift of sight and all that. He'd make progress, he'd start talking about getting married, and then—it was like Charlie Brown and the football, you know? How Lucy always cons him into kicking the football, promising that she won't pull it away at the last second? Well, he was Lucy, and I was Charlie Brown, and no matter how many times I ended up lying on my back, humiliated, I still fuckin' *wanted* the guy." She shook her head.

"I was like that all through high school, all through college."

"And you're not any more?"

"I haven't been in love in so long. But I don't think so. I have less tolerance now. And enormous pride."

"That's how I want to be. But, see, I'm extremely ill, mentally; like, for instance, I didn't leave that guy in New York my phone number, and he doesn't know where I live, but every time I go into town and see a green Beetle, I think, 'He's found me, he's come to *claim* me, he's come to his senses'; and, see, if I had him, if I got him, I don't think I'd really want him. He's not good enough for me. But shit, man, I don't know—like, for instance, right now, if the phone rang here, at your house, I'd have this rush of adrenaline, I'd start having palpitations, I'd think he'd tracked me down somehow. . . ." Rae threw back her head and laughed.

Elizabeth smiled. She liked Rae, a lot. God, what she would give to be jolly.

"So where are your folks?"

"Dead. I'm an orphan. What about you?"

"My dad died in Korea. My mom's in Los Angeles, same house I grew up in."

"Do you like her?"

"I *adore* her. She's a sweetheart. I just can't stand to be in the same room with her for more than ten minutes."

"Yeah?"

"Oh, yeah, man, I start climbing the *walls*. Then I end up hating myself for being such a shit. But I swear to God, she's afraid of *every*thing: she's afraid of men, mice, cars, food poisoning; she's afraid of losing her hand in the washing machine; she's afraid of escalators; she's afraid when she buys toilet paper the clerk will think she's going to use it to wipe herself; she's afraid of drowning; she's afraid of planes—when I flew up here to look for a place, she called the airlines and asked if the pilot's biorhythm chart was available."

"No."

"I swear to God. What did your mother die of?"

"Old age. At forty. Cirrhosis."

"Oh."

"Ready for another?"

"Sure." Rae gave Elizabeth her empty glass, smiling.

Rae was smoking again when Elizabeth returned with the drinks. "Did your dad drink too?"

"Yeah. They both drank like there was no tomorrow. He left my mother for another lady when I was ten."

"What a wipe-out. For your mother."

"Yeah. She went nuts. A week after he left she went out and started buying animals. A beagle, two cats, two white doves and two diamond doves, a guinea pig, a rabbit, and a tankful of tropical fish. It gave her something to do, something to take care of. It made her feel needed. But the house stank. I'd never liked animals all that much. My dad said he ought to buy me a boa constrictor."

Rae laughed.

"And a parrot, that he'd train to say, 'Daddy loves Elizabeth, he'll explain it all someday!' "

Rae looked suddenly mournful, like Stan Laurel. Elizabeth shrugged, took a sip, sighed.

"Were you and he close?"

"Oh, yeah, like that." Elizabeth crossed her fingers. "I used to cut his hair, rub his feet. . . . I was the apple of his eye. And I thought my mother was pitiful for not being able to compete successfully."

"God—mothers. Where would we be without them?"

"I don't know. My mother only loved me when I was doing something she could brag about."

"My mother brags about stuff like—well, for instance, she says to this boyfriend of mine, 'Rae had the talent to be a concert pianist'—which I didn't—'only she was lazy. I pushed her and pushed her to practice, I'd beat the stuffing out of her trying to get her to practice,' like, you know, it speaks of her devotion and wisdom, only to me and the boyfriend it's like she's bragging about having stolen money from orphans—no offense—to pay for my lessons."

They shook their heads, smiled at each other.

"I wonder what Rosie will tell her psychiatrist about me when she's twenty, all this lurid, compelling, rewritten stuff about my lovers and neuroses and clothes and mannerisms"

"Nah. I bet you're a great mother."

"What does that have to do with anything?"

"A lot."

"I don't know. I find myself doing all these things that my mother used to do, things I swore I'd never do."

"Like what?"

"I don't know." Like drinking, for instance—as if there were no tomorrow. Which there very well might not be. Elizabeth stared wistfully at Rosie's bicycle. In this morning's paper, Jerry Brown had likened the arms race to a bunch of small boys standing in a basement, knee-deep in kerosene, bragging about how many matches each of them had.

"Like what, Elizabeth?"

Oh. You still here? "Like, I use lines on Rosie that used to drive me crazy when my mother used them on me. Like 'matters of principle.' Or 'I'm so mad I can't see straight,' or 'I'm so mad I'm seeing red.' And little mannerisms: sometimes I'll watch myself do something she used to do, rub my nose a certain way when I'm nervous, or rub my eyes with a thumb and forefinger when someone is getting on my nerves while making this little sniffly sound—as soon as I notice I'm doing it, my heart stops."

"Yeah, yeah, I know exactly what you mean. When will Rosie be home?"

"Any minute." God willing, she's still alive, every distant siren might . . . "Shall we have one more drink?"

"Oh, *let's*, dammit," Rae beamed. Rae beamed a lot. "Do you like to go to movies?"

"It's my only amusement. Well, besides books, and—"

"Oh, me, too. I figure we'll be inseparable."

They got to their feet and walked inside just as the phone rang.

"It's him, it's him!" Rae shouted. Elizabeth laughed and cracked her hipbone on the corner of the hutch in the dining room.

"Hello?" she asked, picking up the phone.

"Hi, Mama. I'm playing at my new friend's house."

"Good. What's her name?"

"Sharon Thackery."
"Why are you whispering?"
"Because she's standing right here."

Rosie's first day back at school had been all her good dreams come true: she hadn't farted green bubbles. One kid joyously told Mrs. Gravinski that Rosie was the smartest kid in the class, another volunteered that she was the class clown. The smell of chalk dust on blackboard erasers excited and reassured her. The morning passed in a flash.

Recess was a whole new ball game; no more taunts of "Kindergarten baby, born in the gravy." Now Rosie and her classmates had the kindergarten babies to lord it over.

Rosie won at two-square more often than anyone else; the *boing* of the red rubber ball jazzed her, and she exhibited a sadistic competence. But the new girl, Sharon Thackery, was almost as good.

When the whistle blew ending recess and class resumed, it turned out that Sharon Thackery was *almost* as good at reading and writing. Rosie eyed her fretfully, eyed the long thick brown braids, tied with purple ribbons, wanted long brown braids more than she'd ever wanted anything before, and wanting them so badly made her stomach buckle, made it blush in misery, and in her mind's eye she watched herself hack Sharon's off with scissors, saw her*self* with long brown braids. "Rosie! Rosie!"

"Pssst," hissed Sharon Thackery, in the seat beside her.

"*Rosie,*" Mrs. Gravinsky said again. Rosie jerked, looked at the blackboard—A a B b C c—as if it were *The Revelation.* Some of the kids giggled, and Rosie turned red.

"I could read when I was four," Sharon said to Rosie after the lunch bell rang.

"Big deal. I could read when I was three."

"Liar."

"Oh, yeah?"

"Yeah."

"You can ask my mother." They sat at their desks, taking Saran-wrapped food out of their lunch boxes. Rosie's exuded a faint air of rust, banana, musty sweet decay, and a hint of grapes. Sharon's was new. Her mother had cut her sandwich the right way, so that the halves were triangles. Sharon's apple looked like Snow White's. Rosie's had been cut into fourths and the meat was brown. Sharon had—oh, God, Rosie could hardly stand it— Hostess cupcakes, while *she* had these totally gross perforated raisin bars, flat and dry.

"You wanna trade?" Sharon asked her, holding up a cupcake, eyeing the raisin bars. Rosie couldn't believe her ears. What's the catch?

Rosie looked at the chocolate cupcake, iced, with whipped cream inside, shrugged her shoulders, and said, "I guess."

She gave Sharon two raisin bars. The cupcake was the best thing she had eaten in her life. She asked Sharon if she wanted to play outside when they finished their lunches. Sharon did.

Boys were playing basketball, P-I-G, and Around the World; girls hung and spun on the rings and bars, played jacks, hop-scotch, jump rope; mixed groups of children played Red Light Green Light, tag, Mother May I, four-square, two-square, dodge ball. Red rubber balls boinging on the blacktop. Scalloped and missing teeth, scabby elbows, new clothes, shrieking, laughter, tears, the shrill whistles of authority. Some kids too shy to talk or play with anyone tried to blend into walls or hid in the johns. Rosie and Sharon jumped rope.

> Cinderella, dressed in yella,
> Went upstairs to kiss her fella,
> Mayda mistake and kissed a snake,
> How many doctors did it take?
> One, two, three, four. . . .

Rosie got to thirty-one doctors. Holding her breath, she watched, growing subtly but visibly agitated when Sharon got as far as twenty—please God please don't let her do better—up and down, up and down, twenty-five, twenty-six, twenty-sev— Sharon's sneaker caught the rope, brought it down. Rosie didn't crack a smile.

"Too bad," she said kindly.

🍂

Sharon invited her home after school. Rosie couldn't wait to have a shot at her kitchen. She lived a block away, in a two-story mansion with hedges, lawn, fruit trees, all carefully tended. The house, outside and in, was picture perfect. When they stepped inside, Rosie nearly swooned at the chandeliers, Persian rugs, Chinese vases, velvet chairs, and the perfect mother who greeted them at the door, Timmy's mother on *Lassie,* a picture-perfect mother whose voice is so nice it sounds like she's crying, and she's so happy to meet Rosie, she says; come on into the kitchen.

Oreos and milk. Rosie had to pinch herself.

Rosie fell in love—with the house, the mother (nylons, perfume, lipstick)—wanted to play here with Sharon every day for the rest of her life.

The girls played with troll dolls all afternoon in Sharon's pink princess bedroom, dressing and undressing them, brushing and braiding the comical hair. The bedroom was so perfect, so enviable—pink gingham curtains and bedspreads, a vanity covered with bottles of toilet water and Barrettes and hair ribbons, plastic lipsticks, a jewelry box that played music when you opened it: inside, a ballerina spun on a pedestal surrounded by rubies, emeralds, pearls; porcelain geisha dolls under glass boxes, *clean* stuffed animals—it was almost more than Rosie could take. Giggling with Sharon, blissed out, excited, she imagined smashing the geisha dolls' heads off with a hammer, stealing the jewels, a lipstick, the ribbons. Pangs of bad conscience skittered through her mind, but mostly she was very, very happy.

At four they watched *Creature Features* in the den: a roaring dinosaur was advancing upon a pretty woman in a leopard-skin bathing suit.

And now, along with everything else she is afraid of at six years old, Rosie will live in terror of dinosaurs. She is afraid of falling through outer space forever, of going blind, of being bitten on the bottom by a poisonous snake when she sits on the toilet, of a man coming into her room to kill her (her plan is to lie still without breathing and pretend she is already dead), of turning into a black person, of going bald, of falling out the window of her dentist's fourteenth-story office, of the long, cold, bony white arm that will reach out from under the bed and grab her ankle if she gets up; and now, on top of all this: dinosaurs.

At six, when Mrs. Thackery said kindly that Sharon's daddy was on his way home and that Rosie must be going, she called her mother to ask for a ride.

"Oh, honey, I don't think I ought to drive. I've—uh, been having a drink with a new neighbor who dropped in today. . . ."

"God!" Rosie was stung with humiliation.

"Is it far?"

"No. Can't you even drive to *Hilton?*"

"You're on Hilton? Baby, that's only about ten blocks away. And it's still light out."

"Goodbye."

Rosie hung up, fighting back tears unsuccessfully.

"She can't come get me, because she's sick."

"She'll be all right," said Mrs. Thackery tenderly. *"Don't* worry."

"Her dad's dead!" Sharon announced in alarm.

Now tears were streaming down Rosie's face, and she was turning red.

"I'd drive you home but my car's in the shop. And Daddy will be too tired." Mrs. Thackery's weepy voice and sweetness made Rosie all the more miserable and ashamed and jealous.

"It's not very far," Rosie said bravely, sniffling, needing to be alone. "It's only over on Willow." But Rosie did not believe that she would make it home alive. "I better go. Thank you for a very nice time."

"We *loved* having you, dear."

"See you tomorrow," said Sharon anxiously.

"Yeah. See you in school."

"Goodbye."

"Goodbye."

"Goodbye."

She ran for her life, scanning the hillside beyond the row of houses, the hillside where she walked with her mother, where they collected wildflowers and looked for robins' nests in the cypress trees, and the cypress trees were moving, were not really cypresses but camouflaged dinosaurs, and the stream which ran downhill through cypress and oaks, a stream full of guppies and frogs and water skeeters, was filled with blood, and behind the boulders were leering, slavering, huge reptiles, waiting for it to be dark enough to go hunting for little girls; please God please God, save me, save me. Finally she arrived on Willow and tore through the white lattice gate out of breath, eyes shining, up the porch steps two at a time, burst through the front door, slammed it, locked it, and stood panting against it, home.

She took a deep breath, looked around. Where was her mother?

"Mama? Mama? I'm home."

And Elizabeth walked unsteadily out from the warm aromatic kitchen to hug her child, to hear the details of her day.

Chapter
✿3

One starry night a year later, Elizabeth was reading *Huckleberry Finn* to her daughter on the blue velvet couch in the fire-warmed living room. Rosie held her mother's feet in her lap, rubbing them lazily, laughing when her mother laughed, frowning when Elizabeth stopped to sip cognac from a Waterford snifter.

Elizabeth closed the book. "Time for bed, sweetheart."

"Noooooooo."

Rosie rubbed the feet more determinedly and Elizabeth purred. Her mind traveled back in time to nights when she had massaged her father's bony white feet, after removing the wing-tips, the garters, and the thin black socks; massaged them, honored, while her mother did the dishes or sat in the armchair reading. And now she lay, an aging young woman with a seven-year-old girl pressing tiny strong thumbs into her falling arches.

"I'm going to close my eyes for a moment. Will you keep rubbing my feet? And then I'll tuck you in."

Rosie nodded. Her mother's breathing grew soft, and Rosie rubbed more gently.

"Mama?"

No answer but the faintest snore.

"Psssst. Mama?"

She resumed the foot-rub, looked around the room, out the window where a white crescent moon hung, then up at the ceiling, down and sideways to the empty crystal snifter, into her mother's peaceful face, down into her lap, at the gypsy-red toenails. She began tapping rhythms with her forefingers on her mother's toes, as if they were a keyboard, whispering "Deedle deedle deedle" to a melody she heard in her head. After a while, she said again, "Mama?"

"Uh."

"Let's go tuck me in."

Elizabeth opened one eye, closed it, nodded her head.

"Why don't you go put on your nightie. I'll come up in a minute and listen to your prayers. Okay?"

Rosie squinted her eyes and mouth at Elizabeth (whose eyes remained closed), stuck out her tongue, lifted her mother's feet, and slid out from under them.

Twenty minutes later Elizabeth went upstairs to Rosie's room and found her child glowering out from under the covers, her face hard and sleepy.

"Hi, sweetie."

"Hi."

"Sorry I fell asleep."

"Tssss."

"Don't be mad at me."

"I'm not."

"Good." Elizabeth walked to the bed and sat down.

"I would be, if you were my real mother."

"Oh."

Elizabeth nodded her head; she stroked Rosie's back and bottom.

"Can I stretch out with you for a minute?"

"Okay." Rosie slid over, and Elizabeth lay down. "But my mother will be coming to get me tonight."

"Did you tell her where the front door key is?"

"Yep."

"Good." Elizabeth could smell stale cognac reflecting off Rosie's head and wished she had brushed her teeth.

"Do you want me to listen to your prayers?"

Andrew had taught his daughter to pray, Andrew who believed in God. Rosie's prayers could last for fifteen minutes, because anybody left off of her God Bless list was in danger, might be dead in the morning, and it would be Rosie's fault. She prayed as if dictating a letter: Dear God, Thank you very much for the very nice day; I am trying to be good; say hello to Daddy for me and God bless Mama. . . .

But tonight she had already said her prayers by the time Elizabeth came to her room: she had first asked God to smite her mother, and then panicked and begged him to keep her alive.

Rosie closed her eyes, pretending to fall asleep. Elizabeth lay beside her, nuzzling the soft black curls. "I sure love you," she said.

Rosie snored. Elizabeth smiled.

She returned to the living room couch, read at *Middlemarch,* sipped brandy until she could hardly keep her eyes open, then went upstairs to wash her face and rub cold cream around her eyes and mouth, on her neck, into her hands, yawning again and again. Dragged herself down the hall to her bedroom, removed and draped her clothes over the back of a chair, barely had the strength to pull back the comforter and crawl into bed. She turned off the lamp, yawned, stretched out, and closed her eyes. Goddammit, had she remembered to turn off the oven? Had she locked the front door? Had she put the screen in front of the fireplace? Her mind raced with small anxieties. Her eyes popped open.

Shit. It was going to be one of those nights.

If only she had a man beside her. Even Gordon, who had begun to get on her nerves, with his "marvelous"es, his racist riddles, his constant references to the European cities he had visited. If only Rosie were at Sharon's, so that she could go to the bar in town for a nightcap and find a male body to bring home. She would have to call out for one.

 41

She recited the List of Reasons why she wanted to drop Gordon ... but he *was* a terrific lover. She turned on the light, picked up the receiver by her bed, hung it up, frustrated, sad, empty, horny, wired: mad Uncle Theo high in the branches of a monstrous oak crying "I want a wooooooman" until the dwarf nun climbed a ladder and led him down. She nuzzled her shoulder with pouted lips and clapped her eyes shut.

Moments later, eyes open, unrequited: Who do I think I'm kidding?

She climbed out of bed, wrapped herself in her white kimono, and went downstairs to see if the living room was in flames. It wasn't. The front door was unlocked. Goddammit, Elizabeth! She locked the door, fiercely. The oven was off, and in the living room the fire was low, the screen in place. She poured some more cognac into the snifter, picked *Middlemarch* up off the floor, and went upstairs to her bedroom. And then wondered: Are you absolutely positive that the fire was safe and the oven *all* the way off? Relax. Read.

Propped up on pillows, naked, she read; Fred Vincy had gone to see Mrs. Garth, the mother of the girl he wanted to marry, who was rolling out pastry in the kitchen.

> Looking at the mother, you might hope that the daughter would become like her, which is a prospective advantage equal to a dowry—the mother too often standing behind the daughter like a malignant prophecy—"Such as I am, she will shortly be."

Jesus. Relax. Keep reading.

She took a gulp of cognac and read until her eyes itched, read until she was almost too tired to switch off the lamp, but the effort roused her, and she exhaled deeply. It was one fifteen by the luminous clock; if she fell asleep soon she could still get almost six hours' sleep before she had to get Rosie up for school.

If you fall asleep right now, you can still get five and a half hours. She turned the light back on, picked up the book, but couldn't concentrate.

If you fall asleep *now*, you can still get five ... shit.

ROSIE

"A malignant prophecy." There, in the projector of her mind, was her mother, beautiful and ambitious in her youth, in a bed at the St. Helena detox hospital, needing a "hummer" every four hours, needing an ounce and a half of whiskey to avoid delirium tremens: dead at forty.

You have got to stop drinking so much. Tomorrow. If you fall asleep right now, you can still get four hours and forty minutes of sleep.

The pillow was hot and scratchy, and she turned it over, resting her face on the cool cotton. The sheets itched, felt as sandy as her eyes, and she flopped around the bed. She hugged a pillow, one end between her legs: her teddy bear, her lover. Four hours would be fine.

But no, her mind races with images of her mother and Rosie, of more malignant prophecies. What is Rosie learning by example? On the one hand, she is learning the art of amusing conversation and the pleasure and knowledge to be found in books. On the other, she is learning how to kill time, use men and drink; watching her mother who, when the pain or boredom or nostalgia gets too bad, anesthetizes herself; watching her mother be sneaky and critical and depressed. Rosie does not see examples of a mother's commitment to romantic love and work, to change and growth. These she sees in crazy Rae, whom Rosie adores, Rae who shoots for the moon, works hard at her art, and drives herself crazy with obsession, madly in love with Brian the bartender, who keeps successfully conning her into kicking the football—Charlie Brown and Lucy—yet again.

But otherwise Rae is a great, loving, honest example. Elizabeth will change, in every way, will become more like Rae by osmosis. Intellectually, they're so alike, but attitudinally couldn't be more opposite. And Rae tells the truth—always, it seems; secrets and confessions. She cries sometimes, remembering a vast humiliation or foolishness, but more often has Elizabeth and herself weeping tears of laughter, while Elizabeth's verbalized history is embellished, polished and rewritten so that she can hardly remember how it really was, and therefore who she really is.

Once Rae came over to borrow Elizabeth's vacuum cleaner and confided, "I had a vacuum cleaner once. I'd sent away for these magic weight-loss shorts that you hooked up to a vacuum cleaner—only I didn't *have* a vacuum cleaner. So I go to a secondhand appliance store and buy one.

"I take it home, and my roommate is stunned. I mean, I was an even worse slob back then—I had a mattress on the floor that a stranger would have felt perfectly comfortable walking across with his or her shoes on—and here I've just shelled out fifty bucks for a vacuum cleaner.

"But I take it upstairs to my bedroom and lock the door. I get my magic shorts from underneath the bed. They're like elasticized pedal pushers—they're plaid, and they're made out of rubber, and they've got this opening at the hip, like an ostomy. So I put them on, read the instructions, plug in the vacuum cleaner, attach it to the opening, turn on the motor, and start running in place for fifteen minutes, holding the nozzle to my side while it sucks all the air out of my shorts, trying to run on tiptoes so my roommate won't come up to investigate. . . ." Elizabeth treasured the image, could summon it when she needed to laugh. Like now. She smiled.

Rae has such a simple, compassionate heart. They saw Hepburn on television recently: beautiful, but with those tremors. Elizabeth grew disconcerted; Rae grew sentimental. "Doesn't she remind you of a little sparrow?" she asked.

And last year, at a gallery in the city, studying a print of Winslow Homer's "Gulf Stream," Rae pointed out the ghostly ship in the distant waves and thought that it was coming to save the nonchalant black sailor on the broken ship—around which sharks are swimming. "Jesus, Rae," Elizabeth said, with some irritation. "That is one dead darkie."

Oh, Rae.

Oh, Rosie, I swear it: I'm ready to change. I'm ready to grow up some more. I'll be kinder, sober and strong, more like Rae and your dad. You'll have happy memories of growing up with me.

I have lost my childhood. And I am losing my adulthood, it passes too quickly, but I won't, won't, won't lose my child.

Is there a biochemical flaw in me that is making me become my mother, increasingly boozy and insane? Relax, relax. If you fall asleep right now, you can still get three hours. . . .

But she feels crazier and more scared as dawn approaches, the moments between night and day, the hour of the wolf, the hour of the black dogs. She will nearly die waiting for sunrise—and then will spend the day waiting for it to be time for bed. . . . God!

She travels back ten years, is sitting at the Boston airport having just attended her roommate's wedding, desperate to be home with Andrew who had of all things German measles. Over the intercom Elizabeth hears the announcement that her flight has been delayed two hours, and she has a flash flood of panic, profoundly convinced that she cannot survive those two impossible hours, will lose her mind. She has to sit shock still, staring straight ahead the entire time; her mind is Edvard Munch's "The Scream." And this is how she feels now.

The projector in her mind now shows a clip from a New Year's Eve party when she was roughly Rosie's age, in a nightgown, unseen at the top of the stairs, where she sits and listens to the plastered grown-ups sing. Her mother is at the piano, playing songs from the *Fireside Book of Folk Songs*: "Drink to Me Only with Thine Eyes," "Annie Laurie," "Cockles and Mussels." Back in bed, she cries herself to sleep, waking just after dawn to hear a blood-chilling sound, a stage-whispered fight between her parents, which seeps through the wall into her bedroom: her mother hissing that he'd done something in the garden with Backen's wife, her father denying it. Elizabeth can perfectly remember cringing with guilt and rage, her stomach flushed, the back of her throat hot and rashy, the back of her eyes hot and rashy too. . . .

Relax. Try to stop flapping around so much. If you just wait it out long enough, it will be day; wait a few more hours, rest your eyes.

Right now, Rae would be lying wrapped around Brian; an emotional arsonist is better than nothing as the hour of the wolf approaches. Oh, God, *I* want a man here now. Grace and Charles Adderly, in their seventies, still lie together, holding one another as they sleep. Why don't I get to have one, why do I have to keep waiting to find a good man? One with fire in his heart, to sleep with every night?

Because you don't deserve one. Because you treat them badly, because you are weird and manipulative and selfish—selfish, selfish, her mother always telling her how selfish she was. All her loves, except for the miracle of Rosie, have been in vain, totally in vain—no, there is also Rae—and the Adderlys, but they don't know how nasty she can be with men: if they could see the devious workings of her mind, they wouldn't want her either. They think she is noble, an excellent mother, a devoted friend although she hardly ever makes the effort to see them. The last time Grace came for tea, Rosie made them laugh so hard that Grace, standing, had to cross her legs, and pee ran down them, forming a puddle on the floor, which made the three of them laugh even harder. Oh, God, in pain and compassion and embarrassment, Rosie was on the verge of tears. Grace said, "I've piddled." And Elizabeth, touching her shoulder, went for paper towels and wiped it up as graciously, as nonchalantly as if a puppy—her own puppy—had peed.

See, Elizabeth, see? That you are kind, too?

But her mother continues to haunt her tonight. Easter, thirty years ago, her father had promised to buy Easter egg dyes on his way home from the office, but didn't come home until six in the morning, by which time her mother had painted hardboiled eggs by wetting jelly beans, etching faint watery pictures on the white shells, but only the red and the black beans showed up well. Upon seeing them, it was her mother whom Elizabeth hated that Easter Sunday. Not her father.

Her eyes burn, the back of her throat burns, the space behind her eyes burns.

Morning is barely breaking, and she finds she has fallen through into the dreamy burrow just above true sleep, fading, floating. Finally she sleeps.

The alarm went off an hour later. She felt as though she had been asleep for five minutes, her exhaustion such that she was pinned to the bed by centrifugal force; there was no point in trying to raise her right arm to quiet the alarm because her arm would be slammed back to her side. There would be no energy this morning, there would only be the killing of an entire day, the waiting for it to be over, a nothingness. The alarm wore down. She would read the paper, weed, maybe do some laundry.

Rosie opened the bedroom door, already dressed in worn blue-jean overalls, sneakers, and a purple T-shirt.

"Hi, Mama." Elizabeth could barely keep her eyes open and felt like a woman who had barely lived to regret it: bloated, bleary, sad. "God!" said her daughter and stomped off, slamming the door. Elizabeth exhaled loudly.

She went to the bathroom, splashed freezing water on her face, studied the flatness, bags, wrinkles in and around her hazel eyes. She went downstairs to make breakfast for her daughter, who was pouring a half-full bottle of Remy Martin down the sink. Elizabeth rubbed her face and eyes and slumped down at the table.

"I didn't drink that much, Rosie. I just never fell asleep."

"You got so drunk you fell asleep on the couch."

"But I didn't have much more after you went to bed."

"Oh, yeah?"

"Yeah."

"You swear on a stack of Bibles?"

Elizabeth nodded.

Rosie stalked out of the kitchen and up the stairs to her mother's room, retrieved the incriminating snifter from the night table, and returned to the kitchen, glaring. Elizabeth looked back at her levelly.

"What do you have to say about this?" Rosie asked.

Elizabeth did not hear her own voice: She heard the tone of her mother's. "Come here."

Rosie shook her head, looked away.

"I promise you. On my honor. I didn't get drunker after you went to bed. I had a short glass of brandy while I was reading in bed, and I stayed awake all night, just tossing and turning."

"How come?"

"Because I have insomnia. I'm not a good sleeper. It's just part of my nature. I can't seem to change it; like I can't change the color of my eyes."

Rosie looked at the ground, scowling, tracing letters on the linoleum with the toe of her shoe.

"Come *here,* baby. I just want to hold you."

Rosie continued to look at the floor. Her bottom lip was trembling, and the rich blue eyes were wet. Elizabeth could have died with love for that scrawny body, for the tiny succulent bottom, for that person.

"Rosie." I swear to you, things will be different. . . .

"Mama. What is to become of us?"

Oh, *Rosie.*

Elizabeth spent the morning swathed not in gauze but in cotton batting. The front page was filled with disastrous news—Israel had been bombing its neighbors again, and the superpowers were in yet another nervous frenzy (boys in the kerosene-filled basement), and it gave her a thrill she would have admitted to no one. Maybe this time all hell was going to break loose. All her life, all hell—nuclear war—had threatened to break out. But suppose, say, *Russia* dropped a nice conventional bomb on Israel; it would put life into a state of suspended animation, would legitimize hanging out all day waiting to see where the chips would fall, would justify spending all day overeating, drinking, watching movies, playing with Rae, making love. It would get her off many hooks. And it would give her and Rae, who followed and discussed major international difficulties with the involvement and enthusiasm with which other people followed *Dallas,* great comic-tragic material.

"We do not leave the world to our children," she read on page five, in an interview with a world-renowned pacifist. "We borrow it from them."

But Elizabeth, with all the free time in the world, couldn't bring herself to work for pacific groups; the world was too far gone, too ghastly and demented, almost fictional, almost boring. And the people in town fighting the great good fights drove her up the wall.

She had attended one antinuclear meeting and spent the entire time waiting for it to be over. The man seated beside Elizabeth had tapped the shoulder of the equally white woman in front of him and asked, "I've seen you somewhere—aren't you a Nicaragua person?" Elizabeth had hardly been able to wait to tell Rae, who sent peace and women's groups money.

Forget it. The thing was to take care of your children and the people you loved and your life. Personal grooviness *über alles.*

She made poached eggs and toast for breakfast but, with too much coffee and too little sleep, and having survived a night that felt like a nervous breakdown, she found that the food was unable to find a foothold anywhere in her stomach or intestines.

Back at the kitchen table, reading the Help Wanteds, infused with the desire to change her life on every level, in every way— to get moving, forward—she idly lifted a bottle of nail polish and, with a forlorn look on her face and a gaping, heavy hole in her chest, spent the next half hour slowly tipping the bottle back and forth, watching the swaths cut in the polish by the silver stir beads, the silvery etchings in crimson.

Chapter
4

Miss Lacey, the second-grade teacher, was tall and thin, with a long red nose and an abounding interest in the genius and struggles of Rosie Ferguson. She had arranged for Rosie to study reading and arithmetic with the third-graders, gave her fourth-grade grammar workbooks and a blank notebook in which to keep a journal. She comforted her with hugs the day in music class when, upon hearing midway through "Aunt Rhody" that the goslings were crying because the old gray goose was dead, Rosie wept inconsolably. And she prefaced almost all her phone calls to Elizabeth by saying that it wasn't that she didn't treasure having Rosie in her class, but . . .

She had called when Rosie brought Elizabeth's checkbook to Show-and-Tell, when Rosie sold a blackish-green penny to David Harper several weeks later for a quarter, claiming it was worth three hundred dollars, and again when Rosie interrupted art class with an impression of Mrs. Brewster, the obese and loudly allergic principal.

"Hello, Elizabeth," Miss Lacey said over the phone one afternoon.

Oh, Christ. What now? "Hello, Eileen."

Eileen Lacey exhaled loudly.

"This morning, for Show-and-Tell, Rosie brought in a big black rock and claimed it was a chunk of a star that fell into your garden the other night."

"Well, she's got an active imagination—"

"Elizabeth, she said that the star fell onto your boyfriend and killed him."

"Oh."

"In your garden. And the garbagemen took his body away this morning."

"I see. Can you hang on a moment, please? I've left the water running."

Elizabeth had been waiting all afternoon for it to be late enough for a beer. In a fit of resolve following her white night, she had poured all the hard liquor out and now drank only beer and wine.

She returned to the phone with a Mickey's Big Mouth ale.

"I'll talk to her when she gets home. I appreciate your calling me."

"She has *such* a great mind, Elizabeth. I think it's so important that she learn to tell only the truth."

"I couldn't agree more."

"Doesn't she like your boyfriend?"

"I thought she did. Maybe she's jealous of him." Elizabeth rolled her eyes.

"That's probably it. You'll talk to her about it though, won't you?"

"Yes, of course."

Rae called half an hour later to announce an impending collapse, brought on by Brian's not having called for three days.

"Oh, Rae. The guy's an asshole. Drop him."

"But I'm in love with him."

"Spare me the details."

"But—"

"His behavior is continually bad."

"What does that have to do with anything?"

"Are you crying?"

"Yeah, but it's just because I'm so tired."

"Ah."

"I stayed up until five this morning."

"Coke?"

"I wish."

"Speed?"

"Mice. I swear to God, Elizabeth, they're driving me nuts; they're in the cupboards, the eaves, and the kitchen. As soon as I turn off the lights, they begin scritching away—*just* to push me over the edge. They go *scritch, scritch,* then they put their hands over their mouths to stifle their titters; I swear to God, they're snickering into their chests. While I pace around till all hours. About three this morning I made the mistake of looking in a mirror, and I had this eerie, wasted look on my face, like the guy in 'The Tell-Tale Heart.' "

"Get a cat."

"I don't like cats," she said mournfully. "They're too *hairy.*"

"Then set traps. Or poison them."

"I did. I put d-Con wherever I suspected mouse encampments, then I swept it all back up. Don't laugh at me. I couldn't deal with opening a cupboard in the morning and finding all those mousey little corpses, the mamas clutching their babies like a little mouse Jonestown."

"Oh, for Christ's sake, Rae."

"I don't think I can get through the day—"

"Weave. And then come eat dinner with us."

"Nah—"

"Goddammit, Rae, you won't leave the house because *he* might call, right? You could be over here with the woman who rejoices in being your best friend, with your adopted niece who always makes you happy, eating some wondrous dinner, listening to music, laughing, but you can't say yes because *he* might call and invite you to go on a dump run with him. Rae, he has the emotional range and expressiveness of a mean, well-trained dog."

There was a long silence.

"Now I want you to get your voluptuous self over here at five."

"Okay. Thanks."

Poor Rae, thought Elizabeth. Despite my own grave faults, self-centeredness, laziness, aloofness, at *least* I've gotten over the dump-run syndrome, at *least* I've learned to learn to stop letting men jerk my leash.

Rae, with a heart that filled her entire chest cavity, loved Brian with a blind, selfless obsession. She made the common and devastating mistake of interpreting excellent lovemaking for love, of confusing sexual chemistry with loving. She sat around waiting for Brian to call, and when he didn't, she played records to summon him through telepathy, playing them loudly so he'd hear three miles away: "Love and Affection," "Desperado," "All of Me," "If I Could Only Win Your Love."

"You're kidding me," said Elizabeth, when Rae told her. "Is it like 'This song goes out to Brian from Rae: *Please* call'?"

"Exactly."

"Jesus."

Rosie and Sharon went into town after school, first to the post office, where they studied the Wanted posters in the glass display case, casting anxious eyes on the male customers who came and went. They stopped by the dime store to leer at the bras. They ran to the bakery, burst into the sweet yeasty room, and waited patiently for old Gio to give them a hot butter cookie, which he did. Then they crept stealthily to the boardwalk outside, tiptoeing past store windows, whispering in pig Latin, whirling around from time to time to see who might be on their trail.

They combed the dirt recess underneath the boardwalk for coins that inevitably fell through the slats, paced the dark earthy corridor, dimly lit by thin ribs of sunshine which filtered down along with the sounds of footsteps and voices, their eyes as sharp as hawks for flashes in the dirt. Three nickels, a dime, and a penny. They went back to the dimestore, bought twenty-six cents' worth of chocolate stars, and consumed them, one by one, on the curb, with their feet in the gutter, chins on their knees, eyes peering upward at the passing parade.

"This is like looking out of a crib," said Sharon.

"Rully."

"There's that retarded guy."

"Mongo-brain."

"They all look like brothers and sisters," said Sharon.

"I wonder if they know they're retarded, or if they're too retarded to know."

A third-grader rode past on a dirt bike, sneering *"Cur*ly girl" at Rosie.

"Oh, smell off," she shouted at him, stung almost to the point of tears, the hot blood rushing to her face.

"That guy's a *to*tal dog dick," said Sharon.

They giggled hysterically for a moment.

"Look, Rosie! There's a nun!"

"She's coming right at us."

"Yoiks!"

"Raaaaaaid!"

They got up and tore, giggling, to the beach. They pried starfish off the wet boulders, threw them into the surf, caught and freed a dozen black-red crabs, skipped flat stones across the water.

"I'm starving to death," said Rosie.

"Me too," said Sharon.

Let's go to your house and raid the refrigerator, let's go to your house and raid the cupboards, let's go play with your mother, your trolls—

"Wull, we can't go to my house because my mother isn't there," Rosie lied.

"We can't go to my house either. My dad's working there alone."

"So who said I wanted to, stupid?" Rats. "You want to go to the lagoon fort?"

"Yeah, I guess."

"We can think of ways to get money."

They left the beach, cut through the railroad yard, and headed for the lagoon where, months ago, they had found a hollow in the dense brush near the shore on a deserted lot. They had borrowed planks, nails, bricks, and cardboard boxes from the construction site on an adjacent lot and made a fort with wooden and brick benches into which they occasionally pounded a nail, using a rock as a hammer. Rosie sat on a canvas bag of cement mix which they planned to use to cover the wooden frame of the fort once they got around to constructing the wooden frame, after which they would begin work on the moat and the drawbridge.

They had had to abandon the lagoon fort for a month recently. A big carp had washed up on shore, which they determined by mysterious means to be a boy. They christened him Fred and buried him in a shallow grave right outside the entrance to the clearing. Fred was their mascot. Within two days the fort was unapproachable, the stench having beckoned flies from miles around to a luau of decomposing carp.

It was good to be back. When they got bored sitting in the fort—which is to say, when they found themselves in the fort without candy—they went to watch the carpenters hammer and measure and pour concrete.

"How we gonna get some money?" Sharon asked, sitting on a bench made of a plank and two bricks.

"Let me think."

Half an hour later the girls were standing outside Safeway, sorrowfully explaining to adult passersby that they were collecting money because their puppy needed an operation for leukemia, and their parents were going to put it to sleep if they didn't come up with the money soon. The puppy's name, Rosie sadly confided to each grown-up, was Little Maggie.

Within ten minutes they had enough money to buy two bottles of Coke and two small bags of ruffled dip chips. They opened the twist-off caps and tore the foil bags with their teeth, which served them in as many ways as Swiss Army knives: scissors, bottle openers, pliers.

"Hi, Mama."

"Hi, baby."

"What's for dinner?"

"Macaroni and cheese."

"Oh, thrills."

"Rae's coming over in a few minutes."

"Good!"

"Miss Lacey called again."

Rosie looked off into space and bit her lip.

"Any idea what she might have called about?"

Rosie closed one eye, thought hard, shrugged.

"None at all?"

Rosie pushed back in her chair so that it was on a two-legged diagonal.

"Straighten up."

Rosie slowly lowered the front legs to the ground. "Was it about Andrea Kinkaid?"

"No. Why? What did you do to Andrea Kinkaid?"

"Nothing. She's just a total crybaby."

Elizabeth looked exasperated.

"Miss Lacey called about the falling star you took to Show-and-Tell." Rosie nodded glumly. "And the dead man in our garden." Nod, nod. "Is this ringing a bell?" Nod, nod, eyes averted. "Care to comment?"

"Well, I had to bring *some*thing."

"But you didn't have to lie."

Rosie looked bored.

"See how stupid you feel when you get caught? That's one good reason not to lie. And for another thing, if you tell the truth, you don't have to keep track of what you said. It gives you a lot more freedom. And for another thing, it doesn't reflect well on me—"

"Wull, *you* lie."

"Like when?"

"Like when you tell someone on the phone you have to hang up because there's something on the stove when THERE ISN'T ANYTHING ON THE STOVE AT ALL." Rosie, fierce, continued. "Or you tell some guy you can't go out with him because you already have plans, and then we just hang out here all night reading."

"Good. Good point."

"I mean," said Rosie, "what sort of example do you think that sets for me?"

Oh, Rosie. You're becoming a scapegoater, like me. "See, sometimes I think it's all right to lie if the truth would hurt someone's feelings about something that they've already done—like if someone gets a terrible haircut, or an expensive and ugly dress. Or, say, if some perfectly nice man wants to be with me and I'm not interested, I think it's better to lie to save *his* face, instead of saying, 'I don't want to hang out with you because you're so fucking boring it sets my teeth on edge!' But! When you lie to make yourself look more impressive, or you have betrayed someone's trust or broken a promise, or if someone else is going to have to take the blame for something *you* did—"

"But, but—"

"Let me finish. I know you didn't hurt anyone by lying to the class, but maybe they won't believe you next time, when you're telling the truth. And *I* know you lied because you wanted your life to seem more exciting than theirs. . . ."

"Noooo. I did it 'cause people bring the stupidest, most boringest stuff, and you have to listen to them for about an *hour* talk about some stupid *acorn* or something, or some stupid *sea gull* feathers."

Elizabeth smiled. "Yeah, I know, I know how you feel, but there's funny stuff in your room you could take—that fake blood Rae gave you, or—"

"I brought that in two *weeks* ago."

Elizabeth exhaled, looked intently at her daughter. "Look, I really just want you to tell the truth—I want *me* to tell the truth—as much as possible."

"Okay."

"Rosie?"

"Ah-yeh?"

"Did the star kill Gordon?"

"Yep."

"Don't you like him?"

"Not very much. He thinks he's so big. Do *you*?"

"Sometimes. Sometimes I like him all right."

"Mama, but you know what? Sometimes when you tell Rae a

story about something we did, it didn't really *happen* that way. I mean, it mostly did, but when you tell the story, there's all this extra stuff."

"Yeah. You got me. It's called embellishment, it's sprucing up a story to make it more interesting, or funny, or vivid." Embellishment is the story of my life, embellishment and revising, like I never tell anyone that my first love left me for someone less moody, I tell them we just grew tired of each other. And that *I* initiated the breakup.

When Elizabeth turned her eyes and attention back to Rosie, Rosie smiled her rougish, lopsided, knowing smile.

"Deal? We try not to lie? And we always keep our promises?"

"Deal."

Elizabeth was drinking considerably less while Rosie was awake. Three or four glasses of wine, at most. Later, with Rosie asleep, two or three glasses more. That evening she waited for her first glass until Rae swept through the house, unexpectedly cheerful, Margaret Rutherford in *Blithe Spirit* again. Elizabeth attributed it to their phone conversation earlier in the day and felt herself glow within.

"Hey, baby," she said to Rae.

"Hey, Mama."

Okay. You become more like me, proud; I'll become more like you, great-hearted, jolly and honest.

Rae taught Rosie to make macaroni and cheese, while Elizabeth prepared a salad with herbs she had grown herself.

"Now *every*thing's ready to assemble," said Rae, in her singsong Julia Child voice, "so we'll just butter up the casserole dish before adding the noodles—now, we *never* use Saffola, it has to be butter. Saffola sticks to the bottom of pans, so *think* what it would do in your stomach."

Rosie giggled.

"Now, pour in those noodles—there you go—and stir in the cheese and cream, till it's *all* nestly and nice, and we'll pop it into the oven."

Elizabeth watched them work and watched herself make salad,

tall, thin, and regal. She was vaguely jealous of Rosie and Rae, who had been in love since the day they'd met. They were so alike in many ways. Hypersensitive and somewhat waifish: 99th percentile in the Walter Harrington Factor—he had been the four-eyed genius in Elizabeth's elementary school classes who wore mismatched shoes (sometimes on the wrong feet) and returned from the boys' bathroom with toilet-paper streamers hanging from his pants: a comical, earnest space puppy.

Rosie and Rae were both prone to long verbal bouts of free-floating anxiety looking for a place to roost, while Elizabeth kept the bulk of her anxieties to herself. When Rosie and Rae were anxious, they were wired and teary, whereas Elizabeth did her Mount Rushmore pose. Rosie and Rae expressed their bouts with the clammy blind-dreads, which, coupled with their day-dreaming and accident proneness, made them worry about things like being somehow *drawn* to walk into oncoming traffic, or into climbing out the window of a skyscraper. Rae worried that a stranger might rush up to her on the street and poke a fork into her eyes; Rosie that, holding a fork, she might absentmindedly poke it through her hand. And they both believed in God.

"How's Hanuman?"

"The pride of Cucamonga? Back to being a cork on the river."

"Yeah?"

"Yep. This morning, before I talked to you, I was sitting in the sun, all bummed and woozy, and she comes home from a walk and asks what's wrong, and I said, 'I'm obsessively and morbidly in love with an asshole,' and she says, and I quote, 'The description is never the described.' "

" 'The description is never the described'?"

"Yes. And then she walked away muttering, 'Sri ram jai ram.' "

"Let's eat."

"Why don't you move?" asked Rosie.

"Because I'm poor. And I'm sort of fond of her. Every so often she makes sense. She turned me on to Ram Dass, who's good. And she'll make good copy in my biography."

Elizabeth lit the candles on the living room table.

"Mama? Can we say grace?"

"*I* can't say grace. Maybe Rae can."

Rae did.

> "Brahman is the ritual,
> Brahman is the offering,
> Brahman is she who offers
> To the fire that is Brahman.
> If a person sees Brahman
> In every action
> She will find Brahman. Amen."

"Amen," said Rosie. "What's Brahman?"

"God."

"Red or white, Rae?"

"Red. No, wait: white. No, wait: red."

Elizabeth poured her a glass of red wine and one for herself. Rosie blew bubbles into her milk.

"Knock it off, honey."

"Yes, Miss Mother."

"Oh, my God, this is wonderful; Rosie, we've done it again."

They ate in silence for a minute, perfectly happy.

"Rae? How come you have such crinkly-crunkly hair?"

"Because my mother did."

"Did your mother have proton nobulators?"

"Did she have what?"

"Those pinches at the end of your nose?"

"Yes."

"What did your father have?"

"He was fat."

"Did he have——?"

"Rosie, *chew*. You're wolfing down your food."

"I'm starving to death."

"You know how Hanuman eats? Ancient Hindu method. I think she got it from Ram Dass, where everything becomes an instrument of enlightenment if you focus your mind on it. So, eating, she's going 'Cutting cutting, lifting lifting, chewing chewing, tasting tasting. . . .'"

"Starving starving," said Elizabeth.

"Guess what, Elizabeth?"

"What?"

"You know how you kept saying I ought to be making more big weavings, try to con some gallery into showing them?"

"Yeah?"

"Well, I've been doing them, at night. And today I called this guy in San Francisco who has a gallery, and I made an appointment to show my stuff to him next Saturday."

"You did? Well, goddammit! Good for you, Rae."

"I wouldn't have had the courage if you hadn't been kicking me in the ass."

"Sure, you would." Elizabeth reached for her wine. She had swallowed a golf ball. It was unraveling in her stomach: jealous, wormy rubber bands.

Rae was smiling down into her food, pleased and embarrassed.

"Gee, Rae! That's great."

"Thanks. They probably won't take any of them—"

"Oh, shut up. Everything I've seen of yours is gorgeous."

"Oh, Elizabeth. I think the guy was just patronizing me, because I'm fat."

"How would he know you were fat over the phone?" asked Rosie.

"I think I told him."

"Oh, Rae, for God's sake, what did you say? 'Hello, my name is Rae and I'm extremely fat so will you please take a look at my weavings?' "

"You think I'm *extremely* fat?"

"No." The golf ball had gone away. Elizabeth pulled at her nose. "I'd like to propose a toast." The three of them lifted their glasses. "To your success." They clinked their drinks together. "They're very, very good, Rae." Elizabeth *wanted* to want Rae to succeed, but part of her was miserable.

"Are you just saying that?"

"Now you're fishing."

"No, I'm not. I just need reassurance."

"They're so good—you're so good at what you do—that I'm jealous."

"Really?"

Elizabeth nodded, smiled.

Rae beamed. "Oh, thanks."

And the weavings *were* beautiful: portraits in varying textures of wool, pictures of northern California's land and ocean and mountains and sky, sun, moon, stars, birds; deep green trees, light blues, china blues, rich blues, indigos, suspiciously religious-looking white lights and sunshine, and train tracks, clouds, and boats.

"You know what I'd like to do one of these days, Elizabeth?"

"What's that. Want some more wine?" Rae shook her head. Elizabeth poured herself half a glass.

"I'd like to take you backpacking. I know this spectacular *easy* hike from Pretty Boy Trailhead. . . . Why not?"

"I'd hate it. I'm positive."

"I'll take my chances. *I'm* positive you'd love it."

"Forget it."

"Take me! Take me!" Rosie begged.

"No, no. Next year, maybe, when you're bigger."

"Can Sharon come?"

"Sure."

"I should go call her and—"

"Rosie, sit down. You can tell her tomorrow."

"But she's going to start having to work on her dad."

"A year in advance? Sit down. Finish your dinner."

"Tsssssst."

"What's he like?" Rae asked, eager to break the momentary tension.

Rosie shrugged. "He's all right, I guess."

"Is he funny?"

"No."

Elizabeth was out of it, wrestling with her bad conscience, with one train of thought that was scared to death the gallery would take Rae's work, show it, make her famous. If the tables were turned, Rae would be pulling for her. And if they were Rosie's weavings, Rae and Elizabeth would be pulling so hard that . . .

"Rae? Do you want us to go to the gallery with you Saturday? For moral support?"

"Oh, *yeah*. But not into the gallery, I want to go there alone. In case they say no. But with me to the city that day, that would be great."

What an act of courage for Rae to have made the appointment. Elizabeth smiled, forced herself to breathe.

"Mama?"

"Yeah?"

"Why don't you learn to weave."

"I don't particularly want to."

"What *do* you want to do?" asked Rae.

Elizabeth shrugged.

"Don't you get bored? Weren't you thinking of trying to write?"

"Yeah. For about three hours, one day. The day we met, in fact."

"Then what happened?"

"I don't know. I wrote three great paragraphs. Then? It's like that old joke about Billy Rose: This man comes up to him, says he can dive head first from a ladder three stories up into a small tub of water. Billy Rose doesn't believe him, so the guy sets it all up, does it—dives head first into a tub of water from three stories up. Billy Rose offers him a hundred a week to join the show; the guy refuses. Billy Rose offers him two hundred, then three hundred; the man says he's not interested. 'How come?' asks Billy Rose. 'It was the first time I did it, and I didn't like it at all.' "

Rae smiled, but sadly. "So what would you most like to do?"

Elizabeth held her palms upward and shrugged. "Something. With books or movies. Something hard and entertaining."

She stared off at the measuring wall, where Rosie's height had been recorded in pencil and pens—red, green, blue—since she was three years old and thirty inches high. All those instants in between had passed as quickly as vertically lined-up dominoes falling in a ripple, passing like the earth revolved and rotated, where you couldn't see it happen but knew via changes, night and day and seasons, that it had. Something hard and entertaining—that would fall into her lap.

"Don't worry," she said. "I'll think of something soon. Maybe

I could—no—I don't know." She lifted her shoulders, let them drop, smiling at Rosie and Rae.

"Do we have dessert, Mama?"

"Yeah. I got a pineapple."

"Rae! We got a pineapple!"

Rae raised her hands to her ears and opened her eyes and mouth wide, as if she had just won *big* on a game show. Rosie smiled. Rae took a pack of cigarettes out of her pants pocket, shook one out, and lit it. Rosie held her nose, glaring.

"I've got to go home fairly soon. I'll help with the dishes."

"How come?"

"Well." Rae got a look on her face that suggested shuffling and said, "I could lie and say I'm exhausted. I could start yawning like mad—"

"We're on a new truth kick around here," said Rosie.

"But if I tell the truth, Elizabeth will get all weird and hostile."

"Tell the truth," said Rosie.

"Brian's coming over to talk."

Elizabeth got all weird and hostile: shook her head, refused to comment.

"See? I told you so."

Elizabeth looked at her with disgust. "I thought you were going to ditch him."

"I am. But I'm going to talk to him first."

"Talk! Hah. Rae, in deference to your modesty and duplicity, I—"

"It's *my* life."

"Brian's going to be one of the grisliest chapters in your biography."

"Stay with us, Rae," said Rosie. "We *love* you."

"Rae?"

"Yeah?"

"What is it going to take for you to get free of this man?"

The two women looked into each other's eyes. "Death," Rae said firmly, inhaling. "Or someone new."

Chapter
5

Saturday, Elizabeth came to with an evil-tasting, mooing groan. Eyes opened a fraction of an inch, she lay feeling like the man in *Johnny Got His Gun* until her mind cleared enough to register pain. She covered her forehead with a shaking hand, with no idea and only a vague curiosity as to whom she might have been sleeping with. Taking a deep breath, she turned her head to the center of the mattress: she was alone.

Oh, Elizabeth. Goddamn you. Don't *drive*, at least. Drink yourself to death if you can't help it, but don't drive. Bile, hate, and fear ran through her bloodstream. Rosie was knocking on her door.

"Come in."

"Hi, Mama." Rosie had brought her a tall glass of orange juice. "You hung over?" Rosie walked to her, set the glass on the night table.

"No." I'm living on past lives.

"Insomnia?"

Elizabeth nodded, heard and felt several small bones snap in her neck, and knew that Rosie could smell the sour wine wafting up from her stomach.

"What time are we going to the city?"

"Rae's going to pick us up around noon."

"Mrs. Thackery said it would be fine if Sharon came. So is it okay with you?"

"It's okay with me. Call Rae, though, and ask."

"Okay. I'll be back in about an hour."

"Thanks for the juice."

Rosie and Sharon walked into town to buy M&M's with their allowances, then walked to their newest fort, the basement of the old Murphy house, which had gone unsold since the midnight a year ago when Mrs. Murphy passed out smoking in bed. No one had locked the door to the now empty basement, a low dark room that was dank and dusty at the same time; the floor was dirt and the rafters were filled with cobwebs and spiders.

They ate their M&M's one at a time, savoring them, sucking through the thin sugar crust into the melting chocolate, proclaiming the red ones the best, the green ones a close second, the orange ones almost inedible. When the candies were gone, they spent a few minutes turning their eyelids inside out. And then they took turns helping each other pass out.

Long ago they had discovered the wonders of dizziness, the altered state that could be achieved by winding up a rope swing tightly and unspinning at a wild, exhilarating pace, the pleasure of giddy confusion, of staggering around drunkenly until their heads cleared. But passing out for the weirdness of the coming-to was much more scary and fun.

As usual, Rosie went first. She hyperventilated until she was woozy, then nodded to Sharon and lifted her arms so that Sharon could give her one hard, quick squeeze in the stomach from behind. Rosie crumpled onto the soft dirt, out for seconds, then began spinning back to earth through a long tunnel of whirling colors—feather-headed, intoxicated, out of her mind, blissfully confused. As she opened her eyes, a vision of Sharon swam before her, but gradually the distortion slowed down, like the end of a carousel ride. Sharon's image was clear as a bell, and Rosie was smiling drunkenly.

Sharon set her broad jaw into a grimace and began the staccato breathing, scared to death; she nodded, was squeezed, and passed out, began the long swim through the tunnel back to earth, high as a kite. Rosie panicked each time Sharon crumpled to the ground—no sign of life, she was dead, she was dead—and hardly breathed until Sharon opened her unfocusing eyes with a faraway smile.

The third-grader who had taught them how to do this had told them that each time you did it, billions of brain cells were killed, but they did it over and over again anyway.

Three aspirin, a shower, more juice, coffee, vitamins, toast, and sunshine eased Elizabeth's pain. It was a clear blue day and she listened, on the porch swing with the *Chronicle,* to the din of birdsong, towhees and swallows, the uproar of crickets, an occasional car, a faraway siren. White butterflies flew past, and a hummingbird, blue as the eyes on a peacock's feathers, zipped onto the porch, hung suspended, vibrating, not far from her, and then dipped away to a scarlet bud of ginger root, from which it drank, iridescent blue against the red. When it flew away, she opened the newspaper.

I swear I am pulling for Rae's success, I swear I'll be happy if her weavings get hung, really and truly I want her to win. But whenever she thought about Rae's career soaring, she swallowed the golf ball and felt it unravel.

She looked up from the news at her old white Chevy, parked outside the gate; she had apparently driven herself home: golf ball. Goddammit, don't drive. Stay home and drink. It's perfectly legal and logical to have a craving to pour a highly flammable liquid depressant onto the tender pink tissue of your mouth and stomach, no one can stop you from permanently dulling your blade, and it's one way to get through the night. But *please* don't drive, don't risk killing someone with your car; think of Rosie. Okay?

The Pentagon had plans for a missile system that circled the earth. Russia was definitely not working out well. A test-tube baby was thriving. *Brave New World.* Israel was another thing that was not working out well. The boys knee-deep in kerosene. . . .

Okay, here's my plan.

Elizabeth went inside, filled with paranoia and lethargy, and commanded herself to pull for Rae's success. She straightened up the house with opera blaring from the stereo: *Traviata.* Disgusted with herself, she watched herself go through the motions, as if observing an actor playing Elizabeth Ferguson, saw herself as Anouk Aimée playing the lead in *Days of Wine and Roses,* although a kinder viewer might have seen Gena Rowlands' dazed, simple performance in *A Woman Under the Influence.* She cleaned the black hairs from the brushes in the upstairs bathroom and took them down to the kitchen, where she set a pan of soapy water to boil on the stove. She was stirring the brushes with a wooden spoon when Rosie and Sharon burst through the door.

"Hi, Mama!"

"Hi, sweetheart. Hi, Sharon."

"Hi, Elizabeth. Thank you very much for letting me come."

"I'm glad you're coming. Did you check with Rae, Rosie?"

Rosie nodded. "Is it almost time to go?" She walked to the stove and peered into the pot her mother was stirring. "That looks good."

Elizabeth smiled. "Get yourselves some bowls. Rae'll be over in an hour."

They helped themselves to some bread, peanut butter, and raspberry jam instead. Smiling, Elizabeth watched them eat. Everything was going to be all right. The girls had energized the room, made it alive. Sharon looked up and found Elizabeth studying her.

"What," she said.

Elizabeth winked, no longer tired of life.

Rae pulled up outside the house at noon and honked. The girls tore out the door, while Elizabeth went through the house making sure that she had turned off the oven and iron. I swear I'm pulling for you, Rae, I swear I'm hoping for the best. When she stepped out and waved to Rae, behind the wheel of the greenest hatchback imaginable, she took a long deep breath.

Rae and Elizabeth kissed in the car. Elizabeth gave her the thumbs up sign and Rae drove off, babbling cheerfully, while Elizabeth began to worry, no longer positive that she had turned off the iron, that . . . that . . . stop it!

The paneling inside was the same traffic-light green as the exterior, and Elizabeth had the sense that she was wearing an enormous sun visor. She extricated the seatbelt handle, crossed it over her chest, plugged it into the lock. She moved her chest forward against the belt rapidly, testing to make sure it worked. It didn't, and she settled back, with her long legs bent to fit into the passenger seat, feeling as though she were sitting in a baby's swing.

"This is a truly green car," she told Rae.

"Isn't it?"

"It's like we're in a flying saucer. All this green paneling. . . ."

"I always feel that this car is attracting extraterrestrial attention."

"Thank you for letting me come," said Sharon.

"Letting you? I am honored by your presence."

"Did you remember the weavings?" asked Rosie.

"You think I'm retarded, don't you?" Rosie smiled at Rae's face in the rearview mirror. "God, I'm climbing the walls, Elizabeth. What if they don't like them?"

"They will." I swear I am pulling that they will. "And if they don't, we'll just keep trying."

"I'm going to die if they don't."

"Nooooooo," Rosie wailed.

"You guys want to hear Bing and Louis?"

"Yeah." Rae pushed a cassette into the tape deck, and they drove along listening to "Muskrat Ramble," "Sugar." Rosie did her woolly, growly Louis Armstrong imitation.

"If they don't take the weavings," said Elizabeth, "which they will—"

"Hey, hey, hey, I'll be all right. I'm like a cat, you know, I always land on my feet."

Elizabeth smiled at her. It was one of the things Rae liked to say about herself, and to some extent it was true, but Rae stumbled and tripped more than anyone else Elizabeth had ever known. Once, as they walked to the beach, Rae had waved to a passing car and lost her balance and had actually fallen over.

Another thing Rae liked to say about herself was that her mind was like a steel trap, but it was more like a damp paper bag in functional ways. She was so forgetful, so spaced out, that Elizabeth sometimes wanted to ask if it wasn't rather dangerous for her to carry money in her purse—or to carry a purse at all, for that matter. Oh, Rae, thought Elizabeth fondly, turning to look at her best friend, whose knuckles were white on the wheel.

"Lambs!" said Sharon, pointing to a meadow off to the left.

"Oh, *God.* They're so cute," said Rosie, craning for a better view.

"We forgot the mint *jelly,*" said Elizabeth, smiting her forehead.

Rae smiled.

"Mama!"

The girls found a wadded up section of the *Chronicle,* unfolded it, and began to read together, leaving the women to talk. "Way Down Yonder in New Orleans" was playing, and Elizabeth, feeling like an old lizard basking in the sun, reached over and tweaked Rae's cheek.

"Don't be nervous."

"Oh. Okay."

"Your weavings are beautiful. I keep telling you they make me totally jealous."

"Really?"

"Yeah."

"Mama?"

"Yeah?"

"What does well-appointed mean?"

"Read me the sentence."

"His ex, who starred with him in a dozen movies, added, 'Physically, he was not well-appointed.' "

"It means he had a small penis." The two women laughed.

"It means he has a tiny little popo," said Rae.

"It does?"

Elizabeth nodded.

The girls threw themselves against the back of the car seat as if recoiling from bullets. They blushed, giggled, whispered.

"Remember that time Brian and I—"

"I'll give you a buck if we don't have to talk about Brian."

"Okay. You can pay the bridge fare."

"That's two bucks. So you can't talk about him on the way home, either."

Rae didn't say anything.

There were sudden, loud gasps from the back seat as Rae drove through the Waldo Tunnel. The girls held their breaths all the way to the other end, exhaled, gasped, and turned to look back at the rainbow painted above the tunnel's arc.

"Mama?"

"What."

"Are we gonna go with Rae to the gallery?"

"No!" shouted Rae. "I have to go alone, in case they turn me down."

The city glistened white under the blue sky, sitting with decorum on hills behind the bay, behind freighters and barges at the piers, and ketches, sloops, tugboats, ferries on the scintillant water, on the choppy blue waters of San Francisco Bay.

"I love San Francisco," said Rae in her mournful voice.

"It's like Oz," said Rosie, "but white."

Crossing the terra-cotta bridge, the girls half hoping to see someone jump off, they stared at lonely Alcatraz, shuddering, then, to the right, at a schooner outside the Gate on the ocean, the Pacific Ocean.

"I've got such bad butterflies," said Rae.

"Relax." Elizabeth reached for her great old leather purse, extracted two dollars from her wallet, handed it to Rae. "So, you're sure you don't want us to go to the gallery with you?"

"Noooooooo," said Rae, and looked about to cry.

"What're we gonna do, Mama?"

"We'll walk around, look into store windows."

"We gonna eat?"

"We'll wait for Rae."

"Are we gonna buy anything?"

"I can't think of anything we need."

"Oh, my God, we need a *million* things."

"Such as?"

"We need a television set."

"No."

"Please? You *said* you needed a swimsuit."

Elizabeth shook her head.

"Chhhhhhh."

A minute later, Rae missed the Lombard exit.

"Rae? You missed the exit."

"We'll go on Bay. I know a shortcut."

"This should be good," said Rosie.

Elizabeth smiled. They passed the Palace of Fine Arts, its pond filled with ducks; drove along the beautiful green marina: kites, joggers, boats.

"Trust me. I know this city like the back of my hand."

"Every single time you say that, we have to stop at a gas station at least once, usually twice, or we end up so far away from where we want to go that when we ask people directions, they don't speak English or they've never heard of where we're going."

Rae, with her big brown eyes fixed on the road, said grimly, "Trust me."

Her shortcut involved a detour through North Beach, fifteen minutes of neon sleaziness that the girls stared at in wondering disgust. Rae drove past Stockton.

"That was Stockton!" said Elizabeth. "That's the street we wanted."

In a few minutes Rae had driven them into the financial district. The girls ogled at the Transamerica Pyramid; Rae said, "Oops." Elizabeth gritted her teeth but didn't say a thing, just stared out the window on her right.

"Don't worry." Rae turned on Washington, drove to Kearny, to Portsmouth Square, and then turned left into a one-way street (going the wrong way, of course) and hastily backed away from the oncoming cars. Elizabeth felt rage welling up inside her.

"Shit. Okay." Rae turned left onto Clay and drove down to Montgomery again.

"We're back in the goddamn financial district!" Elizabeth said.

The girls were hushed. If Elizabeth's mood went, the day would be shot.

"Shut up, Elizabeth, don't say another word."

Elizabeth glowered.

Rae turned right on Montgomery, right again on Sacramento, past Kearny to Grant, where she had to turn right, because it was one-way.

"Fucking goddamn A, Rae! We're in Chinatown!" Elizabeth folded her arms across her chest, hardly blinking, clenching her teeth.

Rae turned right on Grant, and Elizabeth knew that they were headed back to the wired congestion of North Beach, but by this time she was not speaking to Rae; the rage had rushed past her stomach, up her spine, and it took all her concentration not to start pounding the dashboard or the windows.

Rae turned right on Columbus, Elizabeth now vibrating with anger, as Rae drove them back down to the financial district.

It is *No Exit*. Elizabeth could not believe it when, after a right on Washington, they were back at Portsmouth Square.

"This is like Pac-Man," said Rosie, in awe.

Sharon was hardly breathing.

Rae's eyes were filling with tears.

"Rae," Elizabeth said, as gently as possible. "You want to cross Kearny, then Grant, and then, when we get to Stockton, turn left. Okay?"

Rae nodded, teary and miserable.

"Shit," said Elizabeth, looking away, then back to her friend, whose day it was to have been. "Tssss," she said, sideways out of her mouth, smiling. "Some great shortcut."

Rae followed Elizabeth's instructions, wiping at her eyes. Five minutes later they were at their destination, the Union Square garage.

Please pull for Rae's success, please in your heart wish her well. But as they cruised looking for a parking space on the third, fourth, and fifth levels of the garage, Elizabeth swallowed another golf ball. And then Rae found a space, which she pulled into, one of many available on Level Five, with a big Cadillac on her side and a column five inches away from Elizabeth.

Rae heaved a sigh of relief, looked at Elizabeth, and got out of the car. Elizabeth stared dully at the column. The girls scrambled out on Rae's side, then looked in at Elizabeth, as did Rae. Elizabeth turned to them and asked wearily, *"Why* did you park so close to the column? I'm stuck."

"Can't you climb over the stick shift? Sorry about that. Oh, God, I'm such an idiot. It's just that I'm so *nervous!*" She went to the back of the car.

Elizabeth felt very, very tired. She continued to look at the column and then, forcing herself, for all their sakes, to be a good sport, she finally climbed, cramped and awkward, over the stick shift, into Rae's seat, and then out the door.

The girls, holding hands, looked about ready to jump up and down. Rae, clutching her portfolio, looked orphaned and hunted.

After numerous pats and kisses, Rae headed toward the gallery on Post. The girls skipped alongside Elizabeth, pausing to find openings in the human traffic, gaping at the fattest women, the tiniest men, the drunks, hoods, punks, dudes, whores, and glamorous women. People turned to admire Elizabeth, tall, striking, regal, haughty—even famous, maybe.

Rosie and Sharon each bought a pencil from the legless pencil man who sat on a dolly in front of Macy's, the same man, or so it seemed, from whom Elizabeth had bought countless pencils twenty-five and more years ago, when her shiny black hair was in braids, a girl as skinny as Rosie but taller, in white gloves and camel's hair coat, headed for patty melts at Blum's, or the City of Paris Christmas tree, or the dentist at the 450 Sutter Building. It was coming back as they walked down Stockton, triggered by sounds and smells, voices, cable cars, sweat, perfume, sweets, cigars, sirens, gasoline, car horns, an accordion. When the girls were lost in the moving crowd for a moment, Elizabeth's heart stopped. There they were, seemingly oblivious to her, tiny but growing so fast. She remembered the harsh and distressed way her mother rubbed at her face with a lipstick-streaked Kleenex smelling of Chanel, remembered how she hated being swabbed off with her mother's spit; how delighted, sentimental, and scared of the cable cars her mother was, mushy even, and panicked that Elizabeth would be crushed by one of them. "Rosie! Stay closer." And the way her mother approached the escalators, as if she were leading Elizabeth through fire on a tightrope, stepping past the crack and the first step onto the second step as carefully as stepping over dog do because if your foot touched the crack, the escalator would suck you down, take you around on its treadmill until it spat you out, flat as a pancake with long vertical grooves running the length of your body, flat as a character in a cartoon who's been run over by a steamroller.

"Mama, let's go in a store. Okay?"

Macy's. The dreaded escalator. The girls, well-behaved, quiet, taking in the wealth, the blacks, the shimmers, hysterical on seeing girdles and bras. Elizabeth laughed at their silliness, and at a memory of her mother, tall and stout, grimly wrestling her way into a girdle, sucking in her breath as she pulled and tugged the formidable elastic encasement over each successive dune of fat on her thighs, hips, butt, and belly, until the girdle finally swallowed the highest roll at her waist and gave up with a *whoomph* of resignation, like a sea bass taking its last breath on a boat after one hell of a fight.

"Can I help you find something?" The smell of the girdle, the smell of her mother's lap when Elizabeth pressed her face against it.

"*Ma*ma. Can she help you?"

"No. No, thank you."

"Earth calling Elizabeth, come in, please."

Elizabeth smiled. Sharon was embarrassed, shy, her pencil jammed up behind her top lip.

"I know what you wanted, Mama."

"What."

"A swim suit."

"I don't want to buy it today."

"How come? They're right over there."

"I don't know, Rosie, I'm feeling fat these days; I need to exercise for a while before I wear a suit."

"How come?"

"My legs—my thighs, anyway—look like shit."

"What?"

"I don't want to buy a suit today, is all,"

The Look came across Rosie's face, blue eyes flashing fire, hands on hips, revving her head in stiff circles of scornful, indignant sarcasm. Oh, no, thought Elizabeth, why is she doing this to me now, here?

"Listen, listen," she said.

"Don't you listen *me,*" said her daughter. People were turning to stare at this little girl, as tall as the rack of clothes she stood by, people were giving Elizabeth what she always thought of as the "Don't you feed her?" look.

"Rosie, I'm warning you. . . ."

Rosie was sneering at her. Sharon had gone into the trance where she looked like Gilda Radner doing a young Christina Crawford, wide eyes not focused, tremors of burnt-out anxiety. . . .

Oh, dear God, now Rosie has raised her eyebrows as far as they will go, while keeping her lids shut and her mouth puckered as if, a split second away from whistling, she has bitten down on a lemon; she learned the look from Mrs. Haas. What on earth is going on?

"I'm going to kill you, Rosie," Elizabeth whispered.

Rosie felt the many eyes upon her. She wanted her mother to buy a suit, badly. She wanted her to *buy something,* she wanted Elizabeth to shell out some money. She shook her pencil at her angry mother and said, loud and clear, "Wull, why don't you ask the pencil man how *his* legs look?"

Elizabeth could not believe this was going on. Hot blood rushed to her face and she saw red.

"Let's go," she said.

"Oh, no. Unh-unh. Why can't you just be happy that you don't have BLOODY STUMPS FOR LEGS?"

"What the *hell* has gotten into you? Come on, Sharon."

Sharon was frozen. Elizabeth took her hand and began

to steer her toward the Stockton Street exit.

"You coming, Rosie?"

Rosie shook her head. Elizabeth led Sharon away. Sharon looked back, wide-eyed, over her shoulder at her transformed friend, who had now begun to tap her foot with impatience, holding her ground. . . .

Five minutes later Rosie dashed past unfamiliar coats and legs, in a curving path between clothes racks and shoppers and cashier's booths, surrounded by a sea of strangers and alien smells: synthetics, perfumes, waists she didn't recognize, "Herman" characters everywhere she looked. Her heart was pounding in her throat, her mind raced faster than her legs; she'd never see her mother again, would be adopted by sinister freaks. . . .

And then, after what felt like forever in a bad dream, she saw her mother and Sharon standing with their backs against the wall by the exit, smiling at her. Sharon waved. Elizabeth shook her head.

"What the hell was that all about?"

"I just wanted you to buy a suit."

"Why? Why did it matter so much?"

Rosie shrugged, embarrassed and defiant. Elizabeth did not understand.

Outside in the fresh air, they heaved a collective sigh of relief. Stockton Street was crawling with tourists and natives. Rae had told them to meet her in forty-five minutes in Union Square.

"You guys want an ice-cream cone?"

"Yeah!"

"Yeah." So they headed down Stockton toward Market Street; all was right with the world again. The girls held hands, walked ahead of Elizabeth, whispering, and Elizabeth took in the busy sights and sounds and smells. Head held high, she observed the human traffic with some disdain; many people looked half destroyed by one thing or another. When elegant couples passed, arm in arm, pangs of isolation went through her stomach. As she and the girls stood waiting for the light to change at O'Farrell, behind a cowboy of perhaps thirty, crouched in the gutter waiting to push his Tonka firetruck across the street, pangs of identification went through her—the malignant prophecy. Matrons, businessmen, businesswomen, punks, tourists, hippies, bums, teenagers, blacks, whites, orientals, children, babies, hookers, gathered together at this intersection. . . . How was everyone hanging on so well?

Elizabeth took one of Rosie's hands, one of Sharon's hands, and they walked to an ice-cream shop. Carrying cones on their way back to Macy's, they stopped at a flower stand and Elizabeth bought win-or-lose tea roses for Rae.

"Mama, I have a good idea," Rosie whispered as they approached the pencil man. "Let's take the pencil man home and let him live in Daddy's old study! We could take *care* of him."

"Don't be silly."

"Pleeeze, Mama," she wheedled. "We could push him on his cart to Rae's car. . . ."

"Shhhhh!"

"Please, can we take him home?"

"Shhhhh. You make another scene and there's going to be trouble."

Rosie stopped and handed her cone to Sharon as if she were removing her gloves for a duel.

"Rosie?"

Rosie ignored the edge in her mother's voice, strode purposefully to the old brown man with the mashed-in eye who sat on the dolly. Oh, good Christ, thought Elizabeth, don't let her . . .

"Hello," said Rosie.

"Hello," said the pencil man.

"I just wanted to tell you how well I think your jacket fits."

He smiled, she smiled. That was all.

Rae was sniffling and teary when they met her. The gallery had taken her weavings.

Chapter
✿6

The early June sun shone on Elizabeth's red toenails as she sat on the porch swing reading *My Ántonia* for the second time, a cup of tea beside her. She had cleaned the house, worked in the garden for an hour, washed some sweaters, paid some bills. It had been a dreamy day, a day when she felt glad to be alone, glad to be the elegant, easygoing lady of leisure. She put her book down and went inside to call Rae, but no one answered and Elizabeth went back out to the porch, where she found Rae standing desolately on the doormat, staring into her chubby cupped hands as if they held something precious, and dying.

They looked at each other for a moment. Elizabeth craned her long neck forward and peeked into Rae's hands, which held nothing, and then straightened up to look at her.

"Hi," said Elizabeth. "I was just trying to reach you."

"Hi," said Rae, and jammed her hands into the front pockets of her faded Levi's. "I'm bummed."

"I gather."

"I'm not having a day of power."

"You gotta stop reading Castaneda."

"It's my only amusement."

"What's the matter?"

"Ohhhhh."

"Is it late enough for a drink?"

Rae shrugged.

"Well, let's. We're the adults here. And Gordon brought some brandy over last night."

"I just want to be with you."

"Well. You've come to the right place. How about a hot toddy?"

"I don't know."

Elizabeth led her into the kitchen and turned the flame on under the teakettle. "I'm going to have one," she said.

"Okay, then. Make me one too. I hate to see you drinking alone."

"What are you so depressed about?"

"Everything! I thought, 'If only a gallery would show my work, then I'd be happy.' Well, they sold three of the weavings they took that day, and"—she threw up her hands—"I'm still all fucked up over Brian. Don't be mad at me."

"I'm not mad at you."

"And now that someone wants my work, I'm clutching. I've got weaver's block. I'm sick of San Francisco Bay and the ocean, it's too easy to make the Bay or the Pacific look beautiful; I'm sick of being hung up on Brian. I'm in a rut."

Elizabeth poured two generous shots of brandy into clear glass mugs, cut two thin lemon cartwheels, and drizzled a teaspoon of honey into each cup.

"Ditch him."

She placed a mug in front of Rae, who stared at it listlessly, sighed, and pushed the lemon slice around the amber liquid.

"Rae? His behavior is bad. He is not a good man."

Rae groaned.

"I just don't think you have to hurt so much," Elizabeth said.

"I would kill, practically, to have him out of my mind, you know, out of my heart."

"Cut him off."

"See, Elizabeth, everything is very black and white to you.

Because you're a purist. But I'm a funkie. Purists have all these principles and pride, they're all very secretive and tidy about their garbage. Well, funkies are laxer, funkies are compost heaps."

"Funkies?" said Elizabeth. "Purists? Compost heaps? Do you really believe what you're saying?"

"Of course I do," Rae replied. "Otherwise I would be saying something else. Hey, I thought you were sticking to beer and wine!"

"Don't change the subject. Back to the problems at hand."

"Okay. Problem one: obsession with Brian, inability to say no when he calls, inability to summon pride, consequent feelings of insanity, a growing white emptiness in my chest, and a black consuming depression. Problem two: weaver's block, which right now feels like it's going to be permanent."

They sat in the kitchen, nursing their drinks.

"Okay," said Elizabeth. "Solution: Tell Brian it's over. Then get away, leave town. There is no problem so large it can't be run away from. Pack up your loom, your yarns, your whatever; get on a train, and go stay with someone in a new environment. Go stay with that friend in New Mexico, one thousand miles away. No Brian; new colors, new skies. New landscapes."

Rae put her cup down and looked at Elizabeth. "God. Maybe you're—I have some money from the weavings the gallery's sold, enough to pay Hanuman for a couple of month's rent. I can send potholders to the boutiques from . . . it's a brilliant idea. But wait . . . wait. I can't go."

"Why not?"

"I'll have a *break*down if I can't be near you and Rosie for two months."

"No, you won't."

"But what about *you?* How would you survive without *me?*"

"Well, I did before."

"I don't know."

Elizabeth toyed with a long strand of hair and took a sip of toddy.

"I know it's a good idea. Maybe I should just *do* it. No, wait—oh, shit, I don't know. I wanted to go backpacking at the end of June, but I could go next weekend—no, wait—okay. Wait a minute. I think it's the perfect solution. Would you really be okay without me?"

"Sure. I'd miss you. But we'd write."

"You wouldn't just sit around drinking, pining for my company?"

"No."

"Really? I worry about you, Elizabeth. Sometimes you drink too much."

"I don't think you should worry about it."

"I can't help it."

"Try."

After a moment, Rae said, "New Mexico's a great plan, now that I think of it. How come you're so good at solving everyone else's problems?"

"Everyone else! Everyone else is a list of about two."

"I *love* you, Elizabeth."

"I know."

"I'd give you one of anything I have two of—you ask for it, you've got it: a kidney, an arm. . . ." Elizabeth smiled. "Hey. Why don't you and *I* go backpacking next weekend?"

"Nooooo way."

"You'd love it. . . ."

"I'd hate it."

"But you've never done it, right?"

Elizabeth looked bored.

"Now, see? This is a classic example of the green-eggs-and-ham syndrome. Remember? You keep saying, 'I do not like them, Sam I Am, I do not like green eggs and ham,' but you've never tried them. And then, remember, at the end of the book, the little Dr. Seuss guy *does* like green eggs and ham, he says, 'I do, I *like* them, Sam I Am.' "

"Take a break. . . ."

" 'I *do,* I like green eggs and ham.' " Rae looked smug, palms outstretched. "Don't look at me like that."

"How old did you say you were again?"

"It's so goddamn beautiful there in those mountains," Rae went on. "It would make you believe in God, under the stars, with the river right beside us—owls, food, we'll take rum and—"

"No."

"See, Elizabeth? Your problem is that you never try anything new, you go around saying, 'No, no, no.' "

"Rae?"

"Will you at least think about it?"

"No. I don't want to go backpacking."

"God, you just say no to everything."

"I'm saying no to this."

Rae looked hurt. "Okay. Wait a minute then." She got up to leave the kitchen.

"You want another drink?"

"Yeah. I guess."

Elizabeth filled the teakettle again, set it on the stove to boil.

Rae returned with a paperback book from the living room, sat back down at the table, and reached into her pocket for her cigarettes. She took one out, lit the filter end, and extinguished the stinking flame of burning plastic and paper by dipping it into her drink, all very nonchalantly, as if it were a routine variation on smoking.

Elizabeth looked at her in annoyance, sniffed disdainfully, went to the table to pick up Rae's mug, and said, "They're going to revoke your smoking privileges at the Home."

Rae lit another one. "Okay, listen to this. Cavafy. Okay? One of the people you've foisted on me?" Elizabeth nodded, bored.

> "For some people there's a day
> when they have to come out with the great Yes
> or the great No. It's clear at once
> who has the Yes ready in him; and saying it,
>
> he goes on to find honor, strong in his conviction.
> He who refuses never repents. Asked again,
> he'd still say no. Yet that no—the right answer—
> defeats him the whole of his life."

Rae looked up from the book. "Well?"

"No."

"You're kidding."

"I don't think Cavafy had backpacking in mind when he wrote it."

"But that's not my point."

"Rae. I'd be miserable company. I'd bring you down. I'd whine."

"You'd love it. You think I would risk being stuck with the thing we call Elizabeth Ferguson if I thought you'd be in a bad mood? No way. It's all of four lousy miles."

"I don't know."

'Will you at least think about it?"

"Okay."

Rae got up and went to hover over the teakettle, drumming her fingers on the enamel.

"Hey, Rae. You know what they say? 'A watched pot never boils.' " Rae smiled, but continued staring at the teakettle. *"Get away from there."*

Rae sat back down.

"I think you've hit upon the perfect solution. I can go in a couple of weeks. A veritable brainstorm, Elizabeth."

"Good."

"I'm sort of hungry."

"Well, help yourself to anything you can find."

Rae thought about this for a minute.

"Is there any meat loaf?"

Elizabeth looked at Rae as if she were out of her mind. "Of course there isn't any meat loaf; why would there—"

"I was just *asking*. Geez, you don't have to jump all over me."

"There's some salad from last night, undressed. And some green goddess dressing."

"Uggggg. *Watership Down.*"

"Well, see what you can find."

"What do you think the odds are that you'll go backpacking with me?"

"About ten to one."

"Oh, yeah? That's not so bad."

Rae ambled over to the refrigerator, inspected its contents.

"Do you want me to make you a sandwich too while I'm at it?"

"No, thanks."

"You're anorexic, Elizabeth. What are you, five-ten?" Elizabeth nodded. "And you weigh about one-thirty?" Elizabeth nodded again. "Well, I'm five-nine and you know what I weigh?" Elizabeth shook her head, pouring brandy into mugs. "One seventy-five. See," she said, spreading mayonnaise on rye bread, "I eat like you drink. I don't drink as often or as much as you do, but you eat a lot less. We're both 'One is too many and a dozen isn't enough.' Like, for instance, you'd never have just one drink, and I'd never have just one egg, I'd have a minimum of two eggs, or none at all. Okay, wait, on occasion I'll have three eggs, like in an omelette, say, but never just one. . . ."

"Will you fucking shut up about eggs? Here's your drink."

"I just feel so *happy* now, now that I'm going away."

Elizabeth sat down at the table with her drink and watched Rae make a liverwurst sandwich, which she brought to the table, uncut, and held for a minute, tenderly.

"I'm on the road to morbid obesity," she announced cheerfully, taking a bite.

"Don't talk with your mouth full."

"I'll tell you, Elizabeth. It's like—my life is like Chutes and Ladders. I move along, mosey along working hard, trying to find romantic love, blah blah blah, small advances, small setbacks. Then I luck out, get to go up a ladder twenty steps—like today, for instance, when I was so down in the dumps and you gave me a pep talk, some sense of direction, hope, reassurance, and I'm totally happy now. I've got you, I've got my toddy and my liverwurst sandwich, I have a plan to end this self-destructive cycle of Brianville—right? I'm twenty steps up from where I was. But then there'll be something, some new small setback, and"—a long whistle, descendant in pitch—"down the chute, fourteen steps backward. At which point it's hard to get up again."

Elizabeth exhaled loudly. "But you keep trying. Rae. You take risks."

"And lose."

"Sometimes. But would you trade your life and mind for anybody else's?"

Rae shook her head. "Would you?"

"Yes, if I could still have Rosie."

"You would? With your mind?"

"I don't know. Doesn't seem to me that I—uh, make the most of this allegedly excellent mind. It's all addled. My dad used to say 'crab salad' about someone's addled mind."

"Crab salad?"

"Yeah. He'd tap his head with his forefinger, or do a spiral with his finger, the 'cuckoo' gesture, and say, 'Crab salad.' "

"Hah!"

"There are all these veils covering my mind, old scar tissue and whatnot. And drinking adds more veils, but it also makes me care less. And hurt less. And think less. About all the things I could be doing with this brain. I . . ." She held out her hands, palms up. "There's something great and useful I could be doing, and that I don't know what it is hangs over me like some major errand I know I'm meant to do."

"It's a rut. . . ."

"No, it's a trench, and all the enemy fire is of my own making. I shoot myself down even before I've gotten my head up to ground level for a good look."

Rae looked about to cry. Elizabeth glanced away, pulling at a strand of hair, black hair, in a daze.

Rae got up from the table and came around to her, pressed her thumbs into the hard muscles of Elizabeth's neck and back. Elizabeth let her head drop into her chest; it felt like a cannonball. She purred as Rae pressed hard, in a circular motion.

"You don't want to write."

"No."

"You don't want to cook."

"No."

"You don't want to teach."

Silence.

"You'd be a great English teacher, loving books so much."

"I don't know. Classrooms are so *loud.*"

"We have *got* to think about what to do with you."

"Judo-chop my shoulders. Thank you. Ohhhhhhh!" Elizabeth moaned, a rich soft vibrating moan.

Elizabeth agreed, for reasons she did not entirely grasp, to go backpacking with Rae the following weekend: maybe an urge to move, one step after another, maybe to try something new for the first time in years. And within minutes of telling an ecstatic Rae that she would go, paranoia and dread set in: she would never return alive. She would spend the entire weekend obsessing that the house had burned down, that Rosie was dead, that she would lose her mind up in the mountains not knowing for sure. Goddammit, why on earth had she agreed to go?

Rosie wailed. "Noooooooo, please. Nooooooooo."

"Mrs. Thackery said she'd love for you to spend Saturday night with them."

"Nooooooooo," Rosie cried, her palm against her forehead, tortured eyes piercingly blue against water and redness, lips stretched outward like a square-mouthed jack-o'-lantern.

"Rosie, for God's sake, stop being so dramatic. You've spent the night with the Thackerys a thousand times."

Rosie leaned against the refrigerator, possessed. "I'm begging you," she whispered.

Elizabeth smiled gently at her. "Come on, baby."

"Don't you Come on baby *me,*" she said, trying another tack. "You could get killed! By wolves! And I'd be an orphan, didja ever stop to think about that?" She saw herself clearly, chained to the wall at an orphanage, eating mush from cracked dirty bowls in between beatings.

"Come here."

"Oh, no, you don't."

"I could get killed crossing the street tomorrow," Elizabeth said in a spirit of ironic reassurance, but Rosie took it for the bitter pill it was. She sank into a chair at the kitchen table.

"I always have nightmares at the Thackerys."

"You've never told me that."

Rosie wouldn't look at her.

"Are you afraid I'm going to desert you?"

"No," she lied.

"You're usually *des*perate to stay overnight with Sharon."

Rosie scowled, tore a paper napkin into tiny pieces.

"You and I have to learn to let go of each other from time to time. I'll miss you, and think of you, and when I'm walking back down the mountain, I'll be thinking how happy I'll be to see you again."

"Tssssst."

Rosie breathed deeply, picturing the night when her mother would be off sleeping in the hills, surrounded by bears and rattlesnakes, one of which might crawl into her sleeping bag. . . . And Rosie with Sharon, lying in the twin beds, whispering their favorite jokes and stories: Johnny Fuckerfaster, and the mummy with the green diamond eyes, and the psycho killer with the hook hand. And Sharon would fall asleep, and she would lie awake in the pitch dark, in a strange house, in a separate bed, alone with the memory of the moment when the teenage girl looks into her rearview mirror at midnight on Lover's Leap, and sees *the mummy with the green diamond eyes.* . . .

"Rosie?"

Rosie awoke from her daydream and, defeated, got up from the table. Evading her mother's arms, she walked forlornly to her room and flopped face down on the bed. She lay feeling sorrow for this poor little girl whose mother might get killed in the mountains, knew, *knew* that if her mother went off, she would never see her again. Maybe the Thackerys would adopt her. That wouldn't be so bad. At least she'd have a father, and she loved Mrs. Thackery; there would be Hostess cupcakes in her lunch box. . . . She started crying. She *did* have nightmares at the Thackerys, dreams of quicksand, dreams of prison. Dreams where she couldn't move her feet when something deadly was approaching; of being mistakenly put in the gas chamber, of being thrown off the Golden Gate Bridge by a madman, or her mother. Once she had dreamed that she was at her own funeral, and no one seemed to see her. Once she'd dreamed that a bandit had her and the Thackerys lined up naked against the living room wall; another where a bandit had a gun pointed at her, and she was sitting on the toilet, and he said he'd kill her if she didn't pee—and she had, in the bed.

❧ ROSIE

She heard her mother's footsteps coming up the stairs.
"Rosie?"
"Go away." Come in. Don't go.
Her mother came in and lay down beside her and stroked her bottom.

Still, her face was hard and imperious Saturday morning when Rae and Elizabeth took her to the Thackerys: little Mount Rushmore, I couldn't care less.
But she bid them goodbye with the sad, wet, apologetic look with which a puppy might look up at the person who has just put it into a burlap sack with some kibble and bricks.

PART
TWO

Chapter
🌿7

The two women stood outside Rae's car in the parking lot of the Pretty Boy Trailhead, staring at the expanse of fir, pines, oaks, magnolias, evergreen, and acacia through which a narrow dirt road ran north. Elizabeth scrutinized the woods as if about to clean up the morning after a dinner party, Rae with the beatific look of a child upon first seeing the Christmas tree. She helped Elizabeth into her backpack, adjusted the shoulder straps, complimented herself on choosing such a well-padded model, then slapped Elizabeth on the ass: "Giddyup."

Elizabeth shifted her weight, acknowledged that it was not nearly as heavy as she had anticipated, and waited for Rae to put on her own pack and lock up the car. The sun shone white in the blue sky, birds sang; infinite greens.

They turned toward the trail and had walked in silence for a hundred feet when Rae remembered something. "Wait here a second."

Elizabeth turned and watched her friend tramp back to the car, where she removed the keys from the trunk lock and returned to where Elizabeth stood.

"*Give* me those."

Surrounded by spring-colored growth, wildflowers, the moist clean smell of new leaf and wet earth, they started up again, walked the slight incline alongside a rushing, rain-swollen creek which would turn into a river near the meadow. Rae bounced along as if she were dribbling a basketball.

Birdsong, crickets, frogs, movements in the brush, sunlight slanting through the treetops in sheets and broad beams, all mesmerized Elizabeth.

"Not bad."

"I'm *so* happy you came with me."

"So am I."

"The best part is being away from the phone.'

"Yeah."

"I wonder how many times Brian's called." Elizabeth said nothing. "I told him I was leaving soon, that it was all over between us."

"Good. About time."

"He didn't understand. He was unhappy. I feel sorry for him."

"You felt sorry for Claude Rains at the end of *Notorious.*"

"Well."

"Try to forget about him. It takes a while for your psychic bones to knit after a breakup, but they will."

"You promise?" Elizabeth nodded. "Right now I feel like I'll never get him out of my mind. Now, in my stomach, when I think of him, I get rocket-fueled butterflies."

"It'll pass. You're addicted—you've got a 'jones' for the guy—it means your habit. Your addicted craving."

"Yeah, I know. I'm hooked. And it was doomed from the start, because he panicked at the idea of commitment."

"Doom is erotic."

"Yeah."

Was the house on fire, Rosie alive, the iron unplugged? She remembered Rosie dawdling that morning, a spoon of honey held six inches over her cereal, creating fine golden coils; Rosie, watching Elizabeth apply mascara; Rosie, watching so intently that she seemed to be memorizing her face; Rosie, flopped on the

easy chair, spindly legs draped over the velvet armrest, baby finger hooked over her bottom lip, reading *A Wrinkle in Time*,
slowly slowly raising her eyes when Rae stepped into the house.

"Last night I almost went crazy," said Rae. "It was very late,
well after midnight. I was totally obsessed and hyped up, scared
that if I went to Santa Fe I'd die. I felt crazy, dangerous, like that
guy in the motel room in Saigon at the beginning of *Apocalypse
Now.* . . . There were so many voices, talking in my head, like,
you know, Nurse Ratchet—no-nonsense, diabolically patient—
and my spiritual director, who's sort of a cross between Hanuman and Lenny Bruce, wise and snappy—you know, like, 'Be
here now, baby, avoid the rush.' And so on. It was like a bunch
of speed freaks doing *Spoon River Anthology.* Then all of a sudden, clear as a bell, I heard my mother's voice; it was like she was
in bed with me, soothing her small worried child. It was so real,
in the way that a hallucination is real, that I felt like crying and
found myself hugging my shoulders. It was unconditional, the
hug: I felt like I was home."

"Yeah? Rosie had one of those bouts with existential dread
the other night. She was scared to go to sleep because she might
have a nightmare, and when she's dreaming it feels exactly like
it's really happening, and she couldn't tell what was real, because
dreams feel real. And so, that night, everything felt meaning-
less."

"What did you do?"

"Lay down beside her and listened."

"You're a wonderful mother."

"Sometimes."

"You hungry yet?"

Elizabeth shook her head.

"Holding up okay?"

Elizabeth nodded. "We there yet?"

Rae smiled. "Not yet."

Elizabeth was looking straight ahead at the path, and did not
see the look of misery that crossed Rae's face. Pretty Boy
Meadow was in fact a good six hours away.

Elizabeth felt strong and free, calm and in awe of the forest,
the creek, the birds, and the flowers, felt that having only just

tasted backpacking, she would never be able to get enough of it.

But she had gotten enough by the end of the second hour, when the straps began digging into her shoulders; her feet, in hiking boots, were on the verge of going numb but were, in the meantime, aching and swelling and probably blistering.

"The honeymoon is over," she announced.

"Then we must stop immediately and eat. You'll see."

"I'm tired."

"We'll sit down for a while, eat chocolates and lunch. You'll get a second wind."

"I hate backpacking."

"There, there."

"I *knew* it would be like carrying boxes to a U-Haul. I can't believe I let myself get sucked into this. When will I learn?"

They had stopped walking. Rae began to help Elizabeth off with her pack. "Matron is here; we'll eat a nice lunch. After we rest, you'll want to go on."

"I seriously doubt that." I have to go home. I *have* to.

Elizabeth sat with her back against the trunk of a massive redwood, hugging her knees to her chest.

"Hors d'oeuvres?" Rae asked, handing a box of See's chocolates to Elizabeth, who shook her head. "Look!" said Rae, withdrawing a tin of smoked oysters from her pack, opening her mouth in happy mock surprise. "And Wheat Thins! And liverwurst! And mayo!" She held up each item and looked at Elizabeth as if they were playing peek-a-boo. "Mandarin oranges! And Italian peppers in wine sauce."

Elizabeth smiled, happier now to be sitting down, weightless, about to eat. Now, here, midway (she thought) between the meadow and trailhead, she simply *was:* she would be a good sport, gracious, adventurous.

After they ate, they lay with their heads touching—thick black coils and soft reddish-brown ripples—staring up at the sky through the treetops, daydreaming. This was, Elizabeth realized, extraordinary.

"Hear that high, melodious bird above the others?" Rae asked. "It's a hermit thrush. But doesn't it sound like a nightingale?"

" 'The nightingales are singing in the orchards of our mothers.' "

Rae sat up and reached for her pack of cigarettes in the side pocket of her backpack, lit one, and inhaled deeply. Elizabeth's eyes were closed; Rae watched her, lovingly and then with panic. Taking a deep breath, she said, "Elizabeth?"

"Yeah."

Rae stared at the silver-white ash and, when she inhaled, at the burning ring of orange. "Nothing."

Elizabeth opened one eye and looked at her.

"Well, I just thought that if you were ready, we should start up again."

"Okay. In a few more minutes."

They helped each other on with their packs and headed north. "This time we'll take it more slowly. And if you get real tired, we'll do the Indian shuffle. My dad taught me how to do it; it's the way the Indians crossed the Bering Strait, thousands of miles."

"But we've only got a couple more to go."

"Anyway, it's like this." Rae stopped, then ever so slowly took a baby step, and then another, for fifteen feet. "See? It's great; takes forever to get anywhere but you're not tired when you do."

They walked along, talking of mothers and Rosie, books, and insanities, and, inevitably, Brian.

"One more thing, Elizabeth. Then, I swear to God, I'll shut up about him."

"Oh, Rae. I'm so sick, *so* sick, of Brian. He's an asshole. And here you've got yourself on trial, and you're the judge, and the prosecution, and the defense, and the audience, and the jury. . . ."

"*And* the media coverage."

"And the media coverage. And your jury is not made up of peers, it's made up of all those voices you heard last night in your head."

Rae walked along silently.

"You just don't have to hurt so much."

"I don't?"

"No! You're like the mad king when you're with him, bursting into spontaneous weeping, first of sorrow, then of joy, celebrating your death and rebirth, over and over again."

Elizabeth began to hate backpacking after another hour on the trail. The pack was too heavy for words. Her back and feet ached. All that kept her going was the thought of rest—and rum. She and Rae had run out of things to say, and Rae looked increasingly nervous, which Elizabeth attributed to her concern with Elizabeth's mood. Be a good sport. It will be over soon. That's it, one step after another. I *really* want to go home, want to be home, but since I'm here, with Rae, I will try not to be a bitch.

"God, the air smells good," she said. "Clean and sweet, like creek water." Half an hour more, I figure, of birds and flowers and trees. "And pine: God, these woods. I know why you love it so much now." Friendly as possible.

"You are undergoing the great rewards of what we call the Backpacking Experience—the air, the freedom, the landscape. Don't you feel you could keep walking forever?"

"No."

Rae's face fell.

"I am suddenly happy with the anticipation of completion; like when I'm stuck for a long time with people who bore me, or who are beginning to get on my nerves. Up until the last fifteen minutes or so, I'm tight and judgmental and desperate to leave, but then, when the end is in sight, I feel such relief that it makes me act friendly."

"Oh." Shit, thought Rae.

"I figure we've got about half an hour to go. I've got exactly thirty-six minutes of backpacking enjoyment left in me."

Rae took the deepest possible breath; Elizabeth didn't notice. They walked along.

"Oh, my aching back," said Elizabeth.

Rae groaned. "Elizabeth?"

"Yeah?"

"I'm afraid I have some bad news."

Elizabeth stopped and looked at her, kindly.

"Yeah?"

"Yeah."

They looked at each other for several moments. Rae looked miserable.

"Did you forget something? *Did you forget the rum, Rae?* Goddamn it—"

"Brought the rum," Rae said hastily.

"Brought the rum?" Rae nodded. "Then it doesn't matter what else you've forgotten."

"We're an hour and a half away," she mumbled.

"What? We're what? Just what the fuck do you mean by that?" She had her hands on her hips. "I don't fucking believe you, Rae."

"I lied. I knew you wouldn't go if I said it was six hours. I was surprised you came at all."

Elizabeth was all but baring her teeth and snarling. "We're an hour and a half away?" she asked coldly. Rae nodded. Elizabeth turned away and began walking quickly forward, so furious that her eyes didn't focus.

Rae jammed her hands in her pockets and walked forlornly behind, with her Stan Laurel face on. Elizabeth was seething, hiking rapidly, angry about the pains in her legs and shoulders and back, at her bad mood, at being trapped with Rae, whom she was temporarily hating, *backpacking,* a million miles from nowhere. She wanted to scream at the top of her lungs.

Rae caught up with her after ten minutes. Her eyes looked as if she had been crying, but Elizabeth didn't soften.

"Don't talk to me."

"Listen."

"No."

"You've got every reason to be mad and I'm sorry."

"Just shut up."

"So we're an hour and a half away, and then we've got a long evening ahead of us, and then a long hike tomorrow, and I'm going to go nuts if you hate me the entire time."

"You should have thought about that before you lied."

"I did think about it, but I lied anyway because I wanted us to do it so badly."

"What if someone did this to you?"

"I'd be mad. But then I'd figure that what was done was done, and I might as well have a decent time instead of a shitty time."

"Well, I feel like having a shitty time."

"It's your funeral."

"Leave me alone."

"Let's stop and have some juice and a few See's Bordeaux, then take the next hour slowly. Then it'll only be as far as walking from your house to town, which we've done dozens of times."

"Never after having walked for four hours with thirty-pound packs on our backs."

"Elizabeth, I am really, really sorry."

"Fuck you."

"I made a mistake. I'm only human."

"Rae, why don't you grow up."

They walked along in silence for a long time.

"Is there anything in the world I could do right now to make it up to you?"

"No."

"Are you ever going to forgive me?"

"I suppose you think it's funny, in some way, one of your cute kooky Rae trips, but I don't. I'm sore. I think I'm going to be sore for quite a while."

"But then dinner will be no fun, and the campfire will be no fun, and walking tomorrow will be no fun. I think you might as well forgive me. It's in your best interests."

"Rae? Shut up."

"I'm throwing myself at you. I'm pleading for mercy."

"I don't think you're funny."

Elizabeth had moved into a more controlled phase of her anger; icy, condescending.

"There's nothing I can say or do to make things better?"

Elizabeth shook her head. Rae reached her arm around and deftly unlaced a side pocket of her pack, from which she extracted the flask of rum. She stopped. Elizabeth continued a few feet and then stopped too, turning to face Rae.

Rae unscrewed the silver top. "This is all the alcohol we have. It is eight ounces of one-fifty-one rum. We will be perfectly high after we finish it. All our troubles will disappear. Imagine that first sip tonight, Elizabeth, how strong it's going to taste, how warm in your stomach." She tilted the flask slightly. Elizabeth watched, disbelieving. "But if you're going to hate me all night, four ounces isn't going to make a dent in how badly I feel. So I am prepared to pour it out."

"Stop it."

"I have nothing to lose. I have been forced to resort to coercion. Either you forgive me or I pour it out." She looked at Elizabeth searchingly. Elizabeth glared.

Rae raised the flask to her nose, inhaled appreciatively, then lowered and slowly tipped it.

"Stop!"

"Do you forgive me?"

"This isn't funny, Rae."

"You keep saying that." Rae tilted the flask until one drop trickled out.

"Give me that!" She stepped and reached toward Rae, both hands out.

"Get away from me," Rae screamed, jumping back, holding the flask as if it were a Molotov cocktail. "I'm just crazy enough to do it!"

She made her eyes look wide and crazy, made her hand shake visibly.

Elizabeth stopped. This is nuts, she thought.

Rae began tipping the bottle again.

"*Stop* it," Elizabeth said. She held her palms open, close to her body. "If you pour that out, I'm going to kill you with my bare hands."

"No, you won't. Say you forgive me."

"But I don't." Rae poured an almost imperceptible amount out. "All right, I do."

"You promise?"

"Yes."

"You're not just saying that?"

Elizabeth shook her head.

"Okay then." Rae screwed the top back on and clutched the flask to her. Then she beamed at Elizabeth.

An hour later, they reached the meadow, a vast expanse of green dotted with flowers alongside the Pretty Boy River, full and rushing, pale icy green in some parts, turquoise in others, whitewater crashing onto rocks on the shore. They were greeted by a hysterical fist-sized bird which dashed to within ten feet of them and then, in a staggering, ground-level flight, dashed twenty feet to the right.

"It's a killdeer," Rae whispered. "See the black and white stripes on its neck?"

"I know killdeer."

The bird was flapping and fluttering and screaming as if in great agony.

"It's the mama—it means the babies are somewhere close. It's trying to distract us." The poor bird seemed to be going out of its mind. Rae tiptoed forward. "Look!" she said in an urgent whisper. Elizabeth crept forward and looked down to where Rae pointed. Two tiny, fuzzy baby killdeer were flopping around in the grass, while over to one side the mother screamed and gyrated. "She thinks we're monsters. Aren't they adorable?" The babies peeped and flopped, and Elizabeth looked at them, in awe, and then over at the mother.

"Come on," she said. "The mom's freaking out."

"You ladies here for the night?" a man behind them asked.

Chapter
❦8

"Rosie, my darling, we're so happy to have you. Come in, come in."

Rosie shuffled despondently behind Sybil Thackery to the kitchen, where Sharon sat at the table eating blueberry pancakes. She waved her fork in greeting, and Rosie instantly forgot her mother's impending death, smiled, and sat down at the place that had been set for her, where a marshmallow was melting on top of some cocoa in a blue Wedgwood teacup. Mrs. Thackery, at the stove, flipped pancakes with the graceful wrists of the former ballerina she was, looking as if she were on the verge of a sweeping plié.

"I hope you're hungry."

"Starving to death." Earlier Rosie had eaten two bowls of Irish oatmeal, but there was a hole in her that needed to be filled, and in a moment a stack of pancakes studded with bright blueberries was placed before her on a floral-etched Wedgwood plate, while Sharon passed her matching pitchers of hot butter and syrup which she poured liberally over the pancakes. Sweet buttery steam and the elegance of the place setting; this must be sort of what Heaven is like, but one bite later Rosie began to mourn the eventual end of breakfast.

"I don't have to go to my violin lesson today, because my teacher's gone to San Diego," Sharon announced. "Mommy? Can we go to the zoo today?"

"No, not today. I'll take you to the pool later. I'm just not feeling up to much. I have—my period."

Oh, God, oh, God. Rosie got a look in her eyes such as a cat gets before a fit, and both girls gobbled their pancakes. She has the Curse. Rosie and Sharon had vowed that they would never do it, have it. The girls had pored over Elizabeth's Tampax instructions, furtively, as if the diagrams were scientific pornography; essentially Rosie viewed the Curse as some sort of recurrent voodoo infirmity rather than a biological function.

"Will you have some more pancakes?" Mrs. Thackery swiftly changed the subject.

"Yeah."

"Not me," said Sharon.

Rosie could see that it pleased Mrs. Thackery to feed her, and she felt moved to making her feel good. "These are the best pancakes I've ever eaten."

Mrs. Thackery sat down with them and ate one pancake, with only the tiniest bit of syrup, and then sat with her plump, pink hands on her rounded belly, which pushed out against her striped shirtdress.

Hyped up on sugar, the girls tore through the house, unable to settle, chattering dervishes who managed to get underfoot even after Mrs. Thackery had sunk into a chair as if her backbone were made of rubber. Her eyes, small and brown, did not quite focus.

"Please, will you play outside?"

"We could make you some tea," said Sharon.

"Yeah!"

"No, thank you. I'll be just fine."

"Can we come back for lunch?"

"Yes, of course. And then we'll go to the pool. Give me a kiss, darlings. Now run along."

❧

They tied one end of Sharon's jump rope to the garage door handle and took turns jumping—"Twenty-four robbers came knocking at my door"—until they grew bored.

"I got two bucks," said Rosie. "Let's go to town."

"I don't have any."

"You can have one of my dollars."

"God. Thanks."

"But you know what we could get if we had three dollars?"

"What."

"Mystic Mints, *and* potato chips, *and* Cokes, and candy lipsticks."

"Yeah, I know, but I don't have *any*."

"Too bad your dad's gone. If he was here, there'd be a fortune in his easy chair."

"And the seat of his car."

"Wull, what about on the dresser?"

"Are you crazy?" Her father's bedroom and study were irrevocably off-limits in their coin searches. If he had not gone so far as to actually rig the rooms with explosives, he had hinted darkly on a number of occasions that it would be mortally inadvisable for the girls to enter his territory.

In town, with Rosie's money, they each bought fifty cents' worth of candy corn from Mavis Lee at the dime store, and took their little white bags outside to the curb, where they ate them one by one, section by section, white tip, orange center, yellow butt, whispering and giggling. Rosie made sure that hers lasted a minute longer than Sharon's. She couldn't stand it when Sharon still had candies left when hers were all gone; on several occasions she had bamboozled Sharon into eating her candies quickly—"Let's see who can finish first"—just to make Sharon wish for what Rosie had, which was—more. But while Sharon hardly seemed to notice, Rosie felt glee and guilt; the original sinner.

"You want to go to the railroad tracks?"

"Let's go to the post office and spy on people."

"Rosie, we could go to the lagoon fort and watch the carpenters."

"They don't work on Saturdays. You know what I'd like to do? You know that old oak tree behind the fire station, I mean way back behind it? Wull. I'd like to make a treehouse, *exactly* like the one in *Swiss Family Robinson*. First we'd just make a floor, put wood across over the branches, but then we'd build stairs, and put in windows, and a bed. . . ."

Rosie's head was filled with the eventual details of their palatial treehouse—curtains, running water, refrigeration—and they walked in the direction of the firehouse but found, carved into the trunk of a pepper tree, FUCK. They spent the morning playing detective. Who had done it? A man. How tall was he? The word was written a foot higher than Sharon could reach her arm, so it was a tall man. How strong was he? Strong, very strong, the word was cut deep into the wood.

It was only at Elizabeth's urging that Sharon had learned to swim last year. Rosie had taken to the water at an early age, but at seven Sharon could not even do the dead man's float.

"You see," Sybil Thackery had explained to Elizabeth, "all the women in my family lack the buoyancy mineral; yes, that's right, there's a mineral responsible for buoyancy, and both my mother and I were tested for it when I was young and unable to swim. And the doctor took our blood, and found it lacking in that mineral, so I'm afraid Sharon's lacking in it too."

Elizabeth had not been able to believe her ears. Room-temperature IQ, she thought. "Uh. Listen. I think that Sharon really ought to learn to swim—and I'm sure I could teach her. Let me at least give it a try."

One year later, Sharon was almost as good a swimmer as Rosie. In the water they were as sleek and silly as sea otters. Mrs. Thackery viewed her daughter's aquatic prowess with stunned pride, as if Sharon had had to triumph over muscular dystrophy.

Today, she sat on a chaise longue sipping a diet orange soda by the side of the pool, nervously observing the little girls swimming the width of the pool underwater on only one breath. Chlorine, salt, the buttery coppery lanolin smell of sun lotions, steaming bodies on cement bleachers, cries, giggles, and the red slaps of bellyflops.

The girls disappeared for a moment. Mrs. Thackery sprang to her feet, located them sitting cross-legged on the floor of the shallow end where, pinkies extended, they sipped from teacups.

Rosie in her red tank suit, all skin and bones, a baby flamingo, every rib clearly defined, glossy black hair uncurled by the water, climbed out, dove back in, and did not surface until she had crossed the pool.

Back at the Thackery house, Chutes and Ladders. Rosie's marker, on space 37, was a red plastic girl, well ahead of Sharon's blue boy.

"I know how to make boobs," Rosie announced, as Sharon rolled a five, just missing a ladder. Phew.

"You do?"

"Uh huh." Rosie rolled a six and advanced up a ladder.

"How?" Sharon rolled, hit a ladder, moved ahead of Rosie, who decided not to tell her how. "Come on."

Rosie rolled and advanced four steps. "Wull, see. You get this glass of milk. Then you pull on your *nip*ple and drink milk at the same time, and the boob fills up with milk."

Sharon just stared at Rosie.

"Come on, your move."

"Are you kidding? You pull on your nipple and drink milk?"

"Yep."

"Who told you?"

"This scientist."

Sharon looked at her skeptically.

"Don't worry. I know how to undo them, too."

They sat on Sharon's carpeted floor, considering the prospects. A movie played in Rosie's mind, where her own boobs filled up while Sharon's remained flat. And then, in the movie, only *one* of Rosie's boobs filled up, to gigantic proportions, and the whole world laughed. . . .

"Rosie?"

"Yeah?" Rosie blinked, back on earth.

"I don't want to make boobs."

"Okay. What do you want to do?"

"Slide down the hill, on cardboard."

"All *right.*"

"Dinner in an hour, girls. So don't be gone long."

Sliding was fun, dinner was fantastic: tuna noodle casserole, with crumpled potato chips on top to make it crunchy. Rosie ate two huge helpings, to Mrs. Thackery's delight. Tuna noodle, oh, God, the food here was so much better than at home, where her mother was apt to have made some disgusting gourmet slop, like curry or dolmas, pâté, ratatouille, pasta with cheese and anchovies, and once—oh, God—*tongue.* Tongue!

"This is *so* wonderful."

"Oh, Rosie. It's the easiest thing in the world."

"It's the best thing I've ever tasted."

Life was fine again: lime sherbet and Toll House cookies for dessert; then *A Thousand Clowns* on the tube. All of them loved the movie and each other, and soon it was time for bed.

" 'Bon voyage, Charlie, have a *won*derful time.' "

" 'Bon voy*age,* Charlie, have a *won*derful time.' "

"Remember Bubbles. . . ."

"Okay, girls. That's enough. It's getting late. Come on, my darlings, into bed."

"When will Daddy be home?"

"Late. His plane arrives at midnight."

Mrs. Thackery gently smoothed down the bed as her daughter lay looking intently up into her face, brown braids on the pink pillow. Rosie watched them put their arms around each other's necks, watched them kiss, and waited for her turn, filled with pangs of jealousy. When Mrs. Thackery came to Rosie's bed and bent to put her arms around her, Rosie inhaled the Ivory soap on her neck, the hint of lemon on her breath, and wanted,

wanted more than anything, for this to be her mother, instead of the woman who lay down beside her every night and smelled like wine.

"Are you sleepy?" Rosie asked when the lights were out.

"Yeah." Faintly. "Are you?"

"Totally," she replied, wide awake.

"Well, good night."

Rosie yawned noisily. "Good night."

She was awake for the next several hours, and in the darkened pink princess room the Chamber of Horrors show began.

The fingernail moon outside the window made terrible shadows, turning shoes and socks into snakes and rats. Faces of men appeared at the window, psycho killers, a cyclops who would gobble her down like a cashew, leering one-eyed through the window. Under the bed was the living dead man, Dracula was in the closet, the mummy with the three diamond eyes was outside the door, and there was just enough moonlight to see the beady red eyes of the tarantulas who were marching toward her bed.

"Sharon?" she whispered, but heard only soft, muffled snoring and the tapping of bloody red fingernails on the windowpane. The light switch by the door was ten feet away, but to get up meant almost certain death; if the cobras and rats didn't get her, something else would. . . . She peered down at the floor beside her, stood and walked the length of the bed, jumped down softly, and saw—*truly* saw—and just barely escaped from the long, bony, phosphorous-white arm whose fingers were reaching for her ankles. Flicking on the light, she stood staring at socks and shoes, at branches that touched the window above Sharon's bed. Sharon murmured in her sleep. Rosie looked around, huddled against the wall, and tiptoed to the closet: took a deep breath, threw open the door, and saw small dresses, skirts, and blouses. She turned off the light, dashed for the foot of her bed, and jumped back in.

She heard Mrs. Thackery go into her bedroom and close the door. She lay dying, soon to be the only person awake in the house, except for the men under her bed and outside the window.

Dear God: Hello, please let me fall asleep. Let Mama be alive still; God bless her and Rae and don't let anything happen to them. Please let me fall asleep, I won't ever cheat again, or lie—this time I really mean it.

She gasped each time the old house creaked, settling down for the night. Mrs. Thackery must be asleep. This must be what Hell is like. Please God, let it be morning.

Finally she dozed, and dreamed. She and her mother were in the checkout line at the supermarket, their shopping cart filled with bananas and wine. Something came over Rosie, anger at the wine maybe, and she punched her mother on the arm, and her mother turned into a fat old woman who didn't seem to recognize her. . . . She awoke, sweating, footsteps on the stairs, creaking toward her.

Ohgodohgodohgodohgod, it's a man with a gun, or a pirate, she knows it. The steps are louder, closer—wait. It's Mr. Thackery, she's almost sure, *please* let it be Mr. Thackery. Just in case, though, she stops breathing and pretends to be dead so if it's a killer he won't have to bother with her. The footsteps have reached the top of the stairs, are approaching Sharon's room, but they pass, and she hears the bathroom door open and close, water running. Surely a killer wouldn't use the bathroom first. The bathroom door opens and the footsteps approach again. The door opens slowly, with a quiet squeak and the strong smell of man, by the shadowy moonlight she sees Mr. Thackery in his bathrobe.

He walked softly to Sharon's bed, his smell strong and soothing, an old, warm, salty smell. She ached for a father.

He bent down and kissed Sharon on the forehead, oh please let him kiss me too. Let him tuck me in. "Hello," she whispered.

He spun around, angrily, but his face softened; in the thin moonlight he looked like Sharon, a roundish, open face, soft brown eyes.

"Hello," he whispered back.

He came to her bed, and she smiled up at him. He tucked the sheet and blanket around her neck, smoothed her cheeks with his fingertips, and left the room.

Sheltered, sleepy, safe, her breath grew soft and she slept.

Chapter
9

Millions of times a year, women turn around at the sound of a strange man's voice and are shot, stabbed, raped. Rae was explaining to two men that this was why she had screamed bloody murder.

Two hours later the four of them were sitting around a campfire that Rae had made; they were drinking Tang screwdrivers which the men had provided. Elizabeth and Rae had eaten by themselves and drunk all the rum. Rae had ventured to the men's campsite and invited them over for a joint.

Now they lay sprawled against the logs which formed a ring around the campfire, smoking dope beneath a crystalline starry sky. The white crescent moon made dappled slanting shadows of the trees, and the air was as crisp as chilled vodka, smelling of leaves and grass, of living and burning wood. Pretty Boy Meadow, bordered on one side by the rushing, rock-filled river, icy blue-green at dusk. The music of river, frogs, crickets, birds, owls, and the crackling fire soothed and enveloped Elizabeth, and she only half listened to Rae chatter on about mosquitoes.

Lank, the one who had first approached them, was tall and fat and talkative. In the moonlight, the bald spot at the crown of his short red hair looked like a silver yamulke. The other man, James, was short and thin, with dark fluffy Einstein hair. He lay smoking silently.

"I swear to God," said Rae. "This Off is amazing." She sprayed every inch of her body, clothed or exposed, with the mosquito repellent, then sprayed some into her fingers and dabbed it behind her ears as if it were Arpège. The men were transfixed.

"Mosquitoes adore me. You'll notice they leave Elizabeth alone; she's got that bad-vibe force field, whereas with me, I mean, I can psychically hear them arrive—no mosquito in sight, but ever so faintly I can hear a plane approach, and then, *neeeee-ow, neeee-yowwwww,* they're buzzing me."

"You want another drink, Rae?"

"Sure. Thanks." Lank stood and walked to her. "Elizabeth?"

"Please."

"James."

"Yeah."

"Drunk again," said Lank. "Two nights running. It's because we're unemployed."

"It's because we're alcoholics," said James.

"No, we're not."

"Pretty damn close."

Elizabeth looked up when Lank handed her the red thermos cup of Tang and vodka. "Thanks."

"You have an extremely aristocratic face. Doesn't she, James?"

"Yes," he said, smoking again.

"Do you guys backpack often?" Rae asked, lighting a cigarette.

"I do. Several times a year. It's James's first—"

" . . . and last—"

"—time."

"Elizabeth's too."

"Were you best friends before?"

Rae nodded, smiled at Elizabeth, who scowled, good-naturedly.

"So were me and James. I thought he would love it."

James and Elizabeth looked at each other cautiously.

"You hate it too?"

She nodded. "I liked the first couple of hours. The next five were as recreational as—I don't know. Chemotherapy."

"You know what James did yesterday? He asked me to carry his pack for him against my chest, like a sandwich board. And when I refused, he got all sulky. Then he decided to abandon his pack on the trail. He thought someone would find it, see my address, and ship it home."

Rae laughed. "You know what Elizabeth did, a few hours ago? Well, see, first of all I should mention that I sort of lied—"

"You didn't *sort of lie,* Rae, you lied, period."

"This is true. I told her it was only four hours to the meadow, and so we have this enormous scene, and she goes into this two-hour sulk, during which, at one point, she suggests that I walk back to the trailhead, call the National Forestry Service, lie, and have them pick her up by helicopter."

Lank laughed, James smiled.

"I haven't felt so bratty in ages," James said.

"Where do you guys live?"

"San Francisco. We live in an apartment building on Sacramento. Where do you live?"

"Bayview. I live down the street from Elizabeth and her daughter."

"What do you do?"

"I'm a weaver. What do you do?"

"I'm an unemployed English teacher," said Lank. "He's a writer."

"Published?" Elizabeth asked.

It came out in a much snottier tone than she had intended, and hung in the air for a moment. She looked at him, saw that he was looking at her with disdain.

"I'm sorry, I just—everyone says they're a writer."

"Isn't she awful?" said Rae. "Sometimes I don't know what I see in her."

Elizabeth shook her head at herself, smiled wryly, apologized again.

"Forget it. And yes, one story in the *Kenyon Review*, one in *Esquire*."

"Yeah? That's great. You write short stories?"

"I'm writing a novel. The stories were chapters from the novel."

"So, do you make enough to live on?"

"Not really. I've been working on and off as a waiter for the last couple of years. Right now I'm living off some savings and the *Esquire* money. I figure it'll last me for the next five or six months, and if I haven't sold anything else by then I'll go back to waiting tables."

"What's the novel about?"

"Me."

"Yeah?"

"It's about trying to live a life which, when I review it at eighty, will not contain too many episodes for which I will kick myself."

"It's pretty funny," said Lank.

"So," said James, and sighed. "Read any good books lately?" And then he and Elizabeth were off and running: *Far Tortuga? Birdy? Under the Volcano? Rabbit, Run? Middlemarch? Milagro Beanfield War? At Play in the Fields of the Lord? Out of Africa? Wapshot Chronicle? One Hundred Years of Solitude? Herzog? White Mule?* Yeah, yeah, yeah.

Passage to India? Yeah.

"How about Schuyler?" she asked.

"What's for Dinner? Loved it."

" 'Pussy pines so,' " she said.

"Yeah, yeah. Remember Biddy, the old lady, sitting in the chair with taloned feet, reminding herself of the Chinese empress who looked like a wise old monkey?"

"Yeah, yeah," she said, and they shared a great laugh.

"Schuyler?" asked Rae.

"Yeah, the poet. You know, James, he spends about half the year in an asylum." He nodded.

"James was headed for one. I rescued him."

"You call backpacking being rescued?"

"I'd come into his room where he's trying to write, only he's like a dog going around in circles before it sits down; he's going, 'Thigh, thigh, is there such a word, Lank?' He thinks it sounds too lispy to exist, so I tell him to look it up, so he goes to the dictionary. 'T,' he says, 'okay, t, huh'; he can't seem to place its order in the alphabet; he's going, 'Ellemenopee, cue, are, ess, and tee . . .'—he's singing the alphabet song—'now I've learned my A B C's, tell me what you think of me.' "

James was laughing.

"So I say, 'Good *boy*, James,' and he's going, 'T-h,' big problem here, with 'h.' 'Aitch? *Aitch* aitch aitch.' "

Everyone was laughing, and the joint, relit, was passed.

"We should string up our food pretty soon," said Lank.

Elizabeth groaned.

"It's not that bad," said Lank.

"Yes, it is," said James.

"But we have to do it. Last night we got pretty loaded and starting hoisting up the pack with food in it, up onto the bear wires—see, Elizabeth, strung between the trees? But then we left the other pack, with a few snack-type items in it, which we thought we might need later that night, outside our tent, ten feet away maybe, and this morning, we hear, *Chuff chuff, chuff chuff chuff,* and this bear is gobbling down our Cheetos. Lucky the pack wasn't closed, or he'd have torn it apart."

"Lucky it wasn't in the tent," said Rae.

"Really. Anyway. We have the equipment, and I have the experience, and if we were to pass out and get ripped off again, I couldn't live with myself."

"Let's have a nightcap," said James. "Then we'll do it." He got up to collect the cups and Elizabeth sized him up: five-foot-four tops—no, maybe five-five. She imagined being in bed with him, wondered if their children would have that crazy hair, if their children would be teased in school, imagined them spending their weekends not backpacking. He had a good voice, beautiful hands, pleasant face, green eyes. But she towered over him. Why did the packaging matter so much? The best men she had known, besides Andrew, the ones with whom new languages were invented, had chipped teeth or pockmarks, were fat or sixty or . . .

"You read *Pigeon Feathers* lately?"

"Yeah," she lied.

"Updike's the master. Sometimes, when I read him, I'm so in awe that I think I'll never write again, that there's no point in my trying to compete. But sometimes I read him because I want to *cringe* with admiration, and somehow it gets me back to the type-writer."

Rae and James lit up another cigarette; Elizabeth watched the silvery wafting smoke.

"So you've got a daughter?" Lank asked.

"Does *she* have a daughter. You'll be reading about her some-day—she may be a writer, or a great comic actress. *Ro*-sie Fer-guson."

"How old?"

"Eight," said Elizabeth.

"Does she look like you?"

"Sort of. She's got black hair, but it's curly. We've got the same features, basically, but her face is heart-shaped, triangular, and she's got these very blue eyes."

"Not to be believed," said her aunt. "And her schtick is amazing."

"Are you divorced?"

"No, widowed."

"Oh."

They sat, the four of them, finishing up their drinks, watching the golden red flames of the campfire.

"Would anybody like to hear me sing?" asked Lank.

"No," said James.

"I would," said Rae.

So under the silver moon, Lank got up, somewhat unsteadily, and cleared his throat. Oh, God, thought Elizabeth, this is going to be awful.

They heard the river, the rustle of leaves, the fire and crickets and owl, the great animated stillness of a meadow at midnight, and then Lank began singing "Stranger in Paradise," in an at-first quavering tenor, not loud but with great feeling: It was beautiful, and chills went up her spine. She wanted him to sing all night.

Rae wept.

"Wasn't that beautiful?" she asked, an hour later, when she and Elizabeth lay side by side in the tent. "The song?"

"Yeah."

"They were terrific. Why don't we ever meet guys like that?"

"We just did."

"Yeah, but they live in the city, and we didn't even give them our numbers."

"Did you want to see Lank again?"

"I'm leaving, remember? For two months. But you and James."

"I *liked* him, but I wasn't at*tracted* to him."

"Why not?"

"He's a dwarf. And a smoker."

"None of your deodorant-commercial men have panned out. . . ."

"I can't stand kissing smokers."

"But—"

"Look. It was a good night, a nice twist of fate. And it was for tonight, and that's all."

"But Andrew was a nice twist of fate. It was a total quirk that you ever met, and the rest is history, the rest is Rosie."

True, she thought. If one day, more than ten years ago, she had not chosen to kill time in Brentano's while waiting for a date to show up in North Beach, and if the Neruda collection Andrew had bought there two days before had not been missing middle pages, they would not have been in the bookstore at the same time. Andrew was at the cash register when Elizabeth went to pay for *The Universe and Dr. Einstein*.

"Can I take a quick look at that?" he asked.

"Sure."

He looked at the cover, flipped through the text, and handed it back. "Can I read it when you're done?" he asked.

Rae fell asleep almost immediately. Elizabeth lay in the tent, alone in the dark, in the woods, and listened to Rae's stomach growl.

"Rae?"

The only response was a death rattle, a grunt, and coughing. Elizabeth thought of Rosie and started to play the tape in her mind called "Rosie and the Dreadful Things": Rosie in a burning house, Rosie being murdered. Something was in Rae's nose, causing an airy wheezing distinct from the snores.

To take her mind off the commotion, Elizabeth replayed parts of the James tape. "Jesus!" he'd said. "I couldn't *stand* the idea that the Russians saw that photo—Reagan looking like an old snapping turtle, lying helpless on his back, flailing; some clown in a cheap rubber Nixon mask; the Madame Tussaud statue of Carter; and Jerry Ford behind them all, mouthing 'Woof woof woof' to amuse a child." She smiled in the dark, heard an owl.

She and James had *recognized* each other. Too bad he smoked. Too bad he didn't look the right part. Too bad he didn't know her last name. Rae stopped snoring and ground her teeth, grunted, wheezed; Jesus, Elizabeth thought unkindly. No wonder she'd never been married.

Maybe he would come to Bayview, looking for her. Maybe in the morning there'd be a note from him in her backpack. But you'd eat him alive, Elizabeth, you'd tear him apart.

Hi, James, she would say when he called, sexy, aloof, and wanting to see him. What a surprise, she would say.

"Hello? Hello!"

"Rae! It's okay, you've been dreaming."

Chapter
10

Birds, singing in the pepper tree, wake her. Who, where, when? A thin ray of consciousness struggles through the smog that envelops her, finds a headache tucked behind her eyes, and it all comes back. I, Elizabeth, am in bed with Gordon in mid-June on Willow. I have a headache. Ergo sum.

Oh, God, you did it again—you drove, you drove home from the bar with one eye closed. It made her sick to her stomach. Please, for God's sake, don't *drive*; one of these days your luck will run out. Or get rid of the car.

Gordon, still asleep, stirred beside her, turned to hold her. She wished he would wake up and leave but knew he wouldn't. Soon he would press his long thin body against hers and want to make love, then he would want to make her breakfast, then he would want to talk, then he would want to do something useful around the house, tack mosquito netting to the windows or something, to justify not leaving, and all these acts of kindness would wear on her nerves, would take too long; he would say "marvelous" too often, would tell stories that dragged on like a child's retelling of a movie, would say "Bah" when he finally left. She felt trapped, oppressed by his dull, handsome face. "Trapped like a trap in a trap," as Dorothy Parker put it. Sometimes when he overstayed his welcome, she could get him to leave by directing beams at him from, as Rae put it, her bad-vibe ray gun. Other times, despite her best efforts, he stayed and stayed and stayed. Last time, Elizabeth patiently explained that in the mornings he always stayed a little too long. He became embarrassed, defensive, morose—and he had stayed, and stayed, and stayed.

Why did he tolerate her bitchiness? Because he was a kind and patient man, and she turned him on. And why did she tolerate such a relationship? Because the pickings in town were slim.

Bitch. Siren. User.

"Hi," he said.

"Hi."

"Boy, do I have a headache."

"Yeah?"

He stroked her prominent hipbone, and she felt her body tighten.

"You want some breakfast?"

"No—I want *you.*"

She feigned a yawn, couldn't bring herself to look into his dumb, trusting face. She shook her head groggily. "I need some food," she said.

He made them an omelette with bacon and cheese, while she sat in her white kimono at the kitchen table reading the *Chronicle;* rococo on the radio, sunlight, bacon cooking, Elizabeth so unhappy about her unhappiness that she couldn't speak to him as they ate.

He finally left an hour later, wounded, mad, and disconcerted.

"I didn't mean to hurt your feelings. I just want to be alone."

"Why don't you just *say* so, then?"

She shrugged, shook her head, pulled at her bangs. "I don't know. I'm sorry."

"No, you're not."

"What can I say, Gordon?"

It was no good, and they both knew it was all but over.

❦

"Mama?"

Elizabeth had been in the bathroom rereading the front page ever since Gordon had left half an hour before. Her body was rejecting the omelette he had made her. And she was, in a big way, sick and tired of her life.

"Hi, sweetheart. Come on in."

"No *way.*" Elizabeth laughed. "Don't get that babysitter again."

"How come?"

" 'Cause she eats too much."

"Okay."

"I need my allowance."

The phone in the hallway rang. "Will you get that?"

"Okay, but can I have two quarters today? One for Sharon?"

"Sure—get the *phone.*"

Elizabeth followed the sound of her daughter's footsteps on the carpet.

"Hello? . . . Yeah. May I help you? . . . Yes, she's here, but she's in the bathroom reading the paper." Oh, no, who was she telling this to? "She's been in there an *hour.* I'm afraid to go in."

Oh, Christ, thought Elizabeth, smiling.

"Okay, I'll tell her you'll call back in a while. . . . You're welcome. Do you know what time it is? . . . Okay. Well, 'bye."

"Who was that?"

"Some guy named James—says he'll call back."

Side by side, Rosie and Sharon rode toward town on their bicycles, rehashing *Psycho,* until they turned downhill on the road which ran like a garden walkway past ice plant, ivy, echium, eucalyptus, wildflowers, and nasturtiums: red, yellow, orange, full of nectar. Their eyes shone and their cheeks turned pink as they sped along to the butterfly grove where for the last few days millions of Monarchs had been flying and nesting in the trees. But today they skidded to a stop when they found the road littered with butterfly corpses, in piles like leaves.

"Oh, my God." They went to investigate. Thousands still flew, but the death toll was awesome. Sharon stood, with eyes lowered, a skinny eight-year-old Renaissance Madonna, beatifically sad. Rosie surveyed the bodies with her arms crossed, sneering, toeing a pile of dead butterflies, Joe Friday.

"You know who did this, don't you?" She glared. "Carbavella."

"Yes," Sharon agreed. It was clear, carbavella, bees as big as guinea pigs.

"*Dead*ly mutants."

Sharon whirled around as a butterfly flew past, looked into the sky as if it might start raining snakes, and covered her head. Rosie did the same. They ran to their bikes, frantic and full of adrenaline, out of breath when they reached the piers that marked the beginning of downtown Bayview.

As with most fears, the fact that carbavella existed only in their imaginations did not diminish the sense of danger, and the relief at having escaped: they were filled with a lively joy.

They returned to the harbor after buying all the candy they could for a dollar, and spent the better part of the morning deciphering the Morse code messages of the pelicans and gulls that flew over the water. Gulls were dots, pelicans dashes. The birds had been trained by two escaped convicts from San Quentin, one hiding on Alcatraz, the other on the loose, quite possibly in Bayview. Dot dot dot dot dash dash: "Kill the blonde." Dash dash dash dash dash dot dot: "Send bullets."

"What's dot dot dash dot dot?"

"Heroin."

Elizabeth cleared her throat when the phone rang. She let it ring. She languidly combed the bangs away from her forehead, picked up the phone finally, and said hello, in a faintly British accent.

"Hello, Elizabeth? This is James Atterbury. Remember me?"

"Yes, of course. How *are* you?"

"Fine, thanks. You?"

"Fine, thanks."

"How's Rae?"

"Oh, fine. She's leaving for New Mexico in a couple of days."

"Oh, yeah?"

"Yeah."

"Hunh."

Elizabeth drummed her fingers on the kitchen table. "How's Lank?"

"Madly in love, with an airhead. And she's madly in love with him. It's almost more than I can take." Elizabeth made her smile audible by exhaling sharply. "How's Rosie?"

"Fine."

"I remembered Rae saying, '*Ro*-sie Ferguson,' so I looked up Ferguson in the phone book, and there you were: E. Ferguson."

"Ah."

"Do you have plans for tonight?"

"Well, yeah, I do, tentatively." She was lying.

"If they don't pan out, would you like to get together for a drink?"

"Listen. Let me call you back in a few minutes. I'll see if I can get out of what I'm supposed to do." She wrote down his number and called Rae.

"*Marmee!* I'm so glad you called. I'm getting cold feet about leaving. I'm having terrible separation anxieties."

"James called."

"What? James called? I'm so happy!"

"Why?"

"Because he's perfect for you."

"Yeah, except that he smokes, and he's a dwarf."

"God, you're a turd, Elizabeth. Come *on,* Mama, think of what duds most of your handsome boys have been. I mean, your tall handsome boys. James has a great face, great sense of humor."

Elizabeth stroked her long straight nose.

"See, it's another classic example of the Green Eggs and Ham syndrome—you never give anything a chance."

"I know what'll happen if I give him a chance. I'll end up eating him alive. Of course, I like him a lot, but he'll start getting on my nerves. Now, see, the syndrome I'm thinking of is Short Man syndrome, gross egotism born of insecurity. . . ."

"Yeah, unlike ourselves."

"I don't know."

"Why don't you have a drink with him, see if you have fun together and want to be friends. Don't forget. You're not going to have me to kick around for two months."

"Good point. Maybe I will have him over, let him audition."

"That's a loving attitude. What are you going to wear?"

"I don't know."

"Wear that green silk blouse. It makes your eyes look wicked."

"Okay."

"And those Levi's you had on the other night."

"I've worn them every day this week. I've got them on now. They're giving me bedsores."

"Well, everything you own looks good on you."

"I don't know."

"You're scared, Elizabeth. You should try to trust yourself like I trust you."

"I can just be so awful to men."

"Well, just don't be. That's easy. Be brave and kind. Give it your best shot."

"Are you leading up to the part where Breaker Morant says—"

" 'Live every day as though it's your last, because one of these days you're bound to be right!' "

"Goodbye, Rae."

"Call me with a full report in the morning."

"Okay."

"Can I call if I have a monstrous anxiety attack?"

"Yes, of course."

She hesitated while dialing James's number, hung up midway. If she invited him over to her house, it would be hard to get rid of him if it didn't go well; but she was much, much more secure on her own turf. She dialed the number all the way through.

"James? Elizabeth. I've rearranged things. Would you like to come over for a drink later?"

"Yeah, sure."

"Good. Say about six?"

"Yeah, perfect. How do I get there?"

"After you take the Bayview exit, stay on the road that goes through the downtown area. Bear left when the old railroad yard ends, which will put you on Cypress; go about a third of a mile; then left on Willow. We're at Thirty-six Willow, halfway down the road; it's a white Victorian, sort of dilapidated, with a white lattice gate and a lot of rosebushes."

"Got it. Shall I bring champagne?"

"Yes, do. See you at six."

She spent an hour in the garden, gathered peach and red and salmon tea-roses for vases in the house, and fantasized; imagined dialogue opening lines, thought about how sad it was that a man who was intellectually her match had finally come along—and he smoked. Maybe, if they fell in love, he would quit.

She spent the rest of the afternoon pretending not to care and getting the house just right. She put on the Beatles white album and cleaned the downstairs, straightened the pile of recent *New Yorkers*, rehashed the campfire scene over and over, dusted and polished the fine antique furniture, arranged the flowers in Chinese vases.

So, tell me more about your book. Oh, by the way, did you ever read *The Ginger Man?* . . . One time, on acid, I thought . . . When I was about six years old . . . Rae and I were at the symphony last year . . . Something or other is—oh, I don't know, as rare as an Englishman with good teeth. . . . It's funny how we become more and more like ourselves as we get older. . . . Yeah, like the old joke about kreplach.

She took a long hot bath, with classical music on the radio. After drying herself off, she stepped into a floral kimono, painted her toenails, nursed a beer, modeled clothes for an hour, and finally settled on the bedsore pants and the green silk blouse and the worn Frye boots. Then she put on mascara, dabbed Chanel behind her ears, and changed the sheets on her bed.

When the phone rang at five thirty, her heart sank and she walked angrily to the phone. James was going to cancel. Good.

"Hello," she said, rather coldly.

"Hi, Mama."

"Oh, hi, doll!"

"Sharon and I are doing a play, so can I spend the night?" Then Rosie's voice changed to an urgent whisper. "Say no!"

"What?"

"Ohhh-kay. I'll come right home."

Elizabeth laughed when she hung up. Rosie would take up whatever slack there might be. She sat down by the phone, daydreaming, waiting, thirty-eight going on fourteen. When the phone rang again, she glared at it, let it ring eight times so that James would know what an inconvenience it was for her to answer the phone, busy professional that she was.

"Yes?"

"Hi, Mama. *Please* change your mind."

Elizabeth laughed again. "Well. All right, then."

"Oh, great, thanks a lot. We get to go to McDonald's for dinner."

"Wow!"

"See ya tomorrow."

Elizabeth stopped off briefly at the mirror in the hallway before heading for the kitchen. She opened an ale and created a still life on the kitchen table—a glass jar of crushed red peppers, tea roses in a Mateus bottle, a tiny bright enameled box, and the darkwood, grandfatherly pepper mill.

In the living room, she put *Duets with the Spanish Guitar* on the stereo and looked admiringly at the coffee table, which her mother's mother had bought in Cairo and on which sat a bowl of fresh fruit—apples, oranges, bananas, kiwi—a blue bowl with gardenias floating on water, *Saul Steinberg,* beeswax candles. The room smelled great, of oranges and beeswax, and the early evening sunshine made the dark woods and rich cloths golden, elegant, alive. Everything was just perfect, and then the phone rang again.

"God!" It couldn't be Rosie again. "Hello?"

"Hello, Elizabeth. I'm afraid I have some very bad news." It was Mrs. Haas. Her voice was grim, but Elizabeth detected some pleasure mixed in.

She had, it seemed, offered Rosie and Sharon each a Fig Newton in town, and Rosie had reached out to take hers. Mrs. Haas gave Rosie a lecture on bad manners and had asked her what the magic word was. And Rosie had answered, "Fuck!"

Elizabeth had to pinch her nostrils shut to keep from laughing.

"The *f*-word," Mrs. Haas said.

"I'll talk to her about it. Thank you for calling"—you foolish nosy bitch.

"Good*bye*."

It was six o'clock. She was glad she'd worn perfume: she could smell that she was there. She had butterflies in her stomach; her heart was pounding: jungle drums. Be brave, be kind. A few minutes later the doorbell rang, and she waited a minute and made him ring it again.

Chapter ❧11

"Hi, Elizabeth," he drawled shyly, extending his right hand, which she shook. In his left was a bottle of champagne, which he thrust at her. His eyes were as green as Rosie's were blue, and his shirt was yellow—bright yellow polyester.

"Come on in," she said. His face was full of anxious good cheer, and she looked down at the overgrowth of brown feathery hair which followed him like a wake. Yellow polyester, Rae; I rest my case.

"Great place," he said, standing close to her. She resisted the temptation to step backward and cross her arms. He smelled of Ivory soap and cigarettes, he smelled like a man, and her perfume protected her like a force field. "You have the best roses in the neighborhood," he said, as she led the way to the living room, to show off its beauty, its woods and bookcases and rich dark colors. He admired it all without speaking, nodded his head, impressed, and shook it in wonder, smiling.

"It's beautiful."

"Thank you. Follow me to the kitchen, if you like. I have some glasses in the freezer."

He jammed his hands into his khaki pants and sighed deeply.

❧ 128

Elizabeth had the impression of being followed by a huge puppy who might at any moment bound or flop into her legs. He leaned against the red wall of the kitchen, standing somewhat pigeon-toed, managing to look as conceited as he did self-conscious.

"Here." She handed him the bottle, picked up the two frosty tulip glasses, and walked past him toward the living room. They sat several feet apart on the blue velvet couch, and she looked at him politely while setting the glasses down in front of him on the table, next to *Saul Steinberg.*

He removed the foil. His hands were beautiful, long and broad, white moons on his big square fingernails. "Laurinda Almeida?" She nodded, pleased. "Martin Ruderman, on the flute." Now he was showing off. She nodded. Now he's going to pretend to have trouble remembering the soprano's name, and would say, questioningly, as if without confidence, perhaps with one eye in a squint, "Sally Terry?" And he did.

He untwisted and removed the wire hood and worked the cork out slowly. Elizabeth was in a state of suspended animation, waiting for a glass of champagne, waiting in fact for the first glass to be gone and the second one poured.

The cork exploded out of the bottle and James deftly poured the first rush of bubbles into a glass, filled the other, then filled the first to the top. He gave one to her with a gentlemanly flourish, picked up his own and held it up to her.

God, you have beautiful eyes, she thought. "Cheers."

"Cheers. Good to see you again."

They poured down long sips. It was airy, pale, and gold.

"Are you and Lank friends again?"

"Oh, yeah. I don't hold a grudge."

" 'Published'?" she asked him, smiling.

He laughed. "Rude! Took my breath away for a second. But I'm glad you said it. I shoehorned it into the book."

"Yeah?" He nodded. "How's the book going?"

"Oh, all right. Up and down. No one's offered me an advance yet, but I'm plugging away. So far, the best line in it is, 'Published?' "

"Good. So, you said, it's a book about you?" He nodded. "What happens in it?"

"I grow up. I go from thinking I'm a uniquely and almost unbelievably fucked-up person to thinking I'm a mostly benevolent crackpot."

"It sounds good."

"Thanks. What did you say you do again?"

"I haven't quite figured out what I want to be yet. I've worked in the publishing world, but it bored me. I've thought about teaching, but I'm not sure I like children in large groups. I'd like to be paid to read and discuss literature, but I get so few job offers in any given week." He smiled. "I spend a lot of the time in the garden, a lot of time with Rosie, a lot of time at the movies."

"Where *is* she?"

"At her best friend's, overnight." Elizabeth told him the best Rosie stories she could think of: today's encounter with Mrs. Haas, the falling star she'd taken to Show-and-Tell, the scene at Macy's when she'd shouted, "Why can't you just be happy that you don't have bloody stumps for legs?"

Elizabeth got up, walked to the fireplace, and lit the newspapers under the kindling.

"When did your husband die?" he asked.

"Four years ago."

"How?"

"In a car accident." She returned to the couch, lowered her long lanky frame onto a cushion. "His car hit a tree, and he was thrown into a pool of water."

"So he died by drowning?" She nodded. "Jesus."

"Well, these things happen." Why did she always say this? To convince herself that the freak accident really had happened? He looked at her with great compassion—there, that was it. She didn't want to appear to feel sorry for herself. No big deal, these things happen.

"Were you totally in love?"

Were we totally in love? Elizabeth looked at the expanding flames, heard them crackle, noticed that the record had ended.

"We were pals."

He had never been married. He had lived with women twice, but hadn't, when push came to shove, wanted to marry either of them. So they had left him. He shrugged. "You know, like the poet said, when one person's whistling 'Ol' Man River,' and the other is whistling 'Trees,' something's got to give."

She looked at him, captivated. His teeth were yellow from smoking, and one of the front ones were chipped. "Where are your parents?"

"Dead," said James.

"Mine too."

"Oh, yeah? My dad died last year."

"Were you and he close?"

"No. Not really. He was the most powerful man in my life though, wanted me to be a businessman like he was, and I was, you know, not into it. I was re*lieved* when he died. It was like, 'Ding, dong the witch is dead . . .' I felt I could breathe for the first time in my life."

"What was his name?"

"James. I was always Jimmy. Now *I* get to be James, and we call him Dead Atterbury."

"Who's we?" she asked, smiling.

"Me."

Dead Atterbury. She had to remember to tell Rae.

"We've just about finished the bottle."

"And we haven't even gotten to *your* parents yet."

"I don't want to," she said, and got up. She turned over the record and put a log on the fire. "There's a bottle of burgundy in the kitchen. Would you like some?"

"Are you going to have some?"

"Yeah."

"Okay, sure, thanks. Can I take you out to dinner?"

"I don't know. Thank you, but—"

"How about if we sent out for a pizza?"

She shrugged. Might as well.

"Do you mind if I smoke?" She shook her head, went to the kitchen to get him an ashtray. He was on the phone in the hall when she returned. "Will you bring us a pizza?" he asked. "Yes, sure," He stared down at his feet, at tennis shoes. "What's your name?" he asked.

"That's a shitty name," he said jovially. Elizabeth laughed.

There was a long, long silence, during which he smiled at her without opening his mouth, and she smiled back.

"Ah, there you are. Okay. We'd like a medium thin-crust pizza with, uh—" he looked at Elizabeth—"sausage and mushrooms?" he asked her and she nodded. "And green peppers?" She nodded again. "Ferguson. We are at Thirty-six Willow, off Cypress."

We.

She opened the bottle of burgundy and poured it into their empty glasses, held it up to the red glow of the fire, and, given a spacious bravery by the champagne, languidly stretched her legs out onto the couch, with her boots draped off the side several inches from the cushion on which he sat. Sultry, elegant, dangerous, she felt like Cleopatra, knew by now that they would go to bed. There was that strong and elusive sense of recognition.

"Are you very ambitious?" she asked.

"I like the questions you ask."

"Well, are you?"

"I want to write an important book. I want it to be a success."

"Would you settle for a modest success? Or do you want to be irretrievably rich?"

He laughed and pulled a spiral notebook from his back pocket, frisked himself, found a pen in his front pocket and opened the notebook to a blank page. "Irretrievably rich," he said, and jotted it down. It pleased her. "I guess, if I were to be perfectly honest, I'd say I want the moon. Wealth, fame, praise from a select few."

"And then you'd be happy?"

"Who knows? I already am fairly happy. I'm sure if I reached that goal, I'd come up with a new crop of desires."

They sipped at their wine, relaxed.

"Who will publish it, ideally? Knopf?"

"Definitely. Although much of it will have appeared in *The New Yorker* previous to publication—but wait, then I wouldn't get an Updike review."

"Sontag will do *The New York Review?*"

"Yes."

"And will there be a David Levine caricature?"

"Yes, yes." He rubbed his hands gleefully.

"And who will direct the movie?"

"Is Buñuel still alive?"

"I don't remember."

"Fellini, Bergman, and Truffaut will collaborate; during the course of our work together, we will become best friends. I will fly them, on silly whims, to Rio: the four of us will sit in my suite, *jamming*. And we will pack our noses from a mayonnaise jar of pharmaceutical cocaine."

"And who will play you in the movie?"

"Clint Eastwood, I think. Or Dudley Moore."

"Yeah?" He nodded. "Well, I don't think that's all too much to ask," she said.

"You haven't mentioned the Nobel Peace Prize yet."

"What about, do you get to be God of All the World, too?"

"Yes, eventually. When I've become modest."

They were laughing, it was fun. The color and irregularities of his teeth began to grow on her. She wanted to feel them against her thighs.

But when the pizza arrived, and they sat on the carpet in front of the fire, with woven placemats, linen napkins, fine silver and red ceramic plates, the glow of the fire on his face and in their glasses, she watched him eat with revulsion. He chewed as quickly as a starving rodent—or her mother. She remembered the sound of her mother eating bacon, the wet crunch. God. It was making her sick. She summoned her noblesse oblige, some- how made it through dinner, but knew for sure now that she could not fall in love with this man. Love is details.

He was so close to her blueprint of the great good man, a lot like Rae in essential ways, full of fire, full of humor, full of kind- ness, but she could not imagine surviving a breakfast, complete with hangover, while he did his starving-rodent routine with fried eggs.

After dinner, he took the dishes into the kitchen and then went through her records, determining that they had most of the same ones: she had more classical, and he had more recent rock- and-roll. "And no opera," he said.

"I love it."

"I gathered. It unnerves me. Where did you get all these old jazz collections?"

"From my father. After he died."

"When was that?"

"A long, long time ago. In my early twenties."

He browsed through the books next, withdrew Malraux's *Antimémoires,* and thumbed through it absently for several minutes.

"Have you read that?" she asked.

"No. Have you?"

"Yes," she lied.

He stood reading it, and finally put it back. "It's an excellent book," he said.

It's an excellent book: how pretentious.

Sunny and warm so recently, now she felt panicked and picky, wasn't sure if she wanted him to stay. But they smoked a joint of hers and listened to sonatas on the floor. They stretched out in front of the fire, a foot apart, and stared into the flames. He lit another cigarette, while she contemplated sex.

"It's nice to just lie here," he said.

"Yeah."

"I ate too much. I'm getting a gut."

"We really *shouldn't* be moved."

After a while he said, "When I was six or so, I had this friend named Denny Hoods, my best friend until I was thirteen. In kindergarten he used to lift me up to the water fountain. And one day—this is when we were six—we were at a swimming pool with his mother. She had just gotten out of the water, in a one-piece suit with a little skirt, and a pink swim cap covered with pink rubber petals. And Denny was talking to her while she dried herself off, and then she lay down on a chaise longue. I was staring, just gaga, at her body, watching her rub Sea and Ski onto her legs. Remember the smell of Sea and Ski? It smells—like pennies taste. And she rubbed it in the length of her legs; oh, God, they were long and brown and I was going nuts inside. I felt desperate, but I didn't know what to do. I think I wanted to *lick* them."

She didn't say anything. He sighed deeply.

She sighed deeply, and they both laughed. She turned to him with a level, bemused look, swept her black hair off her face, and waited.

He took her hand.

A little bit of juice ran through her stomach, butterflies and rocket fuel, golf balls, and affection. They watched each other, and she listened to the runoff in her mind, the streams of worry and judgment. He raised himself on an elbow, bent down, and kissed her. Their eyes were open. They kissed again.

"Well, that's over with," he said, and smiled, embarrassed. She reached out and stroked the side of his face with the back of her finger, tracing its planes, traced the outline of his half smile.

"James?" she asked soon. "Shall we go upstairs and make love?"

"Oh, *God,* yes."

He undressed her in the bedroom and stared in awe at her large, large breasts, touched them tentatively, not breathing. Then he unzipped her jeans and slowly pulled them down. "God, you have a beautiful body." She lay down on the bed, and he pulled off her boots, and pulled off her pants, and pulled off her socks. Then he kicked off his sneakers and sat down beside her, running his fingernails softly from her shoulder to her knees. They smiled, both shy, and he tore off his clothes.

No one had ever licked her neck. He traced the line of her jaw with his wet, warm tongue; electricity flowed through her. He was tender, verbal, aroused. He ate her *alive.*

A long time later he put his warm face between her breasts, nuzzling, while she stroked his soft fluffy hair, absent and happy. "These are the biggest ever for James Atterbury," he said. She burst out laughing.

You are too good to be true.

"You are a lover," he said.

At dawn Elizabeth awoke and for a second had no idea whom she was with, until she noticed that her feet were alone at the bottom of the bed. James. She bent her knees to rub feet with him. She felt as if she were holding a child. Still asleep, he nuzzled her face, and she smelled his breath and blanched. Once Elizabeth had gone to Rae's car to get something, had discovered a smoldering red hot fire in the ashtray, burning butts and gum and paper. This is what his breath reminded her of, and she hoped that he didn't want to make love again.

But he did, soon after, and his breath stopped offending her after the first minute of kissing. The room was warm and sunny, and she loved his face.

"What color are your eyes?" he asked.

"Hazel."

"Flecked with gold."

"I have to get to work now."

"Won't you stay for breakfast?"

"Not today. I have to go home and feed Leon, too."

"Leon who?"

"Leon's my dog."

"Wouldn't Lank feed him?"

"He's at his girl friend's."

"Okay, then."

"Okay. When do I get to see you again?"

She shrugged.

"I like you so much, Elizabeth."

"I like you, too. I'm busy tonight." Alarm flickered across his face. "With Rosie and Rae. Rae is leaving for New Mexico tomorrow."

He bent down to pick up his pants, and his socks fell out.

"Look at your shoes," she said. They were lined up, heel to toe, pigeon-toed and still tied, poised as if about to run off. "Something vaudevillian there," she said.

He smiled and bent down to kiss her. "Tomorrow night then?"

"Call me."

She was unable to fall back to sleep, and lay watching movies of James in her mind. He was an original. They could turn out to be great friends and lovers, and Rosie would love him: but. The smoke, the shirt, his height; the way he chewed and the occasional but glaring pretension. It didn't occur to her to give it time, to play it by ear, to forgive him his trespasses. Instead, to reinforce her ruling, she picked up *Antimémoires* and sat down in the easy chair. Glancing briefly at the pizza crusts in the cardboard box, on the floor by the fire, the butts in the ashtray, she read the first few pages.

At first she inwardly sneered as she remembered James as Alistair Cooke, pronouncing after several minutes that it was an excellent book, then read:

> I have experienced time and again, in humble or dazzling circumstances, those moments when the mystery of life appears to each of us as it appears to almost every woman when she looks into a child's face and to almost every man when he looks into the face of someone dead.

And she reread that sentence, that one sentence, closed the book and looked around. Oh, shit, she thought. It *is* an excellent book.

Chapter
❧12

James had the feeling he was being watched as he strolled up the walkway through the Ferguson garden, but failed to see the small girl's face peering through a parting in the living room curtains, or the high-powered binoculars that had been trained on him ever since he'd driven up in an old Peugeot. (Mrs. Haas was appalled, scandalized by James's bumper sticker. Her face came alive: a baseball bat and ball and, in huge black letters, THOSE FUCKIN' A'S. She had *never*!)

He took in the roses, begonias, azaleas; the hose, coiled up neatly beneath the faucet; the small red bicycle lying on its side in the grass and *The New Yorker* on the porch swing. He cleared his throat several times, patted both his mane and the spiral notebook in the pocket of his jeans, and took a deep breath. He was about to meet Rosie for the first time.

Elizabeth was in the bathroom upstairs, applying yet another coat of mascara. She had bought a new lipstick to match the red silk blouse she wore. The lipstick color was Rose Madras. After she poured down the last of the scotch, she had to rinse the red impression of her bottom lip off the rim of the glass. The glass clattered when she set it down on the porcelain soap dish above the sink; her hands were shaking. She dabbed Chanel behind her ears and on her wrists, brushed her teeth with Aqua-Fresh, reapplied Rose Madras, and studied herself. Not bad. The ivory combs securing the bun in her black hair, the lips, the nose, the modified John L. Lewis brows, good, good. The neck was caving in on itself, needing a quick pressing. Feh. She winked at her reflection, snapped her fingers, Roy Scheider in *All That Jazz*: "It's *show*-time, folks."

She was putting Erase under her eyes when she heard the knocking at the front door. After a moment, she heard Rosie say hello.

"Hello, Rosie. Glad to meet you."

"Come on in. Mama'll be right down. Mama! He's here! What's in the bag?"

"Treats from the deli."

Rosie led him to the living room and flopped into the armchair, dangling her legs over the armrest. James sat at the far edge of the couch, crossed his legs, and put the bag beside him. They heard Elizabeth's footsteps at the top of the stairs. Rosie considered James. He cleared his throat.

"Does your hair singe?" she asked.

Elizabeth grimaced and entered the room. James stood, and they smiled at each other.

"Hi."

"Hi."

"Here are some things for dinner," he said, and held out the bag. She looked in and admired the contents: artichoke hearts, a tin of anchovies, smoked oysters, dolmas, chicken salad, and New York Jewish Rye bread.

"Thank you. Can I get you a drink?"

"Yes, please."

"Scotch?"

"Fine."

"Rosie, get your feet off the armrest."

"Yes, Miss Mother."

Elizabeth turned toward the kitchen. How could he have chosen such an ugly shirt? Beige terrycloth with red pockets. Rae, I swear to you. Zoris and white socks. What was his point?

Elizabeth downed a shot of scotch before pouring them each a drink over ice. She wanted it to be time for bed.

"Have you ever killed anybody?" Rosie asked.

James squinted, trying to remember.

"No, none that I can think of. But I tried to twice, when I was a kid."

Rosie took in a deep loud breath of air. "Who?"

"First, when I was about six, I was sitting on our fence in a cowboy suit, with a holster around my waist, two new guns—*chaps,* even—and a black hat. When all of a sudden this horrible little girl named Debbie Solini—like Margaret in *Dennis the Menace*—comes walking down the sidewalk, and I said, 'Come *here,* Debbie' "—his voice rising at *here*—" 'I have something for you.' " James crooked his finger at Rosie. "And as soon as she got close enough, I whipped one of my pearl-handled revolvers out of the holster and cracked her over the head with the butt of it."

"Oh, my God. Then what happened?"

"I don't remember much about it. My old man belted me—but I don't think Debbie was hurt much."

"And who else?"

Elizabeth headed toward the living room.

"There was this kid named Se*bas*tian in my third grade class who was always tattling on me and getting me and Denny Hoods sent to the principal's—"

"There's a girl just like that in *my* class," said Rosie.

"There's one in every class. Anyway, one day Denny and I decided to kill him."

Elizabeth entered unobtrusively and gave him his drink, taking a seat beside him on the couch.

"Finish the story," Rosie demanded. "He tried to kill this kid named Se*bas*tian in third grade."

James clicked glasses with Elizabeth, and they took sips.

"So," he continued, "my cousin Pete, who was in eighth grade and knew about such things, said the best way to kill someone

was to get them to eat a mixture of aspirin and toothpaste."
Rosie's eyes opened wide; her mind was racing. "So we crushed
an aspirin into a teaspoon of toothpaste and then chased him
around trying to force it down his throat—or to at least fling it at
his mouth—because we thought one *drop* and he'd keel over."
    "So what happened?"
    "We caught up with him, and he beat both of us up."
    "Would it have killed him?"
    "Who knows?"

The three of them sat down at the dining table, in candlelight,
with the moon rising outside the window. A small African floral
tablecloth partly covered her full, cream-colored Irish lace. Chinese plates and laquered bowls held the food James had brought,
along with sliced tomatoes and pesto sauce, crisp hot sourdough,
cheeses, and two kinds of mustard.
    James poured two glasses of Napa Valley Petite Sirah into cut
crystal glasses. "A true maroon." Their glasses reflected candlelight, and Elizabeth felt like a million dollars.
    "Pass me the bright yellow, Mama."
    Elizabeth gave her daughter the mild mustard.
    "James? Can I ask you something?"
    "Sure."
    "How come the police don't just arrest the Mafia? . . .
    "James? Why is there wind? What makes it blow? . . .
    "Are you afraid of quicksand? . . .
    "Boy, I never saw anyone chew as fast in my life. . . .
    "Do you believe in God? . . .
    "Did you ever read *Old Yeller*? Didn't you just *cry*?"
    "Saddest book I ever read," said James. "I'm still getting over
it."
    Elizabeth was watching James as he jotted something in his
spiral notebook. James was watching her when she walked unsteadily to the stereo. Rosie was watching them watch each
other.
    "James? Do you know Andrea Kinkaid?"
    "No. Should I? What album is this, Elizabeth?"

"Bruce Springsteen. 'The River.' Listen to the saxophone player, Clarence Clemons."

James lit a cigarette and turned back to Rosie.

"Well, she's this girl in my class. She's this total drip. And you know what she goes and does? Well, one day, her mother goes over to Sharon's house—"

"Sharon is Rosie's best friend. You'll like Sharon."

"—and she brings Andrea along, and so Sharon gets stuck playing with her, so they go upstairs and Sharon gets out her coloring books, I mean these *new* ones, they're for like adults or something, but they're King Tut and Grimm's Fairy Tales and the Jungle Book. You know?" James, transfixed, nodded. "So, well, like Sharon's the best colorer in our *school*, and she's got this big huge box of felt pens with these *skee*ny little tips, and so she gives Andrea King Tut and Andrea just *ruins* it; she goes totally all over the page—*she doesn't even stay inside the lines!* She goes outside the lines on *three* pages. God. Sharon felt like crying, she said. I was *so* mad."

James glared, clenched his teeth, crossed his arms, *seethed.*

"Here's my plan," he said. "Will you tell Sharon for me?" Rosie nodded gravely. "Okay. She goes to Andrea's some day, and she acts all nicey-nicey at the door, right? Says she's come over to play, but doesn't go inside. You with me so far? Then she says, 'Hey! By the way! Got any new coloring books? and if Andrea nods, then Sharon snarls, '*Git* 'em.' "

The Fergusons laughed.

"Listen," said James, pointing to the stereo where Clarence Clemons was beginning a soaring, exuberant solo. "Listen to that sax, Rosie."

Elizabeth stared off into space. James was too good to be true. "Clarence has something to *say,*" she said.

"It's time for bed, honey."

"No, no, wait, please wait. . . ."

"It's late. You've been up an extra hour. James and I want to talk."

"What do you think we've *been* doing?"

Finally she shook hands with James, gave Elizabeth a reservedly dirty look, and huffily went upstairs.

"I'll be up in a minute," her mother called. She and James exchanged alluring looks.

Elizabeth bit her bottom lip and looked at him.

He licked his lips.

"I'll be right down."

"Are you going to marry him?" asked Rosie, as Elizabeth tucked her in.

"This is our third date, for God's sake."

Elizabeth kissed her daughter's concerned face many times, gave her one last wet kiss on the lips, and told her good night.

She was just about to close the bedroom door when, in a voice that was almost a shout, Rosie called out, "Are you gonna fuck him in the butt?" Elizabeth closed the door, smiling. James was laughing when she got downstairs.

"Well, are you?" he asked.

"Ah, Rosie."

"I would trade writing for a child like that." They sat in front of the fire for a few minutes, giving Rosie time to fall asleep, and then, in an instant, Elizabeth was all over James like a cheap suit. There was magnificent sexual chemistry between them: there were no words. Elizabeth was transported so close to the edge that she thought she might lose consciousness several times, and they were both delirious with pleasure. Later, in bed, several hours later, they made love more tenderly and then lay giggling quietly. Their sexuality was like a drug to Elizabeth; it was crystal clear to her that she was hooked and would pay through the nose for it, and that he would too.

In the ensuing week, Elizabeth worked on repelling disdainful thoughts about his shirts—made of materials banned in the manufacture of baby clothes—and his chain smoking and sometimes succeeded in not caring at all. Other times, though, usually at breakfast, she felt a clamping in her eyes and heard voices in her head listing those things that were, ultimately, unacceptable. Largely on account of conditioning and prejudice, his height remained a problem for her, but it also triggered adolescent memories—a five-foot-eight thirteen-year-old with hideously, embarrassingly large breasts. And then she would be flooded with pictures of her parents.

Her subconscious, which she considered to be working well when it functioned as a lint filter, trapping and stifling old pains and furies, had been acting up since James. Sometimes she thought she might go crazy from the intensity of her feelings and the intensity of the ensuing numbness.

One evening, several days after Rosie and James met, they were playing catch in the back yard with mitts and a softball which James had brought. Elizabeth watched from the upstairs window. Leon, James's retriever, was dashing back and forth between them, as in a game of Monkey in the Middle. Elizabeth thought it was a perfect scene for a movie, a warm summer night's game of catch in an overgrown yard with bright flowers on the side, great trees, birds even, Leon dashing between Rosie, in her overalls and purple T-shirt, and James, who was wearing an A's cap and a black T-shirt. Zoom in on the character in their faces, the agility with which they move, the beauty in the way Rosie runs after the occasional missed ball. Then the camera slowly climbs up the Victorian, and Elizabeth is standing, looking down with wistful sentimentality at her child and her lover. They look up and wave. Rosie does a cartwheel.

Elizabeth opened the window a crack, deep into her movie. She heard the crisp *thwap* of the ball against leather, back to Rosie, back to James, and she went into a trance. She was playing catch with her father on their front lawn, a lawn as cropped as Astro-turf. She could smell the salty worn leather glove he had bought her years before, redolent with dirt and sweat and oil; God, it smelled wonderful. Had her mother been upstairs, looking down from the window?

Elizabeth shook her head to clear it, shook and shook and shook, feeling so homesick and lonesome and disoriented that she walked as quickly as she could downstairs to the kitchen, and stood drinking scotch from the bottle until the black hole in her chest subsided. She screwed the top on, blinked, heaved her shoulders, and returned upstairs to the bathroom to brush her teeth and tongue.

James and Rosie went into the kitchen for orange juice, happy, close, still wearing their mitts, Rosie holding the ball, and the first thing James saw was the waves in the bottle, on the counter, barely in motion. Rosie poured them each a glass of cold bright orange juice and asked him if cave children played catch.

"Absolutely. With rocks and apples."

"But they didn't have mitts."

James shook his head, absently.

He looked sad.

"But they still had *fun,* James," she said consolingly.

He smiled.

One night, when James had said he would be there at dinnertime but had arrived, nonchalantly, at eight thirty, he and Elizabeth sat across from each other drinking beer; he was annoyed that she was annoyed but he was affecting a look of beatific indifference while she sat like a statue of dry ice. She would not need this man more than he would need her.

"You look beautiful when you're mad."

She couldn't believe he had said it and let a glimmer of a sneer pass over her face before looking back at the flames in the fireplace.

"Why be mad, Elizabeth? I'm sorry I was late."

"You should have called."

" 'You should have called,' " he mimicked her. "They've found 'You should have called' on hieroglyphics, on rune stones; I swear, it's been the battle cry of women since Eve."

"It takes *two* minutes. You know what a pain in the ass it is to be kept waiting for two hours."

"I wouldn't do it. I do not wait. I would read."

Elizabeth shook her head. "You can't admit that you fucked up."

"Oh, I can admit it. I said I was sorry."

"And then you sit there smirking because I'm mad."

"There are no words, Elizabeth, for how infuriating it is to deal with women sometimes. I know it is equally infuriating to deal with men. But I can't *stand* how much attention women need, how much reassurance—"

"You're an asshole."

"That's on the rune stones too."

He took his notebook out of his back pocket, located, after some effort, the pencil tucked between his ear and hair, and scribbled for a minute, then replaced the pad and pencil with nods of scholarly interest.

"I'll tell you something," he said after several minutes of a sad, hostile silence from Elizabeth. "I'm not an asshole. I have many frustrating things on my mind, like money, and whether some publisher will buy my book—I'm feeling a lot of pressures right now, and I spend an enormous amount of time with you, which *ought* to indicate how important you are, and I don't want a hard time if I'm late occasionally."

"Okay, okay," said Elizabeth. "Good. Let's drop it."

"No, let's keep talking about it; you're still mad."

"No, I'm not. I just want you to call."

"I will promise to *try* to call."

"Okay, good. Fine. Finished." She raised her glass halfheartedly to him.

"Listen," he said, "let's just keep talking, let's keep clearing the air."

"You know what you are, James?"

He shook his head.

"You're a Communicator. Like Rae." He nodded, beaming. "It's a sickness," she said. He nodded happily.

"I *know*. It's also one of the best things about me."

"Mama?"

They smiled at each other, somewhat embarrassed.

"Mama?"

"Come down here if you want to talk to me."

Rosie appeared in the living room in a minute and flopped over into the easy chair.

"Take your legs off the armrest."

"Yes, Miss Mother."

"Now."

"Right away, Miss Mother."

Elizabeth sighed deeply. James and Rosie immediately sighed just as loudly, and Elizabeth smiled.

"I came down for dessert," said Rosie. "We have *ice* cream, James, here at *our* house."

"Peach."

"Oh," he moaned. "It's *peach* season. And we're going to have peach ice cream, right now, right here." From the look on his face and the rolling motion of his shoulders and face, it seemed to be almost more than he could bear.

They sat on the darkened porch with Japanese bowls full of peach ice cream; the crescent of moon was just short of half way, platinum yellow; the points shone most brightly, and it seemed to Elizabeth that there had never been more stars in the sky. "Remember, Mama, when Mary Poppins pasted stars onto the sky?" Elizabeth nodded. She had poured herself and James a snifter of brandy as a chaser for the creamy peach. It was all so good. James sang "Would You Like to Swing on a Star?" Elizabeth silently rehashed their conversation. The two hours before he arrived had caused exactly those feelings in her which made her suspicious of love: sick, angry, hurt, hateful thoughts.

"James?"

"Yeah?"

"Is Heaven in our solar system?"

James lifted his brandy glass and looked down into it contemplatively. "Yes," he said. "I *think* so."

When the Fergusons had gone to Boston to visit Nana, when Rosie was three and a half, they had flown above the clouds but hadn't seen Heaven, no Emerald City where the sun was always shining.

"Where *is* it?" she had asked Andrew, about to cry.

"Higher up."

"How far?"

"About ten miles."

"Oh."

While Rosie and James continued their discussion of Heaven's situation, Elizabeth's mind raced with old, odd, sad memories of men. A perfect summer night: fragrant, warm, starry.

Rosie was positive, *positive,* that she could see Voyager II hovering alongside Saturn that night. They could hear faraway crickets, a chorus of frogs, an owl, the faint rustle of leaves. Rosie climbed lightly into her lap, and Elizabeth finally came back.

There were days when Rosie quite obviously wasn't getting enough from Elizabeth, who sometimes resented her child's presence when she would have preferred to be alone to savor her obsession with James, to rehearse or rehash dialogues and scenes of their life together so far. Rosie knew that her mother didn't want her around and sometimes got even by being as underfoot and demanding as possible. Other times she performed small retaliatory acts, like stuffing wads of newspaper into the toes of Elizabeth's shoes, shaking up the beer bottles, burying dishes deep in the garbage bag that she deemed simply too disgusting to wash.

Then she lied. *"I* didn't do it."

"Did the mice do it then?"

"How should I know?"

"Stop lying to me."

"Maybe James did it."

"Goddammit, Rosie."

"Goddammit, Rosie."

"Don't you fucking start that repeating bullshit on me."

"Don't you fucking start—" Elizabeth whacked her on the bottom, *hard.*

When James and Elizabeth had been seeing each other very steadily but not every night for a month and a half, they would walk in on one another in the bathroom and make jokes. And, as Elizabeth periodically smelled a just-removed Tampax for (among other reasons) indications of yeast or infection, it was inevitable that one day, without knocking, James entered as Elizabeth was dangling a bloody tampon by the string in front of her nose, sniffing.

"Oh, my God," he said. "Are you going to eat that?"

"Tell me a secret," James asked one morning in bed. "I've told you most of my best ones."

He had told her that he had frequently cheated in school until college, had slept with a man once, had sent away for a bottle of Growing Pills when he was a teenager, had lied about having read *Augie March*, had listened with a glass at the door to his parents' lovemaking; that his greatest fear was of imprisonment, that on his fifth Easter he had run outside to search for eggs, had stepped on a broken milk bottle, and had hidden in the bathroom, bleeding profusely, filled with guilt and the fear of punishment, cowering. He showed her the long thin scar on the bottom of his left foot. He had told that at six he had inadvertently killed a dog. She did not tell him—had never told anyone—that when she was four she put a kitten in the dryer because the kitten was rain-wet and the dryer was warm and that her mother had thrown in a load of wet clothes and the kitten had been dried to death. Elizabeth was in a trance when he told her about the dog; the movie played in her mind when her mother appeared holding the dead kitten, blaming herself, and Elizabeth could remember *exactly* how horrified she had felt at four because she felt it again for seconds, remembering; it knocked the wind out of her.

"Please, Elizabeth, please tell me a secret, please."

They lay looking at each other, wrapped around each other. "What do you want to know?"

"I want to know how you secretly feel about men."

"Okay. . . . Part of me hates them and is afraid of them. They have caused enormous pain in my life, and in the lives of my friends over the years, women and men friends. And I am frequently embarrassed for and by them because they're such self-parodies, strutting their stuff, being so fucking predictable. Are you using this for material?"

"Yes. Go on."

"Sometimes I've felt so revolted by a man, usually one I've had sex with, and so afraid of them fucking with my soul, that I think I must have been molested as a baby by a male relative."

"God."

"And then, see, I was *raised* to think men were dangerous, that any man my parents didn't know extremely well was a threat, a killer or molester or kidnapper. I was raised to be afraid of being touched by men. And then at the same time it was made clear to me that the great good approval would always come from a man, and that men were the ones to impress. And *then* I'm prepubescent and the emphasis is on how pretty and flirty girls are supposed to be—I mean, advertising, conditioning— you boys got off easy, advertising-wise. And then I'm eleven, and these breasts start growing like mad—you know, it was like the instant-pudding scene in *Sleeper*—and the boys go nuts and tease me in what felt like a vicious way, and my mother, who's pushing the nice be-pretty stuff, is freaked out about me and boys; it was causing her to go crazy, I think. I spent years getting these Fast Girl pep talks from her. Her voice would get all furtive and whispery-indignant—she'd put her face up close to mine and she'd feel all tingly, in a bad way. And it would be one word: fastgirl: 'Don't wear lipstick, people will think you're a fastgirl; do you know that awful Kerry Burns, her poor mother, the girl's a tramp, a fastgirl, bleaches her hair and hangs out with the trampy girl with the eyeliner, Marsha Crawford. . . .'"

James was laughing steadily.

"I bring home my eighth-grade yearbook picture; she makes a fuss about how pretty I look and then she's in such a frenzy about my sexuality that she's running a finger all over the page like she's looking in the Yellow Pages, it's like 'Can you find the Six Fastgirls in This Picture?' Mostly they were the popular girls. And in the ensuing twenty-five years my most excruciating pains have been caused by men."

"You're heterosexual, so it's men. If you were gay, the pain would have been from women."

"Maybe."

"You're very cynical about love, aren't you?"

"Yes."

"And you're so secretive—it was such good stuff you told me; it makes me able to understand more, you, and women, and me."

"Good."

"But see, the thing is, Elizabeth, we all know by now that it's all there is. And the world is in such danger and madness, and we have no leaders! We only have the people we're close to, and it's time we learned to love and trust one another—better, I mean, people in general."

"You're raving."

"No, I'm not. I think you can learn to have a loving attitude, like you learn a sport or an instrument. And it's time. . . ."

"Are you going to do the last scene from *The Great Dictator?*"

Hangovers. She had hangovers nearly every morning, although of course she didn't admit it. They left her lethargic, but wired and paranoid. Was James simply using her and Rosie for material? He was always jotting things down in his notebook. Was he using them because, in a few more months, he would have depleted his savings and would have to get a job . . . unless he moved in and sponged off her? What would he do if he knew how much she drank, all the extra shots and sips she took behind his back? There were times when, glancing at his face after she dropped a glass or walked unsteadily, she could tell he knew what he was buying into. Sometimes he watched her drink at dinner with a certain apprehension, as if he had slipped her a Mickey Finn, but he never said a word. If he really loved her, wouldn't he want to help her drink less? Un*less* he needed a progressively alcoholic woman in his novel—stop, stop! Stop being so distrustful, defensive, restrained.

But as much as he poured himself into her, and as much as she loved it, and loved pouring herself into him insofar as possible, she couldn't surrender and could only feel the absence of a thin shield of emotional Plexiglas when they were drunk and making love.

"I love you," he said often.

"Thank you." You're wonderful. You're great. Rosie adores you. I adore you. If you really knew me, knew my worst secrets, you wouldn't. "Oh, James."

"What."

"I am *so* fucked up."

"So am I. So is Rae. So is Jonathan Winters."

"Yeah?"

"Why are you so doleful? I *love* you."

She took his hand, kissed his fingernails. "I know you do."

If Elizabeth got out of bed when James did, he helped her make the bed without being asked, nonchalantly, as if by second nature, as a woman friend would.

But as often as not, Elizabeth slept in, claiming that insomnia had kept her up until all hours, when in fact she had drunk too much again.

"I'm getting a stranglehold on Part Two," he said one morning. "I'm going to write all night."

"Okay."

She missed him all day, couldn't get him out of her mind, missed him at dinner, wished he could taste the trout she'd cooked, wished he could see Rosie in her new overalls.

"Look out for bones, baby."

"Don't you miss James?"

"A little. It's nice to be alone with you, though. All to myself."

"Are you going to marry him?"

"I don't know. I've only known him a little while."

"But he sleeps here all the time. And he's in love with you."

"How do you know?"

"Because he looks at you all—googily."

"Yeah?"

"So do you love him?"

"He makes me feel happy all the time, just to think of him. . . ."

"So why don't you just say you're in love with him?"

"God. I don't know."

They lay reading in the window seat that evening, separately.

Rosie snuggled up beside her, absorbed in *Stuart Little,* and Elizabeth was trying to concentrate on an article in *Esquire.* Every so often she looked into her child's face, at the expression of quizzical nobility, at the baby finger crooked over her bottom lip; sometimes a look passed over Rosie's face, as if she were tasting something rare and delicious.

James was second on Rosie's God Bless list that night.

After tucking her in, Elizabeth returned to the window seat, resumed her reading, and found, in an article about high school, an answer to her unvoiced question: why she was so afraid to fall in love. A class of seniors were studying *Beowulf* in English, and the teacher could not get a discussion off the ground. All the kids were bored. Finally, a boy asked the question which was the answer to Elizabeth's. If Grendel was going to the mead hall all the time and devouring a bunch of men, why did men keep going back to the mead hall?

Elizabeth stared, smiling, at the ceiling.

Rae said, Be brave, be kind. Rae kept going back to the mead hall because it was there, and she needed it, and it was fun. Elizabeth sat upright. She would call James. James was wonderful. She liked him, loved him, trusted him, and wanted him. She was going to tell him now, tonight; she was going to throw her hat into the ring.

She walked, smiling, to the telephone, and dialed his number. A woman with an English accent answered. "Hello?"

Elizabeth, bug-eyed, hung up. What? No! Yes. Her stomach buckled, and her knees grew weak, and she stormed the kitchen, electrified with jealousy and rage. She slooshed scotch in and out of a glass, lifted it to her mouth with shaking hands. Goddamn fucking asshole, I was right: Short Man syndrome, general male shittiness—why didn't you trust your intuition? He was all wrong from the start, it wasn't the smoking and shirts and the dog and the quotes that had put her off; it was an intuitive knowledge that he was not acceptable to her. Close call. Thank God she had never said I love you. Good riddance.

The phone rang, and she let it ring ten times. Finally she answered. "Yes?"

"Hi, sweetheart," he said. "Did you just call?"

"Yeah. As a matter of fact."

"Why did you hang up?"

"Guess."

"Because a *woman* answered, and you thought it was someone I was schtupping, right? You're jealous, aren't you! Great! That means you love me. Lank and his girl friend are here tonight."

Elizabeth didn't say anything, only suddenly felt foolish and distrustful.

"On my honor," he said. She could tell he was smirking. Neither said anything for a moment. She heard a door close. "You was *jeal*-ous." She smiled. "Oh," he said, "I'm so happy. My heart soars like an eagle. You love me, don't you? Admit it."

"Yes."

"Can I come over and play?"

"Yes. James?"

"Yeah?"

"You swear to God that was Lank's girl friend? You didn't mention that she was English."

"It slipped my mind."

"But do you swear to God?"

"Yes."

"And you weren't fucking her?"

"No. I wasn't fucking her."

"And Lank is there?"

"Do you want to talk to him?"

"No. I trust you."

"Good. I'll be there in an hour." An angry blonde, ten years younger than Elizabeth, was glaring at him. He turned his palms upward, tried not to smile too broadly. "Elizabeth?"

"Jeez, I'm sorry, James," she said. And sighed. "I just wanted to know."

Chapter
🌿13

James arrived one drizzly evening with an envelope in the pocket of his jeans. "I got rejected at Putnam's," he said when she opened the door. He was brooding; she looked consolingly at him, felt as she did when Rosie suffered—it made her so sad—but a small voice in her was relieved, *glad* he had been rejected. She led him to the living room and felt so sad for him that she even found his green zip-up sportshirt endearing.

"The editor there said it was stupid and badly written and boring and he hoped I would die."

"Let me see."

James scowled and retrieved the envelope huffily. He thrust it at her, as if daring her to read it. The letter read: "Thank you for letting me take a look at your work. I'm afraid it's not right for us at this time, as we already have two autobiographical novels by men on our upcoming list. My main problem with your writing is that the humor is overdone, it's too show-offy. But please let me see your next book, and good luck. You have a lot of talent."

"Where's the part where he hopes you die?"

"You have to read between the lines."

"I bet it's a wonderful book."

"It's a piece of shit."

"Do you want a drink?"

"Yeah."

Elizabeth went to the kitchen. There was a half-empty bottle of J&B in the cupboard, from which she poured two stiff shots (one was an inch stiffer until she took a big bracing sip). She carried them to the living room, sipping on hers as soon as he could see her; the sip legitimized the whiskey on her breath.

Elizabeth was up to many tricks these days. For instance, now there was always a pint of whiskey in the study closet in case she needed one or two supplementary sips, or in case James was not there for the night. Sometimes it made her remember the scene in *The Lost Weekend*, Ray Milland's second bottle of rye, hidden in the chandelier, its shadow on the ceiling, but she knew she was nowhere near as far gone. This second bottle business was just a phase, but her secret frightened her: a furtive aristocrat who pushed wrapped empty pints down deep in the garbage can. She was drinking too much in the terror that James would find out how much she needed to drink.

But though, granted, a long one, it was a phase, so it would end.

"Here you are."

He exhaled and began to rave. He was having an episode.

Why would anyone care about his version of things? He had no talent, no story to tell. It would be discovered that he was not nearly so bright as his grades and banter suggested. He was going to have to get a job.

He was turning out like his father, was in fact becoming his father, and would consequently grow fat and bald and would need bypass surgery.

One of his molars was abscessed. He would need an expensive crown, and he was running out of money, and when the dentist did the root canal, the tooth would splinter and have to be picked piece by piece out of his gums. It would make *The Deer Hunter* look like child's play.

He had been under such financial and professional stress for so long that he was probably riddled with cancer. Soon his moles would begin to change color; sores wouldn't heal.

Elizabeth brought him a salami and cheese sandwich.

He was incapable of truly loving another human being. He was a hoax. He was depressed and obsessed all the time. He was secretly so furious about so many things—his father, his height—that he couldn't go ahead and let himself feel furious, because it would destroy him; if he let any of the black slime out, a flash flood of terrifying emotional pain and insanity would ensue.

She rubbed his neck.

He was probably going to become impotent pretty soon.

She studied his face, watched him go from animated despair to a wide-eyed numbness, saw the gaze of a dead man in a movie, where you can't imagine how he can keep his eyes open and still for so long. She suspected that he felt like the knight in *The Seventh Seal*. She knew the feeling.

"What can I do to make you feel better?"

"You're doing it. Being with you is helping." He picked up a burnt match, toyed with it, drew a charcoal line down the middle of his index finger.

"Do you want to go to bed?"

"I just want to sit here and brood."

"Okay."

"What if I never sell the book?"

"If you do sell it, you'll be faced with a brand new set of anxieties and doubts. About the reviews, and whether you have another book in you. . . ."

"I don't want to die without having published a book."

"But writing is its own reward. It makes you happy."

"Yeah, because I think I'm good. But if it turns out that no one else does, I have to face facts and start over. I have no idea what I'd like to be if I can't be a writer."

"One thing in your favor is that you work so hard. I think you're going to make it. You're brilliant, you're funny, and you're dedicated. You must put in forty hours a week. You know what Renata Adler said?"

"No."

"That everybody likes to go around saying that writers write. But that, really, writers drink and sleep and talk on the phone, and that she had met very few writers who wrote at all."

James smiled and lit a cigarette.

"So the odds are in your favor."

"Oh, thanks, Elizabeth." He hung his head.

"Now, let's take another drink up to bed."

"I won't be able to get it up."

"I don't care. You look like you feel like crying."

"Men don't cry, Elizabeth." He smiled at her.

A broad wedge of moonlight fell across Elizabeth's bed. She lay on top of him, fully clothed, and told him the story of Rae and her magic weight-loss shorts. He laughed but lapsed back into his brood, so she rolled off and lay watching him. Finally he unbuttoned her blue silk blouse, unhooked and removed her bra, and put his head in the crook of her shoulder.

She stroked his fuzzy hair, ran her fingernails up and down his downy back, and shifted so as to nurse him. He buried his head in her breasts for the longest time.

When they made love, she couldn't kiss him hard enough, would have chewed on his teeth if she could. They grew so slippery and wet together that she felt they were two hands, soaping each other in warm water.

Later, still and intertwined, they talked about nothing in particular. She knew how much better he felt, and it made her full and warm. She must be in love.

"Are you still awake?" she asked when his breathing grew soft.

"Yes," he said drowsily. "I'm listening."

She loved that he needed her. "James?" She felt him twitch.

"Vasco da Gama," he said.

'What?"

"Don't take the pocket off."

"Good night, James."

Several days later, he took the Fergusons to a double bill in the city, at the Surf: *Ninotchka* first and then *I Never Sang for My Father*. Rosie fell in love with Garbo, and the three of them laughed their heads off.

"Wasn't Melvyn Douglas handsome?" James asked.

"Yes."

Rosie dozed off during *I Never Sang for My Father*, awoke with a jerk, tried to watch the movie but couldn't. She fell asleep again, with her chin on her chest, lurched back to consciousness, and finally gave up. Elizabeth put an arm around her shoulders, and Rosie slept against her chest.

James and Elizabeth held hands. Gene Hackman was terrific. Douglas, so tall and debonair in *Ninotchka,* was old and sick and tedious, had settled like the contents of a cereal box. Jesus. Could it really be the same person?

Toward the end, Elizabeth heard faint sniffling, detected a quivering of James's shoulders. She took her hand out of his and put her arm around his shoulders. He sniffed loudly while taking a deep breath, collecting himself. Rosie was snoring softly. Elizabeth, holding them both, felt like a father.

Rosie slept all the way home in the back seat of his car, with his corduroy coat folded up to make a pillow. He lifted and carried her into the house, did not see her eyelids flutter open in the hall and then close again, did not see her small drowsy smile, the smile of a cat that has just had cream.

He smelled like a father to Rosie, smelled like Sharon's, strong and clean. Marry Mama, marry me. Thinking she was asleep, he kissed her eyes. God Bless James, she prayed, and Mama, and Rae. . . .

The next day, he asked Elizabeth if she wanted to read what he'd written so far.

Her heart stopped.

"Well, yeah. Sure." What if it wasn't good—would he truly want, and could she give, criticism? She thought no, on both counts.

"I can give you all but the last chapter of the first part. And I'll be done with that in a week or so."

"Well, for Pete's sake, I can wait a week."

"It'll be scary for both of us. That's what'll make it exciting."

"I know it's good. You work so hard, and you're so good with words."

"The best lines in it are yours."

"What?"

"I'm going to have to share the by-line with you."

It pleased one part of her, the part that was proud to have thoughts worth recording—it wasn't theft, she had no use for them. But part of her worried that this was the reason, that James had an ulterior motive for loving her.

"Is there a kid in it?"

"Yes," he said, "now there is; how did you know?"

"Will you get rid of me when my well runs dry?"

"You and I are inexhaustible."

If so, she thought, then they might marry and live together for a long time, so she absolutely must gain control of her drinking. She must stop letting herself go down the tubes, must not be a slave to it. But how? She meant to, pretended to, even sometimes tried to, but she knew the road to hell was paved with good intentions, and she couldn't stand the reality that inner change was a journey of a thousand miles, one step at a time, like the Indian shuffle. She wanted to get quickly to wherever she was going, wanted to wake up already there. And on some nonconscious level she sensed that something in her had to play itself out—had to snap or hit rock bottom—before she would admit defeat, and change.

So when James proposed that they take "a bit" of acid, for the adventure of it, for the fun of it, and because he wanted to write a section on altered states of consciousness, she said yes. It was pushing her luck, utter lunacy, bad timing, she must be out of her mind. Or would be out of her mind, after the LSD. Which was an attractive prospect at certain moments, when her mind was a dulled battlefield, her worst and only enemy.

And if she could have foreseen the madness, foreseen the horror, foreseen how it would hasten the inevitable and unavoidable day, she would still have said yes.

One bright blue August afternoon, when Rosie was going to sleep at Sharon's, they swallowed a weightless square of celluloid the size of a mica chip. Elizabeth felt great, beautiful and brave. It had been years since her last psychedelic adventure; six, to be exact, with Andrew in a cabin overlooking the Pacific Ocean— great fun, sex and laughter. James said that his friend had said it was the perfect light dose, and, as it turned out, it was.

They sat out on the porch swing half an hour later, waiting for the show to begin.

"Oh, well," said James.

"Oh, well, what?"

"Nothing's happening."

"Famous last words."

"When will we be halfway to Barstow?"

"Soon." She was only a little afraid: *adventure.*

After a few minutes more, he said, "Still not a thing," looked down at his shoe, and asked Elizabeth if she would brush the spiders off it. They laughed. *Boooooooooooooom.*

In a silent roar the world turns every color in the rainbow; Peter Maxian, kaleidoscopic and extravagant. The sky, garden, trees, and smoke from his cigarette are so beautiful and compelling that you have to laugh to have ever despaired: it is Heaven. She laughs.

His eyes are luminous green slats. Love for and trust in him purls in her blood. "I'm deliriously happy," she says.

"So am I. You cannot imagine how beautiful you look."

"It's the drugs."

"No, it's not."

"Well, so do you. Your eyes are so green right now that they're making your lashes green." And so on for six hours. Elizabeth becomes sentimental about the orangeness of an orange, the perfection of smell and sight and—ahhhh—taste; James becomes weepy at the glory of jade green kiwi cartwheels against a china-blue plate. Elizabeth, out loud, ponders the golden mean, *le juste milieu,* whether a human body is equidistant between the infinitesimally small and large, between quarks and stars. James, with much difficulty, manages to write this down in the notebook in his pocket, shows her the previous entry: *Merton, p. 35, the soul's structure: awareness, thought and love.* Awareness, thought and love. Elizabeth's mind is boggled with insight. So *that's* what the soul is, a life-changing revelation. She understands what they mean by *soul,* for the first time in her life; she *has* one. She considers, as she considered the orange, the Elizabethness of Elizabeth: images from the past, major incidents of pain and loss and mortification that she's carried around in her suitcase for all those years, come to her and she cries, thinking about her dead mother and father and husband; and she knows that every single thing that has ever happened to her parents and herself, and to James and his parents—backward in time like a geometric "St. Ives" progression—everything has happened to get her to this place, being with James and Rosie in a fine old house with a garden.

They make love in the sunlit bedroom, stoned out of their minds, requiring more trust than there are words for. The sensations are so intense and pleasurably disconcerting that it's like standing at the edge of the surf, as a child, with the tail end of waves rushing through the sand under and around her feet, water rushing toward shore and back to sea at the same time so that it feels like skiing through water and sand.

Who could have thought up balls, those hairy, bleached figs? Staring lovingly at her lover's wrinkles and blackheads was one thing, and somehow increased her faith and love, but staring from several inches away at his cock and balls and asshole is another: grotesque one second, fabulous in a laughable sort of way the next. The first time she had seen her own asshole, bending forward in a bathroom with mirrored walls, eight years old, repulsed and titillated, she had almost gasped out loud. Oh Jesus, she had forgotten, she had been caught bare-assed, examining the puckered brown hole, by her friend's older brother. The most humiliating event to date. What could she have said: I dropped a contact? She laughs out loud at the memory and it is too loud and maniacal and his cock falls from her mouth and she feels his body stiffen, feels his mouth pulling away from her pussy, and in a split second the variety of terrified alienation and madness which is the reverse side of the LSD coin—the psychotic, demonically insane side—has bitten Elizabeth, and his penis looks obscene and ugly and threatening, and a frenzy starts up inside her and she feels she will forevermore live at the far end of the wind tunnel, in hideous distortion, living on the dark side of her soul, living in hell. . . .

"What's the matter, angel?" His voice brings her back to earth. It is James, James has shown up to save her from herself. She turns around and puts her face next to his, on the pillow, and he holds her, nuzzling. And she's got a grip again by the skin of her teeth, hasn't lost it, hasn't had a great psychic blowout.

"Things got weird there for a second." Boy, I love you, James, she thinks, looking into his peaceful bright-green eyes, into a new sort of inner space, not her own, and she's not in the least bothered by the red fleshy lips on his forehead or the big gold ring in his nose.

"I'll protect you," he says.

Elizabeth has a rare cigarette with James, propped up on the pillows, amazed by the splendor of the room at dusk, at the warmth and softness of his leg against hers, at the silver blue doilies wafting from the Camels, glad to find herself not nearly so stoned as before.

"I'm coming down," he says, looking at the V of his fingers holding the cigarette.

"Me too."

"Cigarettes felt like cigars earlier. That was a day, Elizabeth, one of the favorite days in my life."

"It was *per*fect."

"I love that you giggle so much on acid."

"Yeah?"

"Yeah."

"I felt so happy with you all day that sometimes I couldn't tell where you stopped and I started up."

❦

They came down off the acid as gracefully as a hot air balloon landing safe in the right meadow, a soft, cushioned bump and the wild stonedness was over. Elizabeth, feeling sexy and loved and exhausted, put on her white kimono and suggested Kahlua and cream.

"*Per*fect. Let's bring it back up here to bed. I have a bit of jangles, do you?"

"Just a bit. There's always that little bit of speed."

"I think I'm still stoned; I'm just not tripping anymore."

"Me too."

"You sure look beautiful."

"Stay here," she said. "I'll go down and get it. Keep the bed warm for us."

When she returned with the bottle of Kahlua, cream, and two wineglasses filled with ice, he was reading cummings by candlelight, with the radio turned to the classical station, smoking another cigarette.

"God!" he said. "I missed you so much!"

She set the tray on the table by her side of the bed, and while she poured the thick dark liquor over ice, floated cream, he read to her: " 'Humanity i love you because you/are perpetually putting the secret of/life in your pants and forgetting/it's there and sitting down.' "

"Cheers." They clinked glasses, kissed, drank. He read more cummings to her and they drank several Kahluas on very empty stomachs: Elizabeth had never felt such peace of mind in her life, could now understand what people meant by *peace of mind.*

"Are you still stoned?"

"In a funny way, yes."

"Me too. But I'm so glad to have landed."

"The speed's still making me kind of jangly, though."

"Have another drink," she said.

"I sort of feel like smoking a doobie—you know? Just to take the edge off? Or would that be gilding the lily?"

Elizabeth shrugged. "I don't know."

James put the book on the floor, began pawing through his effects on the night table until he located a hearty roach of sinsemilla and a match. "I want to smoke a little dope, drink another drink, make love, and fall asleep."

"We're out-of-control drug abusers," she said, smiling and taking the joint. "But, you know. The Russians are coming."

Several hits and minutes and half a drink later, listening in silence to a trumpet concerto, he turns to her.

"So," he says, suppressing a smile.

"So," she says, suppressing one too, and is horrified the next second to see that he looks like the devil, that the windstorm in the tunnel has started up again, that her room is a white vacuum with no borders and the walls, when they rematerialize, are crawling with spiders, and suddenly the world has turned inside out and it's *Days of Wine and Roses* meets *The Shining*, and she knows that this time she will truly lose her mind.

It is like being stoned on a strobe light, with every color and texture roaring and flashing; even the silence is roaring and flashing and James's face is frozen with terror, and they look to each other, seeing monsters, and they lie back on the pillows, not blinking, not touching, not loving each other, utterly alone.

James is an enemy! He only pretended to take the acid—if indeed it was acid—so that she would take it and lose her mind; he is on the payroll of a Martian king who has ordered James to seduce her for diabolical purposes. "Give her the Black Chip, then *bring her to me.*"

Breathe, she commands. Breathe. She looks sideways at James, who lies gripping himself tightly, pretending to be silently freaked out. Oh, come off it, I'm on to you, James Bond.

Breathe. It's only the LSD. It will wear off. Please let it wear off. The joint has somehow reactivated it, if it really was a joint . . . *breathe*. Things settle down in her head, and she knows that everything is going to be fine, as soon as the acid wears off (*if* the acid wears off; if it really was acid).

The maniacal alien in bed next to her, a million miles away, the silver-irised saboteur, flails at the air above his rigid face, slaps at the top of his covers (what—spiders, leeches, snakes?)

and then feigns peace and dignity, as if he has been solicitously fanning away cigarette smoke. No help there. She tries to pretend that everything is fine—aren't drugs fun and all?—and that the worst is over, and becomes psychedelically deranged again for a moment. Rae comes to her and says, "Breathe into your belly, now into your heart, as if it has nostrils; breathe into your heart and open it up, over and over and over." She can feel the nostrils in her heart flaring out as air fills them, her heart expands like a lung, the shell of concrete around it starts cracking. "And another thing, Elizabeth. Pretend that you're a friend of yours, whom you're taking care of and talking down from a few bad minutes on LSD. You cannot fake things now, if you want to help you guys get through it."

James slaps at the side of the bed—something is evidently crawling up to get him—and she gets spooked again.

"It'll wear off soon," she says. "Pretty soon we'll stop hallucinating." She is scared and faking it, stiff and alien, her voice high in pitch, and he becomes even more dead to her—the James she knew is no longer in there; it is the scene in *The Shining* when Danny is pacing in the dark in his mother's room saying REDRUM REDRUM REDRUM in his sinister conehead's voice, and Shelley Duvall wakes up and starts shaking him and the hideous conehead voice says, "Danny isn't *here,* Mrs. Torrance."

Elizabeth looks at James.

"Everything's just *fine,* Elizabeth." Danny isn't here, Mrs. Torrance. No, it's just James, in almost unbelievably bad shape, but it is James and they love each other.

She breathes into the nostrils of her heart, and the roaring colors and sounds frighten her less. She stares at the stained-glass mirage above the dresser and tells the truth: "I'm extremely stoned again. I guess the dope reactivated it. And I think it'll wear off soon. I'm glad we love each other so much, and that we're alone. I don't think I've ever been this stoned before. I keep almost freaking myself out, and then I remember having weathered other times on acid. . . ."

"Everything's just fine," he says, forcing a smile.

Fakery. He breathes every couple of minutes, or so it seems

to Elizabeth, who finds it contagious, like someone else's limp.

"I'm too stoned," he says. He is shivering. They lie with their arms stiffly at their sides, but Elizabeth forces herself to look at him, to remind herself that it is *James.*

You've been here before, she thinks. You've been stoned, and you've had crises coming down, where it feels like you'll be stuck in this whirring roaring distorted madness for the rest of your life, and it's always worn off eventually.

"Everything's going to be all right," he says, through clenched teeth, staring up as if at a burning ceiling. His terror terrifies her. Spiders and bees fly at her in brilliant clouds and she doesn't scream, simply watches them, just as she watches the writhing pile of snakes near the door where James's pants and socks had been before, because she pretty much knows they're not real, and she makes herself keep breathing into her belly and into her heart. It's just *acid*; it's Hunter Thompson thinking he needs golf cleats for traction on the blood-sopped carpet of the hotel lobby in Las Vegas.

And it's going to wear off soon.

But it doesn't. James is hardly breathing, continues to slap from time to time at the bed, too cold and distant for her to touch.

"Don't worry," she says tenderly.

"Nothing to worry about," he says in the tight nasal voice of Beldar Conehead: We're from France.

"It'll wear off soon." He flinches when she touches his leg. *"Now* we're two distinct bodies," she says, "but earlier we made love, and we both experienced the two of us being one person, because we love each other so much. We had so much *trust."*

Beldar Conehead says, through gritted teeth, "Everything's just *fine."*

Poor James. She is in better shape, not quite so far out on the edge. *She* is going to have to be the strong one. Fear and an enormous strain flood her. She can't save them both, any more than she could save Rosie from falling out of a tree. She concentrates on slow, steady breathing, but her heart races, and she locates her inner voice in the space behind her eyes, down a bit, behind her sinus cavity, and it—her pain, the tears that she isn't crying—feel like a red prickly rash.

But mushy Rae keeps coaching her: Breathe. Open up your heart. She sits up in bed, pulls the kimono tightly around her, puts her hand on James's warm, taut stomach. He seems small and pathetic, Rosie after a nightmare; she thinks he needs her in the same way, and it takes away some of the blind fear.

She lies back down, but this time she draws him to her, so that he lies with his head on her breasts and she can put her arms around him like in Rosie's poster where the giant panda Madonna cradles her baby; and only faking it a little, she breathes slowly and deeply into her heart, into its nostrils, and commands him telepathically to breathe along with her. I love you, I love you, she breathes: respiratory hypnosis. He takes a long, loud breath and blinks. He looks at her suspiciously and somewhat relaxes, even forces a small smile, and then turns away to flail at the blanket. She smiles, holding him again when he relaxes, tenderly, as if he were her child, for twenty minutes more.

"Jesus," he said finally, sitting up, looking around, smiling sheepishly. They looked at each other. Elizabeth felt tears coming on. They grinned at each other. He shook his head with amazement. "No more *mag*gots," he said.

"We made it," she said.

"Skin of our *teeth*. You saved the day."

She nodded. Her eyes started filling up with tears, because of the way she had held him and because she had found a pocket in herself she could return to that was strong, calm, and maternal; and because she was so exhausted she felt made of thin glass.

"Skin of our teeth," she said. Tears fell down her cheeks, and she wiped them away.

"It's okay if you cry." He wiped her cheeks with the backs of his fingers. Her bottom lip shot out and trembled; tears clotted her long black lashes. James was smiling. "I can see exactly how you looked at six years old."

"I'm just so tired, James."

"I know you are." He put his arm around her shoulders and pulled her down, so that her wet face lay on his sternum, and cradled her until she fell asleep.

Chapter
🌹14

Rosie and James made her happy. Elizabeth, not used to the emotion of being happy for hours in a row, and days in a row, was wary. She felt an unconscious need, on occasion, for some recreational conflict-mongering, and so she nagged about trivial matters, or said no as a matter of principle—Elizabeth, whose mother's most hateful expression had been "Because it's a matter of principle." The possibility of losing this happiness made her feel like the soldier in Vietnam who has a week left of combat before he goes home, a "short-timer" desperate with fear that, having survived so many battles, it, the chance to go home, will be snatched away at the very last minute.

One evening after dinner, the three of them sat on the bench above the cliffs overlooking the bay and watched the sun go down. It hit the dark blue water at the horizon and blew to Kingdom Come in rose colors behind the Golden Gate. The fog to the left looked like a wave barreling sideways across the water, caught by a camera just before it crashed and flattened out.

"I have an idea," said James, who had been scribbling in his spiral notebook. "Let's go to the city tomorrow, on the ferry."

"All *right*," said Rosie.

"We'll see," said her mother.

"I know this great little restaurant, walking distance from the ferry building. Very elegant, little panties on the lamb chops and all that, but not too expensive."

"And a movie too," said Rosie.

"Maybe, yeah. Or we could take a taxi to the opera house and see the ballet. Now that would be great material. And there's a wonderful program this week, sort of a mixed grill of stuff from their major performances."

"You know how expensive that would be?" said Elizabeth, who could easily afford it.

James held out his palms. "It might be our last night on earth."

"Don't even *say* that, James," said Rosie.

"Spare me the details," Elizabeth said wearily.

"Look. We'll just go to the restaurant then. We'll split the bill."

"It's just a matter of principle. You don't have that kind of money right now."

"Hey, listen, that's my business. If I want to spend twenty bucks in the city, I'm going to."

"Mama, we can afford it."

Elizabeth bristled. What did he plan to do when his savings ran out? Give up the book and go back to work? Or would he want to move in with her, so she'd pay the bulk of the bills?

"Come on, honey." Elizabeth bristled again. "I have my heart set on taking the ferry with you and Rosie—it would be so much fun. It could be a great adventure."

"I have my heart set on it too," Rosie mourned. *"Lamb* chops with little panties."

"Look, I said we'll see."

"We'll see means no. Why don't you just say no?"

"Okay. No, then."

"Please, Mama?"

"You never want to go anywhere, Elizabeth."

"Oh, good, now you're both whining at me."

"But it's true."

"No, it isn't. In fact, I want to go home. Okay?" James and Rosie exchanged glances.

"I'm sorry," she said wistfully as they trudged home.

"Oh, Mama."

James put his arm around her waist. She was fighting back tears.

Their trip to the city was a rich, fine movie. She watched the extras on the bow of the ferry watch Rosie, stunning and sure of herself, formal in a blue plaid jumper and white knee socks; watched them watch James scribble away in his notebook, dressed in the rare cotton Oxford shirt and tweed jacket, his hair creatively mad. Engines, gulls, chatter, and the rustle of newsprint; Elizabeth smiled with a rueful awareness that she had spent her life under shadows of worry. All those fires and car accidents and humiliations that had never happened, all those hours spent in traffic jams, thinking that her lateness would result in bad fortune. . . . But now, from now on, things would be different.

On the way to the city, James and Rosie talked about W. C. Fields as Pharaoh, Buster Keaton in the lion's den. At one point they had Elizabeth in hysterics. They were, that night, all in love.

And the lamb chops were perfectly rare. See, Elizabeth? All that needless worry? Everything is turning out fine. Okay?

Full of resolve and good intentions, not to worry, not to pick, she found an ad in the paper for a job in a bookstore not far from town. She called the bookstore, learned that it was half-time, noon to five, and made an appointment for several days later.

"Great!"

"God!"

"Don't get your hopes up. All sorts of qualified people will apply." Rosie and James didn't care if she got it, that wasn't the point.

"You'll get it," they said. What bookstore owner could resist this stately learned woman, kind and funny once you got to know her, if you got to know her?

James made sushi for dinner. Elizabeth watched him gravely, knowing now for certain that she was deeply in love. He held a sheet of *nori*—phosphorescent black seaweed, cut like papyrus—over the gas flame until it grew green, laid it down on the counter, put a line of rice and scallion and clean pink *sashimi* and *wasabi* at the bottom of the sheet, rolled it up, and then (waggling his eyebrows) licked the edge and sealed it, as if it were an enormous joint.

"Oh, James," Rosie scolded. She revolved a Möbius strip on her fingers which her mother had just made for her. It was a strip of paper twisted and taped into a loop. Her mother's father used to make them for her mother at the breakfast table. In photographs, her grandfather looked like God, tall, old, silver-haired, or like someone on Mount Rushmore. The paper didn't have two sides anymore—she had drawn one continuous line without lifting her pencil at her mother's request and, sure enough, she had covered "both sides" of the paper.

"Now," said James, "get the scissors and cut it carefully in half down the middle."

When cut into two strips, it sprang into being as one *big* twisted loop.

"Wow!"

"Neat, huh?"

"Do another thing, Mama."

"We're about to eat," said James.

"I can't think of anything right off, anyway."

"What else did Grandpa do?"

"Well, once, at breakfast, he had a cup of soapy water, filled seemingly past the brim, with two pieces of string connected to each side and lying on the water: he pricked between the strings, and they parted."

"Why did he do that?"

"To demonstrate surface tension."

"What's that?"

"It's the molecular bonding on the surface of water, a cohesion that doesn't want to be disrupted."

"It's like your mother when she's in a bad mood. Right, Elizabeth? She has this boundary layer which cannot be broken through."

"That's surface tension: the tension on the surface."

James had set a plate of sushi in the middle of the red tablecloth, whose corners draped triangularly against a second, bigger tablecloth, this one a deep salmon floral. Elizabeth's tables were ephemeral art: the candlesticks, silver, and vases of flowers, wood hot pads, and linen napkins. He brought three enameled Chinese bowls of rice, and dipping sauces, and hot saki, in a Japanese vase, with two enameled vessels.

"Kampai," Elizabeth toasted him.

"Kampai." Empty the cup. The soft heat of the rice wine gave her a capacious strength: tonight she would tell him *I love you* without being asked. She watched the movie of the three of them eating by candlelight, listened more than talked.

The talk was of Babar and Celeste. Rosie, chattering away, was flourishing in James's company.

They read, separately, in the living room. Elizabeth kept looking off into space, daydreaming. If she said *I love you* they would be stuck with each other: she couldn't wait to tell him.

"Do you want a whiskey?" she said.

"No, thanks."

"I'm going to have a short one." She poured a larger shot than the one with which she appeared in the living room. "What is this, Science in Action?" she asked. James and Rosie were lying side by side over a piece of paper, and James was explaining relativity to her. A picky thought flickered, that he was trying too hard to please Elizabeth with how pleased he made Rosie. She stretched on the couch with the new Peter De Vries.

"One hundred and eighty-six thousand miles a second? God!" You're showing off now, James.

Rosie was stunned by yet another mind-boggling figure, like

how many tons a dinosaur weighed, or how many children had died in the time it took to read this page. James's motives, if any, never crossed her mind.

He had drawn a tram traveling on a beam of light traveling away from a clock inset beneath the steeple of a building. "It's gone one second, okay?" Rosie nodded. Elizabeth judged. "So how far has it gone?"

"How should I know?"

"Because I told you. Light travels one hundred and eighty-six thousand miles a second."

"Oh, okay. So it's gone a hundred and eighty-six thousand miles."

"Good. Now, you're on the tram, facing the clock, and you've been traveling for one second. You with me so far? Okay—now, it was twelve o'clock, according to the clock on the building, when you left. What time would you see now?"

"I couldn't see that far."

"Pretend. You couldn't really travel on a beam of light, either. But pretend you can see the clock."

"Does the clock have a second hand?" James nodded. "Then, twelve o'clock and one second."

"No. Time would have stopped, you see, because the light beam which left your eye and traveled to the clock also took one second—to travel those hundred and eighty-six thousand miles. So they would have, in a sense, canceled each other out—"

"Wait a minute. So what would the clock say?"

"Twelve o'clock exactly."

"But a second passed."

"Relative to someone standing beneath the clock. But in relationship to the time and space you traveled, it hasn't changed at all."

"Oh, God. I don't get it."

"Sweetheart, I finally understood it when I was twenty."

"I sort of get it. What if you were wearing a watch? Would it be twelve o'clock and one second?"

"It wouldn't be that late. But it would be a fraction of a second later than twelve. I think. Good question."

"Great question, doll."

I don't know, I don't know, do I really love you, James? Yes, clumsily, but quite a lot. And for once, these last few days, I haven't felt on the precipice: If you leave or betray me, I will fall over it. My mother did.

She turned to him twice, later, when they lay reading in bed. His clothes were in a pile next to the bed where they read. The rustle of pages, four hands brushing and holding paper; she bent her knees to nuzzle his with hers. When he looked at her kindly, she could not say *I love you.* He stubbed out his cigarette.

"More happy love!" she recalled, when they kissed, but she could not, that night, cross the Rubicon: I love you too, James. Maybe tomorrow.

She slept in after he left to write. She and Rosie went downstairs to make breakfast and found a note on the kitchen table, beneath the vase of white tea roses. She and Rosie read it together. He had typed it on the typewriter in the study, and it looked, as did all his notes, to have been transcribed by e e cummings.

little mother of all the russias: i
will be working on the book all
night, aided by nasally administered medications.
i will call you tonight i love
you. 'i
want to do with you what spring does to the cherry trees':
neruda.

"Don't you just love James so much?"
"Yeah. I guess I do."
"So do I. I think you should marry him."
"Oh, you do, do you?"
"Yes."
"What shall we have for breakfast?"
"Hot dogs."
"Is that what you want?" Rosie nodded. "Okay, I'll make you some."
"So are you going to marry him or not?"
"I don't know. We haven't known each other that long."

"But he's perfect." No, he's not. He talks too much, smokes too much, quotes too much. "And he can fix things, too."

"If I married him because he can fix things, I'd be using him. And I don't want to use him." Don't want to have to break up. . . .

"Wull, I do."

Love fills and creates the blackest voids. The day with its promise of night loomed before her, waiting to be killed. It was this pining obsession she disliked so much about love, he on her mind every second, all the while, suspecting that he was concentrating on his book, with periodic—and brief—fond thoughts of her.

Every car that drove down Willow was James, and every second the phone might ring but didn't. She read the newspaper, twice. Reagan, Begin, Russia—shit! She wrote Rae a long funny letter, urging her on: *Weave. Play. Get over you-know-who. Keep going and don't look back. May God restore your glorious gift of sight.* She planted snapdragons, sweet peas for Christmas, and listened to an opera on the radio at four while cleaning the downstairs, went to the phone several times to call James but didn't, and to call Grace and Charles Adderly but didn't. Waiting for the day to be over, she read on the porch in the sun until six, when Rosie and Sharon arrived for dinner.

The girls disappeared into Rosie's room while Elizabeth fried mushrooms to go on their steaks. Bach and the smell of butter frying soothed her, and she poured herself an Irish whiskey. She must somehow learn to concentrate: when she wasn't with James, she must learn to focus on whatever she was doing— reading, gardening, cleaning, cooking—but even as she thought this the rhythms and smells and therapy of cooking escaped her. I will call him tonight and take the plunge. I will learn to accept him as he is, so we will be lovers and allies. I will throw away the bottle in the study tomorrow, and, *mutatis mutandis,* we will live here together with Rosie. I will grow up, and younger, again. Commitment and compromise go hand in hand, like brother and sister.

"Click." Just when Elizabeth thought that getting through the evening would be as precipitous as that delay long ago in the Boston airport, Rosie and Sharon appeared in the kitchen, brandishing empty soap boxes, with lenses drawn on and shutters cut out. *"Click."* Sharon pulled a drawing out of the box, of Elizabeth in the kitchen at the stove, stirring and smiling.

"God, you draw well, Sharon."

"Click." Rosie handed her a drawing of James and Rosie out in the rose garden, playing Monkey in the Middle with his dog Leon and a Frisbee.

"Rosie! This is wonderful. We'll send some to Rae."

"Click." Rae at her loom. *"Click."* Sharon standing on her head, horizontal motion line suggesting a cartwheel.

"You two knock me out."

"One more, one more!" Rosie said, backing away slowly in a crouch. *"Click."* Elizabeth and James's heads on the pillows in Elizabeth's room, under the covers. Rosie had James's fluffy hair just right, and a heart in a caption balloon above Elizabeth's head.

The little girls giggled hysterically and tore out of the kitchen to compose themselves before dinner.

Everything is going to be fine, remember? Just relax. He will call.

It was quarter to ten when she tucked the girls into Rosie's bed. Everything was going to be fine. He was probably working as hard as he could, trying to finish so he could knock off and surprise her by coming over. The speed or coke or whatever he had would keep him up all night: he would be missing her by now.

She poured some Bushmills into a glass decorated with a drawing of Cruella de Vil and ten dalmatians, drank it pacing in the living room. She put Ry Cooder on the stereo to drown out the Cruella de Vil theme song playing in her mind and put another log on the fire. She sat down stiffly on the couch and studied the part in Cruella's half-black, half-white hair. Unless, after he called, he planned to come over, she was not going to say *I love you* tonight. Too bad for you, James; if only you'd called at a reasonable hour, I would have told you. But if you call in the next—oh, God, this is becoming "A Telephone Call."

This is not progress, she thought. I am almost forty and am anxiously waiting for my goddamn boyfriend to call. She saw herself lying in a hospital bed, weak but beautiful, surrounded by James and Rae and Rosie. She tried not to think about James. A memory blip of him flashed through her mind, and she blocked it by silently singing Cruella de Vil. No, this is not progress, she thought. I should call him. Maybe he's dead! Maybe he's had a heart attack like his dear old dad, or maybe he's—no, not in bed with another. . . . Progress would be to have faith. She got up and poured another shot of whiskey into the glass.

By eleven she felt the fierce disappointment of a fifteen-year-old girl at her parents' house who has been stood up by a boy, or the five-year-old whose goldfish has died. She went to the phone but sat back down. He said he will call, and he will. Cruella de Vil, Cruella de Vil. Fuck progress. Tonight, I want to wallow, in the calculated shallowness that allows men not to make that three-minute phone call which would better the woman's world for a while. But finally, when the phone rang, she smiled, stood up unsteadily, and lurched toward the phone.

Eyes shining, heart pounding, she answered with a note of incipient boredom.

It was Grace Adderly, calling to say she was sorry to be calling so late.

Crushed, Elizabeth said, "Oh, it's all right. God, I haven't seen you two for ages."

"Well, we're just fine, and we miss you. I've been thinking about you all day, wondering if everything was all right. I know it's late, but you're often up till all hours."

"Everything's just fine, Grace." Except for, you see, I'm cracking up. "I'm just lying in the living room, watching the fire and reading."

"We want you to come visit us soon, in the city! We *miss you* and Rosie."

"Hello, Elizabeth," Charles called from somewhere nearby.

"Did you hear him? He said hello."

"Hello! Gee, we both miss you too."

"Why don't you come for dinner soon?"

Oh, God, I've really got to hang up now, I know I haven't seen you for months, but you see my boyfriend is supposed to call, just to say hello, and I haven't seen him for over fifteen hours.

"Well, we'd love to, as soon as I get my car fixed."

"Oh, is it on the blink again?"

"Yes. Again." Not really, but if I come to the city, I'll have to drive home after all that wine or, even worse, stay the night.

How many times had James tried to call since she'd been on the phone with Grace? Rae, waiting for Brian. . . .

"Well, little Walter went and had *babies* on us." Elizabeth grimaced, tightened her fist in frustration. "You know little Walter, don't you, the tiger-stripe with a knot on his tail?"

"Two tacos and a fur hat," said Charles in the background.

"Charles! That's a horrible thing to say about a little cat. Shame on you." She began to tell Elizabeth about the nice movers who had dropped the dishwasher on Walter's tail but Elizabeth cut her off.

"Oh, Grace, it's good to hear your voice. Why don't Rosie and I come in for lunch next weekend?"

"Lovely. Which day?"

"I'll give you a call in the next few days, when I have a better idea of how long the car will take."

Finally Grace hung up.

At midnight, she called his house. No one answered. That was odd, because he couldn't disconnect his phone, could only take it off the hook, in which case she would be getting a busy signal. He must not be home. He had lied, then. Unless he was on his way over here. What if he's in someone else's bed? Golf balls.

That just can't be. He is in love with you. Don't worry. Think of all the disasters which never happened outside your mind. She poured some more Bushmills and stretched out on the couch, old and lonely and duped, waiting for him to arrive. Her loneliness triggered off the memory of twenty-some years ago, when she had awoken one night, well past one, to the sound of a piano and had tiptoed in her flannel nightgown to the top of the stairs, where she could hear her mother playing and singing softly,

"Someone to Watch Over Me," sad as possible, twice in a row.

She exhorted herself to have faith. She imagined marrying him, imagined the family of three they would be, imagined softly scratching his downy back with her nails. She got up and called.

"Hello?" said a woman, before the phone was slammed down, and for just a few moments Elizabeth lost her mind. She wanted to die.

She hated him more than she had hated anyone else. She gulped at her drink, just hanging on. Steady, old girl; good riddance. Better now than after a marriage. She wanted to light into him so vehemently that he would sink to his knees with his hands on his ears, as if she were sounding a drum-busting high note. She splashed whiskey out of the glass, her hand was shaking so hard. I hope you never sell anything else that you write. Rosie and I weren't enough? Asshole! We were the best thing that ever happened to you. She lurched, with fire in her eyes, up the stairs, to her room, holding the bottle, loaded for bear.

At two she passed out, crying, and when she awoke, just before dawn, she wished she could have died somehow, without deserting Rosie.

Chapter 15

Rosie and Sharon played that morning in the murky green stream that ran down a cleft in the ridge and ended in a stagnant pond filled with moss and minnows, willows, frogs, cattails, dragonflies, rushes, and water skeeters. They took off their shoes and stepped into the knee-deep water; Rosie, in baggy red shorts, walked upstream, with Sharon behind her, chewing on a reed, speaking in frog. Green frogs, brown frogs, blackish-red salamanders: they were brave when it came to slimy things, caught and freed dozens. They fought a duel midstream with cattails, then stripped off the brown fuzz and carried the rods to use as spears if the need arose. The stream was the Amazon, and they were its first explorers.

They screamed, giggling, when their tennis shoes, tied at the laces and draped over their shoulders, thumped against their backs—giant leeches, poison-tipped spears. They pointed out monkeys and snakes that hung from the branches beside the water, caught a glimpse of cannibals with bones in their noses and a big pot of boiling water and onions—there, behind that

boulder—stepped over sleeping alligators, and stared into the
bushes for the gleaming gold eyes of jaguars, or of deadly spiders
with jeweled bodies, as black and bright as a witch doctor's mask.

The tropical sun beat down on their backs until, finally, hun-
ger drove them back to the mouth of the mighty river.

"We should have brought a lunch."

"No kidding."

"I'm starving to death."

"So am I."

"We could collect acorns, and make some mush. . . ."

"There's tuna fish at my house."

"Is your dad home?"

"Yeah."

"Is your mom home?"

"Yeah."

"Well, let's go there. There's always money in your dad's easy
chair."

"But if we went to your house, we could get your allowance."

"Well. Maybe we should go to your house for lunch, get the
money from the chair, then go to my house and get my allowance. Then we can go get some candy."

"Okay. But I have to be home at three. I have a violin lesson."

"Okay," said Rosie, and they set off for the Thackery home.

Mrs. Thackery made them tuna fish on Wonder Bread and pink
lemonade. Rosie adored her.

The girls got the giggles soon after lunch, and Mrs. Thackery
asked them nicely to go outside to play.

"YOU'VE GOT FIVE MINUTES TO GET OUT OF
THIS HOUSE," Mr. Thackery bellowed from his study upstairs.

"We're going to go to Rosie's."

"All right, my darling. But be home by two thirty, for—"

"FOUR MINUTES THIRTY SECONDS." Rosie looked
around anxiously, half seeing the Beast upstairs, in his lair, covered with scales and hair.

"Give me a kiss, my darlings." Rosie kissed her soft sweet neck, awkwardly, below the chin.

"TICK TICK TICK!"

Meanwhile, back on Willow, Elizabeth grieved. Her sense of loss and hate wiped out the weeks of happy memories. Her pride was mortally wounded, and a river of jealous, revengeful, and humiliating thoughts occupied her mind. Now she felt certain that he had been with the woman who'd answered his phone, the first time. But she wasn't going to confront him. She thought that it would secretly please him for her to be livid about another woman; he might successfully use it as material. So she took the phone off the hook for the day. When she finally had to face him, she would keep her voice level and let him know that she had cut him off at the root.

She took a quick walk into town to take her mind off the telephone and tried to believe that James was no big loss. Willow was lush and bright, and neighbors looked up from their gardens to wave as she strode past imperiously. These people seemed to take pride in her now, pride in her elegant clothes and looks, as the children in Rosie's class took pride in Rosie's genius: it added certain elevation to their movie. She was silent and friendly, returned waves, nodded as her father once had, with a quiet snort of smily nervousness. Mavis Lee's mother sat weeding a begonia bed, with a can of beer beside her on the earth, wearing a finely woven straw bonnet which had eyelets around the brim through which the sun cast a necklace of tiny light beads on her aged brown chest. When Mavis Lee's mother looked up to toast Elizabeth, the necklace fell across her face.

Beer—she would get some beer, and garden, she would wear a hat for shade: everything was going to be fine. It wasn't the end of the world. The end of the world would be to lose Rosie.

What would Rae say? That everything that happened was supposed to happen, and happened for the best, no matter how disastrous it seemed. You would see this later, farther down the road. Rae would say that God hadn't meant for Elizabeth and

James to be together forever, because He had someone else in the wings for her, who didn't smoke or write or fuck other women.

Walking home with a six-pack of ale and some groceries, her throat ached, her stomach flushed, and the hot red rash flared up behind her eyes. Back home, in the kitchen, she opened an ale to fight back the tears, and her stomach was empty except for coffee and steamed milk. The thought of surviving the next few days—probably, in fact, the next few weeks—filled her with a towering, discouraged agony. She was hopeless, would never be wholly happy again. But the ale lifted her spirits, and a jolt of hatred came to save the day. She opened another ale, at about the time the girls stepped out of the Amazon, and took it out to the garden.

As she gathered sweet williams and snapdragons, she swore she would not honor him with a scornful confrontation, but hostile dialogue spun through her mind, and her lips moved as she bent over the pansies. She caught herself, looked around to see if anyone was watching her go mad, and, finding no one, willed herself to relax. She drank the ale with a vengeance as she watered the morning glories, tried to concentrate on the white pinstripes radiating from their china-blue centers. She talked to herself again, out loud, muttering insults, caught herself, and stopped.

The man was a joke, not worth this misery. She ran through the List again—the smoking, the height, the shirts, the dog, the pretentious quotes, his repellent chewing—and the treachery.

The bright garden blurred for a moment as she stood up with an armful of flowers. He had ripped her off, betrayed her, and she could never trust him again.

She walked fairly steadily to the kitchen and arranged the flowers in three crystal vases, took one to the living room, one to her night table, and one to Rosie's room. She put them on the chest of drawers and stared at the giant panda Madonna, thought first of Rosie in her arms, and then of the times she had held James that way, and then of the times she had felt him hold *her* with the sad composure of the panda Madonna, and couldn't stand the pain.

Halfway through another ale, she felt that she could breathe again. She went back out to the garden and sat down beside a flower bed. Her house and garden and child were stunning; everything was going to be okay. This too, she thought, shall pass. She sat admiring her long thin legs, zeroed in on the gypsy-red toenails, cut to the red blossoms of the ginger root, cut to the beautiful white Victorian under a bright blue sky, cut to the woman with sun on her fine black hair, leisurely drinking a beer in her garden, calm, a woman to envy.

Her blade grew duller and duller. She couldn't remember the names of common items; for instance, she couldn't recall "manuscript" as that thing of James's which she now wouldn't have to read. She snapped her fingers; what was the word? M and N appeared on the screen behind her eyes and she stared at the letters as if having a moment of second sight: manuscript, that was it.

She needed Rae desperately all of a sudden, needed just to hear her voice, and decided to call her in New Mexico. But when she stood to go inside, she swayed forward, regained her equilibrium, and swayed slightly backward. She gagged, surprised, and looked down at her feet, which suddenly seemed not big enough to support her tall frame, and stood swaying in the hot sun, an inflatable punch-down clown on weighted cardboard feet. She walked slowly inside, cradling the flowers, trying not to lurch. The whirlies began on the porch steps, and it took all her resolve to make it inside.

She held on to the wall, holding back vomit: you were a fool to drink three ales on an empty stomach in the midday sun.

Oh, I do not feel well at all, she thought, as she inched along the wall to the living room. She flopped down onto the couch and lay down, swallowing over and over. The couch was on the high seas, and then on the low choppy seas, and she knew she had to vomit, but the bathroom was too far away; even if there was time, she would have to crawl—*urg*, bile rose past her throat and she blearily looked at and reached for the clear glass fruitbowl. *Urgggggg.* She threw up in the bowl, on deflated grapes, over and over, feeling better. When she stopped, her eyes were full of tears. The dry heaves began: there was nothing left to throw up. I am not impressed, she thought. To have reached such a low that the dry heaves are an improvement. At least it is taking my mind off James—oh, shit on toast, I have hit rock bottom. James! See what you made me do?

It was two o'clock and the girls were four blocks away.

"We forgot to look in your father's chair."

"He wasn't in a very good mood." They opened the white lattice gate and stepped into the Ferguson yard. "How come there's never any change in your easy chair?"

"Cause my mama doesn't carry it in her pockets."

"Why?"

"Because it makes her look bulky."

"You think she's going to marry James?"

"Yeah." I hope so.

They burst through the front door and tore into the living room. Elizabeth, on the couch, was dead to the world. She was making the gurgling, hiccupy noise of a person who may be throwing up shortly, and a bowl of vomit and grapes lay on the floor beside her.

Rosie looked as if she had been slapped, hard, out of the blue. Blood rushed to her face. She blinked back tears, nostrils flaring, and ran from the room, up the stairs. Sharon's surprise had passed and she lingered for a moment, taking in the scene with a look of infinite compassion. Elizabeth opened an eye, saw Sharon, and closed it. Sharon turned and bolted upstairs too.

Rosie was in her bedroom, crying, and wouldn't look at Sharon when she first entered. It was all a bad dream. If James could see her mother now, he'd never want to marry her. Sharon would never forget this, would from now on see this scene when thinking of Rosie or Elizabeth.

"It doesn't really matter," said Sharon, kind, sturdy friend that she was. "Maybe she has the flu."

"Of course she has the flu, you think she goes around just throwing up or something?"

"No, I didn't think that."

Rosie stared down at her pigeon-toed feet, brooding but no

longer crying. "Well, I think I'll go into her room and get the money she owes me."

"Okay."

"She owes me a *lot.*"

There were three tens and a one in Elizabeth's wallet. One dollar was not going to make much of a dent in Rosie's hate. A ten, on the other hand . . . and there were three of them, besides. Plenty to go around. Sharon watched in horror as Rosie pocketed a ten and replaced the wallet in the purse. Rosie looked at her defiantly.

"What are you staring at? She owes me ten."

"Rosie! We're gonna get in such trouble."

"I told you. She owes me it."

Sharon looked around the room wildly, holding her breath.

"Let's get out of here," she said.

They tiptoed downstairs, tore out the front door, and ran to town without stopping. Breathless, they entered the five and dime, where Mavis Lee measured out a dollar's worth of candy corn in two small white bags. They stopped at the grocery store for Mystic Mints and Cheetos, bought a can of Coke at the gas station, and went to the fort on the lagoon. They started with the candy corn, gobbling it down like popcorn.

It was a sad, frenzied time they spent, sitting on bricks, the day they ripped off Elizabeth. Plagued by bad conscience, guilty on Elizabeth's behalf, they felt the Mystic Mints grow chalky in their throats and finished only half the box before moving on to the Cheetos, all of which they consumed with the help of the soda.

Rosie's mind reeled with shame. The food helped, in a way, but how could she face her mother, hating her now as she did? She hated the woman from whom she had stolen, hated the woman who'd loved her so much.

Elizabeth woke up at three and eyed the bowl on the floor. It all came back rather quickly: the ale, the whirlies, the retching, and a vague recollection of Sharon. Dread filled her. Rosie and

Sharon had seen her, passed out. Rosie, I swear to God, it will never happen again. You see, James was—James betrayed me, you see, and so—no. I know. I drank too much before, too. Sometimes I feel tired and weak, drinking makes me feel better; but Rosie, I swear to God, I will not embarrass you again.

She got up and went upstairs to wash up. She'd been trying to cut down, and drinking more than ever: it was time to truly get a grip. Rosie was everything in the world to her, the great constant love. That Rosie trust her, from now on, was foremost in her mind as she climbed the stairs to the bathroom. Fuck men, fuck James: the hell with them all. She brushed her teeth, put on mascara, brushed her hair up into a bun, and rubbed blusher onto her cheeks. Rosie, I'm sorry, she thought, and planned the perfect meal to win back her affections: cheeseburgers, potato chips, something special for dessert. Fresh air would do her good. She would walk to the bakery for brownies. That was it, fresh air and brownies.

She breathed deeply, relieved and contrite, went to her purse, and opened the wallet.

Chapter

🌹16

"Well, I gotta go. Come over at four," said Sharon, leaving Rosie off at the boardwalk.

"Okay. See ya." She watched Sharon walk away. There was over five dollars in the pocket of her voluminous shorts, and nearly an hour and a half to kill. And she couldn't go home.

She was lonelier that anyone had ever been before, except for Typhoid Mary. Everything felt wrong, like a creepy dream, and she was afraid she was going to die: Rosie was stoned with fear.

She bought a package of bubble gum at the five and dime, where she saw herself in a full-length mirror: ugly, skinny, evil. Her eyebrows looked like caterpillars. Her heavy black curls and her eyes were devilish, like that lady with snakes for hair, whose face turned you to stone. Don't look! Turn away! But for a moment, she didn't move a muscle.

"Rosie?"

"Yeah?" She whipped around, out of the trance. Mavis Lee was ringing up her purchase at the cash register, normal chubby nice Mavis Lee, who'd known her all her life.

"Here's your change. What's the matter?"

"Nothing."

"Are you sure? Where's your sidekick?"

"At her violin lesson. Until *four.*"

"Is that why the long face?"

"No. Derrr. I have to go," Rosie said glumly, unwrapping a piece of gum.

" 'Bye, Rosie," Mavis Lee said, scowling in imitation. Rosie scowled good-naturedly and dropped her head forward, sticking the gum in her mouth, tracing the letter R on the floor with the toe of one shoe, happily embarrassed. Chubby old Mavis dropped her head, silently stammering.

"Tssss," said Rosie, smiling, and crossed her arms reflexively. Mavis crossed hers and twittered her face like Mrs. Haas did, the look Elizabeth said was gratified indignation, and after a moment looked at an imaginary wristwatch. Rosie giggled, chewing her wad, thoroughly pleased with the attention. Slowly, with her eyes on Mavis, she blew a thick pink bubble. Mavis's brown eyes grew bigger, as did the bubble, now the size of an orange, bulging bigger and bigger; it was tormenting Mavis, and Rosie relished the moment. Mavis thought it was going to burst all over her face. She took it out of her mouth, tied it off, bit a small hole in it, and dangled it before her eyes as it deflated. Then she put it back in her mouth, said goodbye, and left.

By the time she reached the beauty salon, she was glum again. Only ten minutes had passed since Sharon said goodbye. Standing on one foot, she looked into the window at the ladies getting haircuts, or getting curlers, or under the drier. She blew a bubble, and furrowing her brow she gazed vacantly at the coils of blond hair which lay on the linoleum floor beneath a beautiful woman, the most beautiful woman Rosie had ever seen. The blonde read a magazine while a man put her hair in pink curlers. The blonde was Beauty: the daydream began.

Rosie's eyes crossed almost imperceptibly, and her lips parted; a small bubble covered all but her bottom lip, and remained so for the length of her trance: She was grown up, with blond hair, and *so* good, so good that she could love the Beast. She looked deep into his eyes, knew they loved each other, took him by the paw, and led him home. He could live in the study—somehow she would hide him from her mother. One morning she would bring her poor beast a bowl of cereal and find him dead. She and Sharon would drag him outside to the rosebushes and bury him. Rosie would cry, "I finally found my beast, and now I've lost him." Then the prince would fall in love with her, and she would say, "No, I cannot marry you, for I love my beast," and he would say, "Look into my eyes, I *am* your beast." And it turned out he got to be a prince because of Rosie's love. The end.

She snapped to with a blink, and looked at the clock in the beauty salon. It was only *three* minutes later, forty-five to go until she could begin walking to Sharon's. To make the time pass, she forced herself to sing "This Old Man," all the way through till he played ten, he played knicknack again and again, and then made herself move next door, to the record store, where she stared at the records in the window and sang "This Old Man" all the way through again. Then she moved sideways to the next shop, women's clothing, and sang "This Old Man" again. By the clock in the butcher store, sixteen minutes had passed. She glared at the clock; twenty-nine minutes to go, and Sharon's house was only five minutes away. She walked in baby steps for as long as she could toward Sharon's.

Mr. Thackery's car was parked in the driveway, and when she got to the front stairs, she could hear typing from the open window in his study on the second floor. She knew that she and Sharon were not allowed to be in the house with him if Mrs. Thackery wasn't here, because they got on his nerves, so she sat huddled forlornly on the front step. Thick bored time passed. She could stand it no longer: if she could just play with Sharon's toys and trolls, Mrs. Thackery and Sharon would be home before she knew it. But she couldn't go in. Making several braids in a troll's hair took time; she could play with the musical jewelry box, with the jewels and the ballerina who spun when the lid was lifted, or she could color in the King Tut coloring book. She fiddled with a plastic-tipped shoelace, wrote with it on the cement stair, wrote her name in a layer of fine dirt: *Rosie*. She turned her head and peered up at the open window. She shouldn't go in. But she did.

She closed the door softly and walked up the stairs, not making a sound. Her heart began pounding in her throat as she crept to the closed study door. Taking a big swallow, she asked, in a high quavery voice, "Mr. Thackery?"

He didn't answer for a moment. "Yes?"

"It's Rosie."

Again, he didn't answer right away. "Yes?"

"I'm supposed to meet Sharon here at four? But I was wondering if I could play in her room until she gets here?"

"Well, sure. Come on in for a minute."

Rosie opened the door a crack and peeked in.

"Come on in, all the way. That's a girl. Don't be shy."

Mr. Thackery sat at a huge, ancient desk and looked at her in a friendly way.

"Hi."

"Hi, Rosie. I just wanted to say that I'm sorry if I yelled at you two this morning. I was trying to concentrate."

"Oh, that's okay." Rosie looked around in wonder; although she had peeked in once or twice with Sharon, she had never been inside this room. There was a boat like the *Santa Maria* in a bottle, an antique desk with a globe on it, a shelf filled with ivory statues, a great warrior's sword with jewels on the handle, and a huge aromatic leather easy chair that looked like a throne.

"Have you ever been in here?" he asked, not getting up.

His face was kind and roundish, pink and fatherly. She shook her head.

"Well, look around."

She did: a grandfather clock said fifteen minutes till four. A clear glass stallion reared on its hind legs, a large framed photograph showed Mrs. Thackery holding Sharon when she was a baby—Sharon had been the prettiest baby in the world—and an old-fashioned gun was displayed in a glass case on the wall.

"Here's something you'll like," he said, opening his desk. Rosie just looked at him. "Come here. My father gave it to me when I turned eight. Are you eight yet?"

Rosie nodded her head. "Yeah." She walked to his desk to see what he was taking out.

It was a very, very old pocket knife. He pulled it out and

stroked its sleek silver blade, replaced it, dropped it back in the drawer. He got up from his desk, and indicated that Rosie should sit down in his chair. She looked up quizzically into his kind face. He nodded once, and she sat down. She bounced on the cushion, gripping the broad padded arms, pushed back slightly, found courage, and reached for a wrapped cigar on the desk. She inhaled it, leaning backward, smoked it like Groucho Marx. Mr. Thackery laughed, and Rosie blushed, happy again. He was standing close to her, on her side, like a father would, like he was her father. She knew he was smiling down on her. At that moment, she had a tremendous crush on him and sought his approval—another laugh: she straightened up in the chair and reached forward to push an imaginary button on his telephone. "Yes, Mrs. Binsley, will you please send in a dozen donuts?" And he laughed. "Thenk you veddy much," she said. And he laughed again. It was ten of four.

His hands were jammed into the pockets of his suit pants, and she saw, out of the corner of her eyes, what she thought was his hand moving in his pocket. It brushed faintly on her shoulder, and electricity flowed through her. Something was going wrong here; she looked up into his friendly face, and he held her glance, a glance full of the entranced helplessness of a child; and at the bottom of her vision was movement, and slowly her eyes moved downward, and his zipper was undone and coming out of it hard and upright was a—no, no, this couldn't be, she stared at his hand on the huge purplish-red veiny dick, at the hideous tuft of black frizzy hair, and waited to wake up.

He touched it to her arm. It was like hard rubber.

"I show Sharon all the time"—*Row row row your boat*—"it's good for girls to see their fathers naked; it's nothing to be ashamed of"—*gently down the stream,* time is standing still—"if your father were alive"—*life is but a dream.* Life is but a dream. *Row row row your boat, gently. . . .* It was sticking straight out, waving. "Sometimes Sharon touches it." No, Sharon wouldn't touch it.

She's in the nightmare where she can't move, where she's paralyzed, underwater: the top part of it looks like a purple mushroom, and he has his hand wrapped around the rest of it, is moving it up and down like a conductor pulling on the train whistle's string. . . .

"Go to Sharon's room, there's a girl," he said, and stepped away from her chair. His breathing was louder now, and at first she couldn't move, but then slowly, afraid that he would grab her, she inched out of the chair and without looking at him, once again not blinking, she tiptoed toward the door. Two minutes till four.

"Rosie? I think you better not tell anyone. Okay?" Rosie, at the door, with her back turned to him, nodded several times.

It was a dream, but even in a dream you had to run for your life; her mother would be furious at her if she knew. Sharon wouldn't really touch it. It was so ugly that she would never get it out of her mind, everywhere she went she would see it; she would go crazy, like the girl in *The Mummy with the Green Diamond Eyes.* She was taking the stairs two at a time, she had to get out of there before Sharon and her mother got back, she could never come over again . . . but throwing open the front door, Rosie saw Sharon walking toward her, holding a violin case, and Mrs. Thackery struggling with a bag of groceries in the back seat, and she was trapped. Her heart was pounding a million times a minute, and she wanted to run to the back yard, climb over the gate, and escape, but Sharon ran up to her.

Sharon took one look at Rosie, and her eyes grew huge and alarmed, and they both looked as if, if you pushed the right button, they would spring twenty feet in the air.

"I have to go—"

"Wait a minute, wait a minute." Sharon grabbed her hand and pulled her toward the house. Rosie dug her feet in like a mule, and Sharon said, "I just have to put my violin inside," and before Rosie could collect her thoughts, Sharon had dashed to the house, opened the door, stuck her violin inside, and run back to Rosie. They looked at each other, and then over at Sharon's mother, who was walking toward them holding the grocery bag.

Rosie pulled herself together, or so she thought: she had her eyebrows raised all the way up so that her eyes looked half awake, and her mouth was in a tiny tight smile. She moved toward Mrs. Thackery and the gate as if walking on eggshells. "Hi," she said, raising her hand in salute. Sharon was all but tiptoeing too, looking as if she were about to whistle.

"Hi, Rosie, my dear. Did you just arrive?"

"Oh, yes."

"Mommy? We're going to the schoolyard."

Rosie nodded.

"Well, all right. but be home by six, at the latest."

"Well, 'bye," said Rosie, still nodding.

"Goodbye."

They ran, hell bent for leather, past the school, through the town, across the old railroad yard, until they came to the start of the Mexican Trail. They stopped to catch their breath. Straw-colored now, the hills of the ridge ran downward like the knuckles of a lion-paw foot, covered here and there with green patchwork, bunched and nappy from a distance, like fleece. Rosie and Sharon leaned, gasping, against the trunk of a great cypress with fantailed branches that looked like a catcher's mitt: Charles Adderly. had pointed out the resemblance once, in his sprier days. You could watch it catch a northerly, flick its wrist, and fling the wind back toward the bay.

They set out at a fast clip up the trail, bordered on either side by trees through which the afternoon sun lay in slats and sometimes broad beams on the ground. Birdsong, and the crunch of leaves, twigs, and acorns in the dirt beneath their feet.

Rosie looked grim. Now no longer positive that Mr. Thackery had shown her his dick, she was at the same time filled with the dreadful prospect of having the memory of it appear in her mind every few seconds for the rest of her life. The images would haunt her forever: his dick and the knife. And the gun. What if she told, would he hurt her? Who could she tell? Rae was gone, and her mother would do something drunk and humiliating. The Adderlys were too far away, and besides, you weren't supposed to mention dicks in front of old people. She would never be happy again.

"Sharon?"

"Yeah?"

"Nothing." Sharon knew the secret too.

"Jackie Boy?"

"I don't feel like singing," said Rosie.

"Just one song."

"Okay."

"Jackie Boy?"

"Master?"

"Sing ye well?"

"Very well."

"Hey down."

"Ho down."

"Derry derry down, among the leaves so-o green-oh."

Singing, she could block the picture of the penis. "Well, I-i-i've got rings on my fingers, bells on my toes, elephants to ride upon, my little Irish rose": walking and singing in the warm forest took her mind off Mr. Thackery, but each time it flashed through her mind, her stomach fluttered. "Listen," she said suddenly, and they stopped, as did time: somewhere close by, up on the hillside behind them, came a distant crashing, the crackling of twigs and leaves, too fast to run from, and they stood gripping each other's hand, wide-eyed and unblinking, as the cracklings approached, whipped around expecting a werewolf or tiger, and screamed bloody murder at a terrified fawn, which turned and bolted back up the hillside.

They giggled hysterically for several minutes, then set off again, still holding hands.

"Rosie?"

"Yeah?"

"Nothing."

"What."

"Your dad's supposed to let you see it in the shower when you're very little, and then as you get older he wants you to see that it's just this natural thing, so you don't scream when you see your husband's."

"Mama never told me that."

"That's because your father's dead."

"I don't even want to talk about it."

"But you're not supposed to tell anybody, because it's totally private."

"Well, just shut up about it, because I'm not going to tell."

"You promise?"

"Yes."

"You swear to God? . . . Rosie?"

"Yes, I swear to God; now just shut up about it."

"We should go back," said Sharon. "We've walked for so long."

"Just a few minutes longer."

"Okay." After a minute of silence, Rosie began singing:

> "Bell bottom trousers, coat of navy blue,
> She'll climb the riggin' like her daddy used to do.
> If you have a daughter, bounce her on your knee.
> And if you have a son, send that boy-o out to sea,
> Singing bell bottom trousers, coat of navy blue—"

"It's starting to get cold."

"Okay. Let's go back."

"Boy, are we going to get it from your *moth*er."

"Oh, boy." A vision of her mother, loud and furious, filled her head. Cruella de Vil. She was in for a bare-bottomed spanking, there was no doubt of it. Unless James was there. She hated for James to know about the theft, but her mother didn't act so mad when someone else was around. She could sneak upstairs to her room and hide, but if James was there the punishment wouldn't be so bad, her mother wouldn't act so disappointed and tight. "You want to spend the night?"

"I don't know."

"Mama won't be so mad if you're there."

"But I don't know if I can."

"Well, you can call from my house."

"What if *your* mother says no?"

"I don't know. We've gotta walk faster."

"I'm getting the shivers."

"Me too."

They walked along with a sense of rising panic: the forest was getting dark; it was later than they'd thought. Elizabeth was waiting for them. What was Mr. Thackery doing right now? They held hands and walked as fast as they could.

An owl, birds, ominous cracklings. What if a man stepped out from behind a tree? "One hundred bottles of beer on the wall, one hundred bottles of beer. . . ." Their teeth chattered as loudly as red plastic wind-up dentures clacking across a table. When they reached the great old cypress, they broke into a run.

By the time they reached Willow, they were on their last legs, and walked toward the Ferguson house with side aches, skinny brown legs trembling with cold and fear and exhaustion, holding hands, all but limping. They stopped at the white lattice gate to take deep breaths. Rosie crossed herself, and then they stepped into the front yard of the Ferguson house.

PART
THREE

Chapter
17

By a quarter till seven Elizabeth was half out of her mind with worry, and had called the Thackery house a dozen times, but each time the line was busy. She gulped down a shot of whiskey to quell the mounting panic, dialed again, hung up, and sank into a chair at the kitchen table. The girls were hurt, or dead, or lost: she felt so sure of this that she took it to be a premonition rather than an active lack of faith. The thought of James made her hold onto her stomach with both hands. She got up, dialed, and slammed down the phone again. That gossipy airhead!

Hunched over the kitchen table, she wrote out a list of their forts—the lagoon, the railroad yard, the old Murphy house, the dunes on the beach—and their classmates, with the intensity of a myopic amphetamine freak doing scrimshaw. For the police. Oh, God, don't let them be dead. If only they are safe—I will give up anything else.

In the meantime, she poured herself another whiskey and dialed Sharon's number again. But the line was still busy.

She leaned in the direction of the front door and cocked her head. Thinking she heard footsteps, she walked to the front of the house. No one was there; she stood at the opened door and gazed out in a trance. Please let the girls come home. Maybe she was dreaming, would awake to find James beside her. . . . Across the street, a green-trimmed window on the lower level of the Haas house opened and an orange cat flew out onto the lawn. The window slammed shut, and Elizabeth's phone rang, just once. She looked toward the phone on the teak stand in the hall, puzzled. An auditory hallucination? I am losing my head, she thought.

She went toward the kitchen for another glass of scotch. She had a genuine reason to drink (although a week ago, the dog Leon's tenth birthday had seemed a good excuse). Please, she prayed, to no one in particular, let the girls be safe. There *are* no atheists in foxholes, she reflected, and then the phone rang. She had taken three fast steps toward the kitchen when the front door opened. She spun around, lurched to the hallway, and rushed toward the two girls who stood inside the door.

She gaped at their beautiful faces, but the relief was instantly forgotten and she wanted to slap them both silly, wanted Sharon to leave so she could attack her daughter. The phone continued to ring, but no one moved. Sharon held her breath, while Rosie looked back at her mother with an air of casual defiance, which made Elizabeth want to wrench her daughter's arm out of its socket.

It was clear to Rosie that her mother had gone crazy; they clenched their fists and jaws identically, facing off.

The phone stopped ringing.

"I better call my mother," Sharon said, squirming.

"She has to stay over tonight."

"No."

"It's okay, Ros—"

"Mama? She really has to." There was an eerie look in Rosie's eyes, new to Elizabeth, sad and tempered and mature. What on earth has Rosie seen? Death or sex or violence?

"Rosie?"

"Mama?"

"What's going on here?"

Rosie looked skyward for help. Elizabeth looked over at Sharon, who was staring down at her feet and sucking on a baby finger. Slowly, she raised her gaze to Elizabeth's face. After a moment, Elizabeth heaved a sigh.

"Okay. Go call your mother. Tell her you're going to spend the night, and we've been trying to reach her for the last hour. But the line's been busy."

"Thank you."

"Thank you."

Sharon walked to the kitchen. Rosie's shoulders sagged.

"Do you know that it's almost seven?"

"Yeah."

"Do you know what sort of turmoil you caused me and Sybil?"

"   ."

"Where were you?"

"On the trail."

"Goddamn it! What do you have to say for yourself?"

"I'm sorry."

"Sorry isn't good enough."

"I'm *really* sorry."

"You're becoming untrustworthy!"

"   !"

Sharon had just hung up in the kitchen when Elizabeth stormed in. She got the whiskey out of the cupboard, poured some into a glass, and went to the refrigerator for ice cubes, seeming not to have noticed Sharon.

"Elizabeth?"

"Oh. Yeah?" Elizabeth turned toward her, taking a sip.

"Mommy says it's all right if I stay."

"Good. Why don't you go play with Rosie until dinner?"

Sharon all but tiptoed out the door.

Wobbling somewhat, she sat in a chair, stooped over the kitchen table, holding her glass as if to keep it from floating away. The kids had come home. Teardrops speckled the table-cloth.

Rosie was sitting on the bottom stair, pigeon-toed, hugging her knees to her chest. Sharon sat with her back against the front door, Indian-style.

"Mama was just angry because she was worried about us."

"Mine too."

"How come she let you spend the night?"

"Search me."

Rosie stuck her nose into the air, sniffing. "I smell bacon."

"Me too."

Visions of Mr. Thackery wafted through Rosie's mind, and she shivered, on the stairs. She had to tell, had to tell; why had she sworn to God? If you swore something to God and then broke your promise, you went straight to hell when you died: Satan with a long red tail and pitchfork, standing unharmed in the flames. Did the devil really exist, or was he like Santa Claus? If she went to hell, she'd never see her father again, but if she never told anyone, she'd be crazy with the secret for the rest of her life. Like King Midas's barber. She heard her name being called, turned slowly toward Sharon. "What?"

"I said, your mother wants us."

Rosie stood.

Elizabeth had made grilled cheese sandwiches with bacon and avocado, which she set on plates at the kitchen table, in front of two glasses of milk. She kept them company while they ate, but took nothing for dinner but whiskey.

"I want you girls to go to bed early."

"Okay."

"Tomorrow we need to have a serious talk."

"We'll pay back the money."

Elizabeth didn't say anything for a minute. Then she nodded. "Okay. But let's talk about it tomorrow." Tending to the girls helped take her mind off her dreadful anger, let her forget about James for seconds at a time. She needed them to need her. She didn't know how she would survive the next twelve hours, not to speak of the next few weeks. Or months. Tomorrow would never come, tomorrow never came: by tomorrow, tomorrow morning would have become "today," this morning, and today was insufferable. And she was getting quite drunk, with little decrease in wired unhappiness.

"Is James coming over tonight?"

"No." She shook her head, and her stomach was pitching and wormy.

"God, it's almost nine."

"Can we have some ice cream, Mama?"

"Sure. Why don't you two get your pajamas on, and I'll bring you each a bowl to eat in bed."

"Okay. Will you read us the book?"

"For a while."

"Oh, Mama, thanks."

Washing the dishes, sipping on scotch, Elizabeth felt calmer. The hell with James. The main problem wasn't the loss of the man, it was the sickening obsessive anger: she must station a bouncer at the door to her brain, kick James out the second he entered her consciousness. She dropped her head and shook it.

" 'It's Mrs. Which, Charles Wallace said.' " Elizabeth sat hunched over on Rosie's bed, where the girls lay in Rosie's nightgowns. She wore a worn, sky-blue chamois shirt over a thin, lacy white nightgown from Greece, which she had bought even before she married Andrew. She had begun to slur, but only every so often. Her eyes were bloodshot and sad.

" 'There was a faint gust of wind, the leaves shivered in it, the patterns of moonlight shifted, and in a circle of silver something shimmered, quivered, and the voice said, "I ddo nott thinkk I willl matterrialize completely. I ffindd itt verry ttirinngg, andd wee hhave mmuch ttoo ddoo." ' "

"One more chapter!"

"Nnoo."

"Pllease." Rosie already felt nostalgia for this evening, for grilled cheese and bacon, for Sharon beside her and ice cream in bed, her mother's reading voice, and *A Wrinkle in Time;* like she felt at the last few pages of a perfect book which had no sequel. Had she, earlier today, really seen a dick? What if the police asked her to swear on a stack of Bibles? Was she positive?

No.

After listening to their prayers and kissing them good night, Elizabeth went downstairs. She stood in the living room, stroking her nose as she watched the fire. There were two Elizabeths, one in the lacy white nightdress and sky-blue chamois shirt, black-haired and sad, lit by the golden-red fire, and one who watched this woman. She clutched her stomach with suddenly clammy hands and grimaced. Jolts of sexual jealousy flashed through her, stroboscopic slides of James played in her mind, worms and acid hit her stomach, and turning away from the flames, she set off for the kitchen.

Half an hour later she went to call Rae. It would be an hour later in New Mexico, ten thirty or so. Rae, I'm having a crisis. I don't think I can survive the night. My soul has been thoroughly fucked with, by James, and by, uh, being such a heavy drinker. I mean, close to twenty years' worth, and on top of this, James makes love with other women—Rae, I can't cope. You see, he said he wanted to marry me. I was the love of his life! Fucking A! And I finally decide that he's everything I wanted in a man, and I call to tell him I love him, finally—he's been telling me for weeks, but I've been hedgy and suspicious—and a woman answers the phone! At midnight!

But no one answered the phone. Elizabeth let it ring and ring—thank *God* you were home, Rae, I was losing my *mind*— and ring.

Now what? She would never fall asleep. She had never felt so close to the precipice, would go mad, like her mother, tonight. She took a scotch to the living room to wait in front of the fire for the great, possibly silent blowout.

She held in her hand the trump card, which she had carried since her teens. If all else failed, she could play the breakdown. She would be committed to an institution. She could let out all the screams and the black slime of thirty-eight years; once she got started, it would really be something. She smiled.

But then there would be a cleanup. And she would knit back together, slowly, cleanly, a well-set bone. Rosie would stay with Rae until Elizabeth was well. Finding herself no longer afraid to play the trump made her calm enough so that she didn't have to. Not yet.

She got up and went to the stereo and put on a song from *Blood on the Tracks,* "Idiot Wind," and its scathing, vituperative lyrics gave her the strength of anger, of spite and revenge. Her face came back to life. You're an *id*-iot, James, you're an *id*-iot, James; God, I hope you rot, never sell your book, and mourn the loss of Rosie and me until you die, fat, bald, and alone.

She got up and played the song again.

God save him from her wrath. Sneering with dignity, she rehearsed what she would say if she ever talked to him again. You're malicious, James, and shallow. There is, in your eyes and heart, the glint of a child playing dodge ball, about to nail a friend's ankle: you're an insecure, pathetic shit, James. You are not a good man.

You see, when men act in deceitful, retrograde ways, women sometimes stoop to that level and act just as badly. And I don't want to catch what you have.

It's the worst thing, James, to be a hypocrite. I wouldn't be in your shoes for anything.

The end of love negated all the memories of fun and loving. Conversations lost their value, passion lost all meaning. She had been duped, like Rae had been duped by Brian all those times. There would be nothing to show for her friendship with James except hatred, and much greater caution. It hurt more than anything had before. She hugged herself and began to cry.

Poor Elizabeth. She saw Rosie at the beach on a hot black Fourth of July, the year after Andrew died. When the fireworks above the bay had stopped, someone gave her a sparkler and lit it, and Rosie cut flashing red swirls in the black air, joyously absorbed, until it began to sputter and went out, and Rosie stood holding a piece of burnt wire, on which she then burned a finger. Elizabeth cried and, after a while, felt better.

But then, at midnight, she heard a knock at the door and lifted her head slowly off her chest. She looked like a child roused from sleep, grumpy and bleary, lips swollen into a pout.

Go away.

Knock knock. "Elizabeth?" James. Oh, God, oh, no. Go away. "Elizabeth?" She sat very still. "It's me. Let me in."

The knocking continued. She couldn't let him see her like this, it would diminish his sense of loss. Slowly, with cold dignity, she rose and staggered, with her head held high, to the door.

"Go away." She pushed in the button to lock it.

"What's going on here? I knew you'd be mad, but—I've driven all the way from the city."

"Yer an idiot, James." She stared at the swirling wood grain of the closed door, and she swayed.

"I can explain everything."

"I doubt it." She stood hugging herself.

"I've been sick."

She sneered. "My heart bleeds."

"That doesn't make sense. Are you drunk? Oh, wait, did you say your heart *bleeds?* Oh, never mind. Please let me in."

Elizabeth studied the closed door between them, took several steps backward, and sat clumsily down on the bottom stair. She waited for his next move but heard nothing. Had he left? No, she was sure of it. Still she waited, and there was only silence. It was a trick. If she opened the door, he would leap out at her and push his way in. He would trick her into forgiving him, and she would end up back in love, and he would betray her again somewhere down the road. Was he still on the porch? Had he ever been there? She shook her head to clear it. Finally she stood, wobbling, turned the doorknob, pulled it open an inch, and peered around. It had not been a trick, he was not on the doormat. The stars were glittering dots of gold in the black sky, and James sprang at the door from out of the shadows. She cried out, and he pushed his way inside.

She slugged him in the shoulder, bruising a knuckle. "Don't you *ever* do that again."

He grabbed her wrists so she wouldn't hit him anymore, and she took two steps back, glaring.

"What do you want?" she asked, pulsating with anger.

"What do you think? I want to talk to you."

"I don't want to."

"Tough shit, Elizabeth." They were glowering at each other, like two dogs with a bone dropped equidistant on the ground, an electrical moment, poised on some brink of violence and desire.

"It's me, do you remember?" he said. "I don't know what's going on."

"Bullshit."

He clenched his fist, put it in his pants pocket. "I have *not* done anything wrong, and I have obviously been tried and convicted without a jury. Of my peers. So you had better just goddamn well explain why you're in such a state. Was it because 'You should have called'?" He changed his voice into a fishwife's. "Is that it?" She looked at him as if he had shit on his clothes. "Let me tell you something—okay?—about what's been happening, and then you can run your latest paranoid scenario by me. Yesterday, midmorning, there was a terrible burning when I peed, a terrible feeling in my bladder like it was sucking on a lemon, so I went to a doctor. It turned out to be a urinary tract infection, and he put me on antibiotics. And he *also* put me on this heavy-duty muscle relaxant called Perideum, which makes your pee look like it's a tequila sunrise . . . okay? And it makes you dopey. I slept all day, until about three in the morning. So I got up and wrote until noon or so—I called you but no one answered so I thought I would just show up at six or so, like I always do—but I took another pill and crapped out. I knew you'd be *mad,* but I came over as soon as I got dressed to see if your lights were on. And—hey!" He looked around, up the stairs, and then walked down the short hallway to peer into the living room. "Is anyone else really here? Are they up in your bed?"

"Yes." They were.

"Good. Good for you. So now tell me your problem."

She was holding herself tightly in, and across the chest, enunciating carefully like she did with Rosie when angry. "First of all, you could have called. You're not an adolescent anymore. You're supposed to have grown up. Which is to say, we have been intimately involved for some time, almost every night, to the exclusion of others, and *you hide with embarrassment for two days at my expense because you've got an infection in your tee-tees!* Christ!"

"No one's perfect!"

"I'm not talking 'perfect,'" she said, much too quickly, so that she sounded shrill. "I'm talking faithful, responsible. . . . I called your apartment all night, and no one answered—"

"I was *sleeping*—"

"James! Until midnight, when a woman answered—"

"Not at my place—"

"Oh, *yes,* at your place. . . ." Wait, what?

"You're crazy. You were loaded."

"Get out of my house."

"No," he said. "A woman didn't answer at my house."

"Oh, you fucking liar, James. And you slammed the phone down—"

"Wrong!"

"Right!"

"I give you my word."

"Oh. I dialed wrong and reached another man's house who wasn't supposed to be schtupping—"

"God. You're so paranoid. You shouldn't be on the streets."

Glares, clenched jaws, something beginning to snap in Elizabeth. Had she misd . . . no! But maybe—no! *May*be.

"I swear to God. In whom I believe. And give my word."

The room spun for a moment; the thing snapping inside had cut off her wind. Her eyes softened. She was going mad.

James took a step toward her, with his arms out tentatively as if coaxing a half-tamed wild animal, but she held onto herself and slid with her back against the wall a few feet farther from him. Help me, someone. I don't know which end is up.

"Let's sit by the fire," he said. After a minute she followed him to the living room, where he stood leaning against the mantel. "There's no one else here, is there, besides Rosie?"

"Sharon." She stopped at a bookcase and leaned against it, eyeing him.

"Is there brandy?" She nodded. "I'll get us one. Okay?" After a pause, she nodded, and he left. The living room was warm and lit by one small light and golden-red flames. Her scotch was on

the coffee table. Had she misdialed? She knew she hadn't. But
decided she might have. Was Rae still alive, was James telling
the truth? Why couldn't she know for sure, how could she live
not knowing for sure? She couldn't. She was shivering in the
warm room, having what she took to be an alcoholic breakdown;
tonight a lot of air had escaped from her tires, which had perhaps
been patched too many times. She was in fact having a blowout.
She daydreamed of hospitalization: a tearful Rae would fly home
. . . James would never leave her side . . . but Rosie—oh, God.
She was pinching the flesh on her upper arm when James arrived
with the silver decanter and two Baccarat snifters.

She took a drink from him and slid away, tearful mewing
noises escaping even as a stern voice in her head commanded her
to pull herself together.

"What can I get you?" he asked. Dilaudid. Committed.
"Can't I hold you?" She shook her head, backing away. He
poured an inch of brandy for himself and sat down on the couch,
swirled it in his glass, poured down half of it and set it down. He
watched her with great concern; finally he lit a cigarette and held
the pack out to her, but she didn't meet his eyes, and after a moment he put them back in his vest. Elizabeth, in a hundred-
pound backpack, stood shivering, with tears pouring out of her
eyes.

"God, I feel so helpless."

She had never fallen to pieces before in front of another person. She had held out for almost forty years. In the darkest moments of her soul she had always been alone, or the only person
awake (near dawn, the hours of the wolf), and so much despair
and disarray and need were welling up and spilling into the open
that she would never recover—would only be faking whatever
sense of equilibrium she could muster.

"Come here," he said gently.

No; she shook her head.

"Do you want me to leave?" She stared at her feet. "Not that
I care, because I'm not leaving you."

She walked unsteadily to the mantel with her drink and laid
her head on her hand on the wood, feeling a bit stronger as the
fire warmed her up. Tears ran lengthwise across her eyes, ran

down her fingers and cheek, and she became aware of tears in her ear.

"Come here," he said. No. "Do you just want to cry for a while?" Yes, she nodded, with her head sideways on the mantel. "You sure look beautiful in that kimono. I sure love you, Elizabeth. Do you believe that?" After a minute she nodded. "I want to get married someday. But you gotta trust me more. *I* trust you with everything I have. And there's no reason—I give you my word—you can't trust me."

And so Elizabeth, at that moment, lifts her head off the mantel and *decides* to trust him, decides that he was telling the truth and that she was a faithless foolish old woman. When she looks at him, and he can see he has won, *he* decides that from that moment on he will be faithful to Elizabeth, will give up—and it was an easy decision—the other, occasional women.

"I really love you," he said. "I want to hold you all night."

She nodded. They took long sips of their brandies.

"Now, get over here," he said, snapping his finger at the space beside him on the couch. "Come on. Here, boy." He snapped his fingers again, patted the empty space. She got irritated and looked away. "Here we go, come on, sit down"—cocking his head, calling a puppy. She finished her drink, put it on the mantel, put her hands in the pockets of her kimono, crossed her feet at the ankles, and waited, reconsidering James. "Okay. Here's my final offer. I *prom*ise to call you, come hell or high water, the next time—I promise to try as hard as I can." She shook her head, smiling faintly for the first time in hours, able to breathe. "And I'll throw in a twenty." He looked up expectantly—she had forgotten his great face; now that she'd turned the projector back on he looked perfect—and reached for his wallet. When she looked over at him again, he waved a bill at her, raised and lowered his eyebrows several times.

Tears came into her eyes again for no particular reason. What if he *had* been making love last night, what if he *was* lying. He was everything she had wanted in a man, all her life. She was utterly terrified that she wanted him so badly. Taking a deep breath, she willed her feet to deliver her to the couch, where she took the money out of his hand and sat beside him.

He beamed at her. She scowled, looking down into her lap at the airy egret and cherry blossoms on the white kimono, pocketed the money. He put his arms around her tense shoulders, laid his head against her neck, turned to kiss it. Slowly, as if she had arthritis, she raised her arms and held him by the shoulders.

"You see," he said, "we've finally met our match. I figure we don't have a chance; we might as well go for it. We're *supposed* to be together. As I see it," he said, leaning forward to pour them more brandy, "we are difficult, *weird* people and we make each other laugh. We're *very* kind to each other, mostly, and we drive each other wild in bed. I wait all day to see you again. You make me so happy, all warm and filled-up inside. It's like other people feel about having *Jesus* on their side. Is this too mushy?"

She nodded, looking down, still feeling rocky, but also saved.

"Do you know you've never said I love you? When I say I love you, you say thank you, or that you're glad. Well, do you, Elizabeth?" She nodded, glanced up at him, looked down.

Why couldn't she say it? He seemed to be in love with this broken down old drunk, red-eyed and snotty. She shook her head in wonder at them both.

"You *do?*" he asked. "Madly?"

She pursed her lips, looking down, nodded, smiled, and then looked up at him.

"Oh," he said, smiling back with a distant and mystical look on his face.

They slept in front of the fire. He held her all night. She was sick in the morning, but happy. Three days later, with boxes of books and clothes, he came to live, with his dog, at the Fergusons' house.

Chapter
🍂18

Rosie, lonely, crazy, and mad, sat in the window seat several days later, thinking of Midas, king in the land of the roses, and of his barber, sworn to keep the secret of the donkey ears. She saw herself on all fours in the garden, whispering into a hole in the earth, saw the grasses which would grow and, when the wind blew, whisper what Sharon's dad had done.

Each time she remembered it, her stomach dropped, hollow and full of dread, full of worms.

She was alone. Her mother was at the library, James and Leon were watching a football game at a friend's house, and Sharon was at her violin lesson. If only Rae were home. If only Rae were her mother. Rae would notice something wrong: Rae would make her confess.

A dog barked, the wind blew, birds sang. She opened her eyes and sat listening, then got up, full of gloom and nervous energy, and skulked into the study.

The desk was covered with papers, a typewriter, pencils, and books: it was her favorite room in the house, since James had moved in. She glanced at the closet: did he know that her mother kept a bottle in there? Rosie flushed.

She carried a stool to the closet door and opened it. The house was still. She climbed onto the stool and reached behind a stack of seed catalogs, where the bottle was hidden. Her heart pounded when her fingers touched the cool glass.

Crrreeakkk: someone at the front door! She whipped her head around—it's Mr. Thackery, come to kill her, or her mother. She scuttled down off the stool, closed the closet door, and ran out of the study.

No one came in. Rosie peeked out the living room window: no one was in the yard.

Back in the study, Rosie eyed the closet but went to the desk and sat down. There were piles of paper everywhere, piles thumbtacked to the wall above it, piles of index cards, and a pile of balled-up typing paper on the floor beside her. She put her legs, crossed at the ankles, on the typewriter, took the nearest stack of index cards, leaned back in the seat, and began to read what James had written.

On the top card was the word "Communicate." On the second card was written "the bleached, bluish-white sky." On the third, "Pelicans, killdeer, wren tits." The fourth read, "Lying on top of Elizabeth, dozing. Face pressed against her neck and into pillow—rooting around for pockets of breathable air instead of stale CO_2." Whaaaaat? The fifth one read, *"Demons,* p. 354, most thoughts are smoke whose fire we are denied." The sixth one said, "Rosie's Lashes." Rosie's lashes? She put the index cards back on the desk and reached for the button on the imaginary phone.

"Yes, Miss Biddley," she said out loud, "bring me some coffee and some Sugar Babies. Right now!"

She put her feet back on the floor, and picked up a pile of envelopes. She set them on the typewriter, except for the top one, from which she extracted the letter. It was on fine paper, with a magazine's name at the top, and it said, "It's a lovely story, but I'm afraid we can't use it." She cringed for James, felt hot in the cheeks for him, hung her head for a moment. Replacing the letter in the envelope, she tried to think of get-rich-quick schemes. Sometimes people found a chest of jewels in their back yard or in caves, treasures which pirates had buried—she stared off into space and stroked her chin. Oh, my God! Was that *hair* she felt? Adrenaline surged through her. She pinched at the downy hairs on her chin, eyes wide, as movie snippets sped in her mind: "Little girl grows beard, read all about it!" "Step right this way, ladies and gentlemen, see *Ro*-sie, the amazing bearded child" . . . She leaped from the chair and ran to the mirror in the hallway, peered at her chin from two inches away, and did not see any hairs. Then the reflection blurred as her eyes widened, and what she saw was the wiry black hair, the sickening dick . . . red, rubbery, touching her.

Rosie gasped, shuddered: help, help! God! She shook her head and looked ready to cry, but didn't. After a moment, she lumbered into the living room.

She walked around the living room, lost and lethargic, looking glumly at the bookshelves, fireplace, and furniture, and the terror began to pass. After a while she stopped at a bookcase, searched for and found *Parade of the Animal Kingdom*, and took it to the window seat.

Soon she is saved, soothed: tigers, owls, cocoons, peacocks, and polar bears fill her crazy mind.

Sometime later she let the book drop to the floor, got up, and plodded into the kitchen. She poured herself a glass of milk, took a stack of graham crackers from the cupboard, returned to the living room, and sat in the middle of the carpet to eat.

In between milk-logged bites, she constructed a house of graham crackers, of golden-brown baked walls. She stared at it with dark stoned eyes, seeing a roof of cake, windows of transparent sugar: old Mrs. Haas popping Hansel into the crate; Rosie sweeping.

Stick out your finger so I can feel it.

Hansel sticks out the goose bone.

Got to fatten you up some more.

Rosie whirls around to push Mrs. Haas into the oven, then frees Hansel from the crate; the birds who ate their trail of bread crumbs show them the way out of the forest, and they run home into their father's loving arms. The father is Andrew. It turns out that he didn't get killed in the car crash, that was a lie told by the nasty stepmother who is—this is terrible, I don't really mean it—Elizabeth.

Rosie's face grew cloudy: I really didn't mean it. She blinked, back in the living room, shaken, and dismantled the house.

Absently, she picked up a book of matches from the coffee table and lit one, held the blue and orange flame close to her eyes so that they crossed, and blew it out. She lit another one and held it to the corner of the last graham cracker, which wouldn't light. She let the third match burn too far, in trying to light the cracker, dropped it when the flame burned her finger, and stuck the finger in her mouth, while meanwhile, in a creamy patch of the oriental carpet, the match continued to burn. . . .

Five minutes later, Elizabeth kicked the front door to summon Rosie, as her arms were full of books.

"Rosie!"

After a minute she heard soft footsteps.

"Let me in, honey."

"Mama?"

"Yeah?"

"I was bad."

"Open the door this second." She lowered the books to the ground.

"Very, very bad."

Elizabeth threw open the door and pushed her way past Rosie, smelling smoke, expecting the worst (burning curtains, charred walls). Wild with adrenaline, sniffing like a basset hound, she came into the living room, spotted the black, wet hole in her six-thousand-dollar carpet, saw the bowl of water with which the fire had been put out, and began to shake so violently that she had to hold onto a bookcase. A thousand times, away from home, fantasies of her house in flames caused by negligence (an iron, a joint, an ember from the fireplace) had nagged and haunted her; today she might have lost a child or house. People did.

She spanked Rosie so hard that her palm burned as red as Rosie's bottom. Rosie sobbed with pain and was sent to her room in disgrace.

"I'm so mad I'm seeing red!" her mother shouted up the stairs at Rosie, who lay face down on her bed, whimpering.

Elizabeth sank into a chair at the kitchen table, badly shaken by a cumulative sense of narrowly averted catastrophes, all the instances when blind luck had been the only determinant. Rosie might have set the house on fire. Children did, children died.

What the hell was wrong with Rosie these days? She was moody, withdrawn, and resisted leaving the house—hardly ever went to Sharon's anymore, spent all day reading, moping . . . like Elizabeth.

Elizabeth looked up at the measuring wall. Rosie was turning out like her, following her example. Elizabeth cradled her chin in her hands, despairing, hating the way she spent her time, waiting all morning for the hangover to wear off, waiting for it to be time to start drinking, waiting all the while for the unavoidable, inevitable day when she couldn't fake it any longer, when she got too—had to give up and get help.

She went outside to work in her garden. She would deal with the carpet and Rosie later. She knelt by a bush of red roses: a breeze rustled trees, bushes, and grass; hidden birds trilled and warbled high, piping songs.

Come on, relax. Tend to your roses and they will tend to you. Here, now, this is it. This is fine. No secrets yet to be discovered. Relax.

She began to dig around in the dirt at the roots, picked out dead leaves and small weeds. Was Rosie jealous of James? No. Face the facts, Elizabeth, it's your drinking. She stared at her dirty fingers. It's tearing her apart, like your mother's did you, when you were small. Remember? She nodded. The solution was to stop drinking, and she would, soon, honest. This time she really meant it!

Feeling a great relief, she resumed weeding, lifted a handful of rich earth to her nose, closed her eyes and inhaled (might have been sniffing coffee beans). She talked softly to the flowers, with affection, promised the rosebushes she'd get them some food in a moment and a nice glass of fungicide. She sprinkled granules of rose food, tamping gently, heeding only soil and roots, buds and branches. The sun broke through to Elizabeth, on her hands and knees, dirty hands and fingernails, aching knees, and her face had lost all isometric tension: she looked radiant.

At two she went upstairs to talk to Rosie, who was lying on her bed reading Hans Christian Andersen, and who looked up at her mother guiltily, scared.

"Hello," said Elizabeth.

"Hi."

"I need to talk to you, okay?" Rosie nodded and closed the book. Elizabeth came over and sat on the bed beside her, draped her arm across Rosie's stomach, and sighed. "I'm sorry I spanked you so hard, okay? Will you accept my apology?" Rosie nodded and let her bottom lip tremble. "But goddamn it, baby, you could have burned down the whole fucking house. You were lucky. *I* was lucky. I might have lost you."

"We can fix the hole somehow. . . ."

"That isn't the point. The point is that you broke your promise not to play with matches, you've wrecked a carpet which was a wedding present from your father's grandmother—can you imagine what that carpet means to me?"

"I'm really, really sorry."

"I know you are. But sorry doesn't undo the damage."

"Wull. You said you were sorry."

"And I was."

"So am *I.*"

"I know, I know, and I forgive you, but this time you were lucky—think about it, Rosie. Don't think of the match, of just lighting one match for fun, think about the house in flames. Everything we own, all of James's writing." Rosie hung her head. *"Promise* that you won't play with matches, and *mean* it."

"I promise."

"I love you, Rosie. I would die if anything happened to you." Rosie nodded. "I must seem like a pretty messed-up mother to have—I *am* a pretty messed-up mother. But. No one could love anyone more than I love you. And: soon, things will—I will— get better."

They looked intently at each other, mother and daughter: The Fergusons. They both tried to smile.

The phone rang while they were eating lunch, and Elizabeth rose from the table to answer it, hoping it was James.

"Hello?"

"I'm home!"

"Rae!"

Rosie's mouth dropped open, and then she beamed.

"When did you get home?"

"Two minutes ago. Can I come over and play?"

"Yes, of course. Hurry."

"Is Rosie there?"

"Yes. Rae! I'm so glad you're back."

"I've been so homesick for you both! I'll be over in five minutes."

Rae's homecoming constituted a small miracle. The Fergusons stood waiting for her on the porch.

"I have to go look down the street," said Rosie, dashing down the stairs and through the garden. "Here she comes," she shouted, tearing through the gate and down the street to the left, leaving Elizabeth standing alone with her hands on her hips.

Rosie and Rae came into sight holding hands. Rae waved. She wore the same old jeans, baggy and faded, and her clogs knocked on the sidewalk, but her sweater was new, fuzzy and gray, and her hair was up, lazily. Elizabeth walked down the stairs and waited at the open gate. Rae. Thinner, it seemed, and tan, dark eyes crinkled up sheepishly. The women walked, silent and grinning, into each other's arms.

Rae smelled of cigarettes, coconut oil, salt, and the alpaca sweater. They stepped apart to kiss. Rosie waited for them to be done.

"You look so pretty, Elizabeth. So do you, Rosie."

"So do you. You've lost weight."

"Fifteen pounds."

"I have a million things to tell you."

"Me too. You must never go away again."

"Rae," said Rosie, "*you* went away. We just stayed here."

"Would you like a beer?"

"Sure."

They sat on the porch, the women with ales, Rosie with grape juice.

"I got you both presents, but I left them in Sante Fe. The friends I stayed with will send them soon."

"James lives here now," said Rosie.

"I know. Elizabeth told me in a letter." Rae looked over at Elizabeth. "You lucky duck."

Elizabeth smiled.

"Is it just—wonderful?"

"Pretty much, yeah."

"I *love* James," said Rosie.

Rae looked suddenly mournful. "I'm so jealous," she said, and grimaced. "I mean, I swear to God, I'm also totally happy for you, really I am. *Really* I am."

Elizabeth nodded.

"I don't think," said Rae, "that I could handle it, if I didn't know you get so jealous of my career." They smiled at each other. "Aren't I a scumbag?"

"Oh, yes," said Elizabeth.

Looking at Rae, Rosie panicked, cringed. No *way* could she tell Rae about the hairy dick. She stared listlessly at her grape juice. No one noticed. *Help!*

"So, tell me about New Mexico."

"God, it was great."

"Are you over Brian?"

"Tsssst. Water off a duck's back."

"Yeah?"

"The guy was an asshole, Elizabeth. I don't know why you kept pushing me into his arms."

Elizabeth smiled. Rae lit a cigarette. The corner of Rosie's mouth turned down: no one noticed.

Rae burst out laughing. The Fergusons watched.

"I gotta tell you both this one thing that happened." Rosie and Elizabeth nodded. "And you're both sworn to secrecy . . . Okay. When I first arrived in Nambe, I was *to*tally depressed about Brian, right? I was shuffling around moaning, I seen sunrise, I seen moonrise, lay dis ole darkie down." Elizabeth smiled, and took a sip: God, I have missed you, Rae.

"But a few days after I got there, my friend introduces me to this guy named Peter, who's pretty funny, and I kept hoping he'd call and ask me out. But he didn't."

"Is this going to be an uddult story?" Rosie asked.

Rae nodded. Rosie got to her feet.

"Oh, don't go, sweetheart," said Rae. "I can tell your mom another time."

"No, that's all right. I have to do this thing inside, and then I'll come back out."

"Promise?" Rosie nodded, and went to the door. Elizabeth shook her head, and took another sip.

"Go on with your story."

"You really want to hear it?"

Elizabeth nodded.

"You're not just saying that?"

Elizabeth smiled.

"Okay, so there I am, down and out in New Mexico. One day I go into town and eat roughly ten pounds of Mexican food, then head for the drugstore for candy—it's one of those savage pig animal days. I buy a bag of M&M's, and a *People* magazine, which I take outside to read in the sun. In it, I learn that anorexics gobble down laxatives to lose weight. My eyes open wide, and I go back into the drugstore, and up to the pharmacist. The store's crowded, and I sort of whisper to her that I need a good strong laxative. Well, she's got a voice you could cut glass with, and she starts screeching laxative suggestions at me." Rae threw back her head and laughed.

"She hands me the kind she uses, and it says, 'the gentle laxative,' but I can't bring myself to say I want something *ruth*less, something called Dyno-Lax or something, so I buy it, and eat most of the box.

"Then I go home to Eileen's, raid the refrigerator, and wait for something to happen. But nothing does, nothing at all. And then, several hours and two snacks later, Peter calls and invites me to dinner that night.

" 'Hope you're hungry,' he says.

" 'Starved,' I say. 'Haven't eaten all day.' "

"Oh, Rae." Elizabeth laughed.

"Okay. To make a long story somewhat shorter, I get all dolled up, my black silk dress, pearls, sexy black heels, lots of makeup . . . and we go out to dinner. Peter and I really hit it off. By now, I've completely forgotten about the laxatives. He invites me home for a nightcap, and we both know I'm going to spend the night.

"When we get there, we have a brandy, and listen to records and then—I swear to God—he says he's got blisters on his feet from jogging, and he's got to soak them for a few minutes. I figure his feet are dirty or something, and we're about to go to bed, so I say, 'Fine, fine.' He pours me another drink, hands me the new *New Yorker,* and goes into the bathroom. Closes the door, runs water in the bathtub. I sit there reading happily, feeling like the sexiest woman alive, when all of a sudden I've got to shit so bad that my eyes are watering."

"Oh, God! What did you do?"

"I sat there praying, squeezing my cheeks together, not blinking. I hear him running more water, he's going to be in there forever, and *I* am dying, Egypt, dying. I am *burst*ing. I have never, in my life, been more desperate."

Rae began honking with laughter.

"So I decide my only chance is to shit in a saucepan or something, and throw it out the window; honest to God, that was my plan. Fuckin' A, mama, I'm thirty-two years old, in silk and pearls, the sexiest woman alive, thinking, He'll never ask me out again if he comes out and I'm squatting over a saucepan. . . .'"

Elizabeth roared.

"But there was no other way! I'm wishing I was dead, I'm worrying that I'll throw the saucepan out the window and it will kill a pedestrian and the police will come knocking at the door."

Elizabeth held her sides.

"And then, miraculously, he emerges, and I smile prettily and say, 'Oh, la-dee-dah, there you are,' and I make it to the bathroom with one or two seconds to spare."

The women sat laughing in the sun.

"Did he ask you out again?"

Rae shook her head. Elizabeth shrugged.

"Oh, well."

"Boy, I missed you. Who else could I tell that story to?"

"It's great to have you home. I missed you too. So did Rosie."

"Is something bothering her? She's *never* left during one of my stories before. Am I losing my touch?"

"Something's on her mind. But she won't tell what it is."

"Well. Sometimes it's just hard, being a kid."

Elizabeth raised her eyebrows in agreement.

"Do you know what the Arabic root for 'child' means?"

"Now, Rae, how the hell would I know what—"

"Well, see, the only reason I know is I read this book called *Arabia* while I was in Santa Fe."

"Oh."

"And 'child' means, among other things, 'to intrude on and sponge off of, to arrive uninvited and impose upon.' And it *also* means softness, and potter's clay, and dawn."

"Yeah?"

Rae nodded.

Elizabeth took a long sip of ale. "Potter's clay." Rosie's turning out like me. "Dawn." A new day, somewhere down the road . . .

"Elizabeth?"

"Yeah?"

"I think that if you were to ask me nicely, I would stay for dinner."

"Good! I'm making lasagne—with sausage. Let's go find Rosie, and cook."

"All *right*."

"Rosie!" Elizabeth called from the bottom of the stairs.

"What?" Rosie was lying face down on her bed.

"Come on down. Rae's going to stay for dinner. Come help us make lasagne."

"I'll be down in a minute."

Rosie shuffled into the kitchen a few minutes later. Rae took one look at her eyes and lifted her off the ground in a hug: Rosie clung to her for dear life.

Elizabeth watched them with a sad look on her face.

Rae set Rosie back down. "What's the matter, sweetheart?"

Rosie scowled, shrugged.

"Don't you want to talk about it? You'll feel better."

Rosie shook her head.

"Well, will you help us make lasagne? I've invited myself to dinner."

"Okay."

Elizabeth assembled the ingredients and together they began to make dinner. Rosie diced tomatoes from the garden for the sauce, while Rae sauteed ten toes of garlic in butter, and then added sausage. Elizabeth minced fresh basil and parsley.

"Would you like a drink, Rae?"

"No, thanks."

"I'm ready for a short one." Elizabeth went to the cupboard, got down the scotch, and poured herself a drink.

Rosie glowered. Rae noticed. Elizabeth got some ice cubes from the freezer, and dropped them into her drink.

"You done with the tomatoes, Rosie?" Rosie nodded glumly. "Then take them to Rae. Now you can help me slice the cheese."

Rosie scowled at the ball of mozzarella. "This stretchy stuff?"

"Yeah. But wait till I get back—I'll just be a minute."

Elizabeth took a sip of scotch and left the room. Rosie sat down at the table, and began tearing a paper towel into confetti-sized pieces. Rae turned to look at her.

"Come on, honey, out with it."

Rosie squirmed, shrugged, said nothing. Staring down at the table, she saw in her mind's eye the hairy purple dick, and flushed. Rae came and stood beside her.

"You're having a hard time these days, aren't you?" After a moment, Rosie nodded. Rae sat next to her and stroked Rosie's cheek. "You look like you're carrying the weight of the world on your shoulders."

Rosie rubbed her eyes, miserable, squirming.

Rae pointed to the whiskey. "Is that what's on your mind?"

Rosie shrugged and sighed deeply.

"You and me gotta talk," Rae whispered. "Okay?" Rosie rubbed her nose. "Really we do—as soon as you're ready. Maybe tomorrow?" Rosie shrugged. "And be nice tonight, okay?"

Rosie looked exasperated. Rae poked her in the stomach. Rosie doubled over, smiled.

Chapter
🌿19

Much later that night, James stood guard beside Rosie while she said her endless prayers, kneeling at the bed. Her head was bowed, so loose black rings barely touched the back of her white flannel nightgown and fell forward across her cheeks to the tips of her fingers. Spindle-like arms draped with flannel jutted out like wings, and she looked as small and fragile as a figurine from a creche, something like a cross between the Little Drummer Boy and the Little Match Girl.

James fingered the penknife in the pocket of his khakis. He was both moved and preoccupied, would watch her with tenderness a moment, stare into space the next. He wore a black T-shirt and argyle socks, one mostly green, one mostly gray.

Downstairs at the kitchen sink, Elizabeth finished up the dishes. She wore her hair up, and the white kimono, and a look of sedated regality.

She was listening to reggae on the radio: Bob Marley—Dead Marley—and Bunny Wailer; singing along softly, sipping unblended scotch. She was drunk enough to have decided that she was about to quit drinking.

She went upstairs to kiss Rosie good night, pushing off from the banister every few steps.

"James?" Rosie was asking.

"Yeah?"

"If the world blew up, would we still go to heaven?"

"Don't think about that before bed."

"But would we?"

"Yes, I think so. I think our souls would survive."

"Would they be burned?"

"What, our souls? Only physical things can be burned."

"But what about in hell? Doesn't just your soul go down?"

"Good question."

"Okay, sweetheart, hop into bed," said Elizabeth, stepping into the room. "It's after ten."

"Hi, Elizabeth."

"Hi, James. Good night, Rosie. I love you."

"Can Leon sleep in my room?"

"No. Leon sleeps outside. You know that."

"But what if a killer comes into my room?"

"What good would Leon be? He'd race around the house, gathering shoes to drop at the killer's feet." Elizabeth laughed.

"Don't worry, Rosie. Your mother locked the door. And if anyone got in, I'd tear them apart."

"Really?"

"Limb from limb," James snarled.

Rosie managed a small smile and climbed under the covers, wiggled around to warm up the sheets, and lay down with her head on the pillow.

Elizabeth kissed her eyes and mouth, James kissed her cheeks. Rosie was fine for about two minutes after they left.

Then, drifting off to sleep, the frizzy black hair appears on the dark screen behind her eyes and she watches the movie where Mr. Thackery touches her arm with his penis; in the movie his face looks eerie, like a retarded ghoul's, and it doesn't stop playing until she's sung "Row Row Row Your Boat" half a dozen times. It was late, and fairly soon, Rosie dozed.

Sometimes, like tonight, when Elizabeth saw the full moon, it looked exactly like Marilyn Monroe's face. James and Elizabeth took off their clothes and climbed into bed. James switched off the lamp. They held each other.

She was about to fall asleep, but her hand brushed against his balls, and she petted them, rolled them between her thumb and forefinger, one at a time, both at once, and he exhaled a deep moan, like a wind from some faraway tropical place inside him.

"James? I want to tell you something." He was scratching her shoulder blades, lightly. "I'm going to go on the wagon. Pretty soon."

James hugged her. "I'll go on the wagon with you."

"Okay. I'll let you know when I'm ready. It's going to be soon."

Elizabeth nuzzled against him and closed her eyes, sleepy, re-lieved, and in a few seconds fell asleep.

She awoke a minute later. James was talking softly. She felt in a swirling fog. "What did you think?" he asked.

She searched through the fog for an answer.

"Two and two thirds Negroes."

James didn't respond. She started to fall back to sleep.

"What did you say, Elizabeth?"

"Oh"—nonchalantly—"never mind."

James was still holding her, snoring, when she woke with a headache at dawn.

Two hours later he was pounding away on the typewriter from behind the closed door of his study, coughing and occasionally laughing out loud. He was listening to KJAZ and perfectly happy without her.

She was depressed and tired as she squeegeed egg yolk off their breakfast plates with a toast crust. She went to the living room to read a book and heard Leon scratching at the front door. She begrudgingly went to let him in, and he tore through the house panting, joyous and hungry. In an actively bad mood now, she went to the kitchen, made him a bowl of Gravy Train, and lured him outside to the front porch with it. He mooed.

Inside, she looked at the closed study door like a hungry kid watching someone eat ice cream, and the clacking—the sound of his life's work—got on her nerves, like a dripping faucet. Walking back to the living room, she slapped at her forehead, mistaking a lock of hair for a spider, and wiped at the corner of her mouth. Rosie stomped down the stairs and into the room, wearing red bermudas and her purple T-shirt.

"Me an' Sharon are going swimming with Mrs. Thackery today. Why didn't you wake me earlier? She's picking me up in an *hour.*"

"Don't whine at me, baby. I'm tired."

"I can't even find my suit," she began, and in the next few minutes had infused the downstairs with frustrated demands and energy as pervasively as food escapes in a space ship, infusing every molecule in the air. "All the towels are wet. Leon took one of my zoris, will you drive me into town to buy some more? I need a dollar, for the snack bar. I don't *want* any breakfast. No, I *hate* eggs. You always make them so they're all snotty. God, I *hate* Raisin Bran, it's all boogery."

And so on until Elizabeth yelled, at the top of her lungs in the kitchen, "Shut up!"

Elizabeth went upstairs to get ready for her interview at the bookstore, but sat on her bed for the longest time, immobilized. She could hear typing downstairs, and birds outside the window. She almost called the bookstore to cancel the interview. She was *so* tired.

Finally, though, for reasons she didn't understand, she put on a dress, and Spanish boots, and combs in her hair, and blusher on her cheeks, mascara on her lashes, and Chanel behind her ears and wrists.

She didn't get the job.

The owner's sister-in-law wanted to give it a try.

"Oh, I see," said Elizabeth. "Well, thanks anyway."

By the time she reached the doorway she was already in tears, and already reporting back to James and Rae that it was a lousy bookstore, mostly diet and cat books, no Faulkner, no Woolf. . . .

She drove to the grocery store, still sniffling, still rehearsing what she would tell her friends: James, *Betrayed by Rita Hayworth*, a novel by Manuel Puig, was in the cinema section. Oh, Rae, I didn't really even want the job. It's just that I wanted it to be me who said no, not them.

She dried her eyes, blew her nose, and went in to shop, with her head held high. She bought the makings for veal piccata, a six-pack of ale, and peaches. She began to feel better, paid, and left.

She wasn't ready to go home. She pulled off the road just past the harbor and looked out to sea. Streamers of silver and red burst through dark sworled clouds and were reflected perfectly on the water. The red spinnaker of an ancient ketch flapped. She opened an ale and watched an aircraft carrier plod toward the Golden Gate Bridge.

When she finished the ale, she opened another.

Her hazel eyes were old and sad in the rearview mirror, and the corners of her mouth drooped. She drank quickly and put the two empties on top of the groceries. They clinked against each other when she started driving home. She should have put them back in their carton.

Hers was the only car on the road. She reached into the glove box for a Certs and, fiddling with the jammed button, saw a gangling blur dash out of a roadside bush, watched a big blond puppy dive beneath her wheels, saw it in slow motion because her mind was speeding ahead of time, and heard a terrible thud— *kathunka kathunka kathunka*—like a book going around in the dryer.

She slammed on the brakes and the car stalled. The top of her head was coming off, and her heart beat in her ears. She slowly turned to see the bloody crumpled dog, felt a whirling revulsion in her guts: it might have been a child. Her thoughts were wild, full of terror, her white knuckles on the steering wheel were trembling, and she started the car and fled. Coward! Go back! Jesus Christ! Go back and deal with it, Elizabeth.

But she simply couldn't.

She parked outside her gate, turned off the engine, and came completely unglued. She was still sobbing ten minutes later when James opened the passenger door and slid in beside her.

"What's the matter? Didn't you get the job?"

She shook her head.

He held her. "There, there," he said, "there, there": Yossarian and Snowden, whose guts are spilling into his flak suit. "I'm cold, I'm cold," "There, there."

When Rosie arrived home at two, she found her mother and James in the window seat, talking. Her mother's eyes were red and wet, with black smudges of mascara underneath.

"What's the *mat*ter, Mama?"

Elizabeth looked at her sadly. "I—didn't get the job."

Rosie winced, reached out to stroke her mother's knee.

God, do I love you, Rosie.

"Oh, Mama. It's okay."

Elizabeth nodded. "I don't know why I'm taking it so hard. I think I'm just very tired."

Rosie nodded gravely. "Wull, why don't we go to the movies?"

"I'm too depressed."

"It would cheer you up."

"No, really, I just don't want to."

Rosie sat down in the easy chair and threw up her hands in exasperation. "God!" she said.

James smiled at her. Rosie crossed her arms.

"You mean we're just going to sit here all day?"

Elizabeth shrugged. "You don't have to, sweetheart. Why don't you give Sharon a call, and see if you can play at her house for a while?"

"No!"

Rosie got up and began pacing, angrily—Sharon's house, Sharon's father. Elizabeth watched her, puzzled.

"Rosie, *what's* been eating you?"

Rosie stopped pacing and looked down at her feet.
"Mama?"
"Yeah?"
There was a long pause. "I think I'll go see Rae."
Elizabeth nodded encouragingly. Rosie felt sick to her stomach.

"Hi, Rosie, what a nice surprise."
"Hi, Rae."
Rae was sitting on newspapers, on her porch, painting a bookcase white. White paint was everywhere, drizzled down the front of a plaid flannel shirt, streaked across her forehead and in her hair, in a puddle to the left of the newspapers, and in footprints which led to the door, where Rae's moccasins lay, soles up.
"I'm just about done here. Jesus, what a mess, hunh? You know what I always say? I always say, if you want something done right, do it yourself."
Rosie smiled and leaned against a white Corinthian column, with her hands jammed into the pockets of her baggy shorts, chewing on the neckline of her purple T-shirt.
"Mama didn't get the job."
"Ohhhh, nuts."
Rae put down the paintbrush.
"Is she depressed?"
Rosie nodded. Rae put the lid on the paint and got to her feet.
"It probably wouldn't have been that interesting for her anyway."
Rosie nodded.
"Hey, are you by any chance hungry?"
Rosie shrugged.
Ten minutes later they were sitting in Rae's breakfast nook, with a pot of lemon grass tea, eating buttery raisin-bread toast.
Rosie looked shaky and sad. Rae studied her.
"So. Do you want to talk about it?"
Rosie shook her head, praying for Rae to make her tell.
"Well, *I* do." Rosie looked up at her. "I know you're feeling

pretty angry about your mother's drinking. I feel upset and helpless about it too. And it's time she and I had a *long*-overdue talk about it. It's *so* hard to mention. . . ."

Rosie shook her head. "There's something so much worse."

"Really?"

Rosie nodded, absolutely terrified.

"What is it?"

"I can't tell you."

"Yes, you can."

"I swore to God I wouldn't."

"You *have* to. It's eating you up."

Rosie hung her head. Sharon's dad showed me his dick. Sharon's dad. Rosie was stricken, trapped and anxious. She looked up at Rae.

Sharon's dad—"Sharon's dad." She stopped.

"Go on."

"I can't."

"Okay, Rosie. Either you tell me what he did, or I call and ask him."

"No!"

"Then tell me."

"Sharon's dad—showed me his dick."

Time stopped. Rae's mouth dropped open. Rosie burst into tears. Rae slammed her fist down on the table.

"God!" she shouted and got to her feet. She grabbed Rosie out of her chair and sat back down, with Rosie in her lap. "That bastard! I'll kill him!"

Rosie buried her head against Rae's breast, sobbing.

"Oh, Rosie."

"He put it on my arm."

"Oh, Rosie."

"In his *study.*"

"Why didn't you tell Elizabeth?"

"I promised Sharon I wouldn't."

"How did Sharon find out?"

"He does it to her all the time. When he did it to me, I ran out of the house, and Sharon got home right then, and she knew. But she said—and he said—that all fathers show it to their daughters, so when they see their *hus*band's—"

"Bullshit, Rosie. Sick men do it. It's a *crime*. Men go to jail for doing it."

"Oh, no."

"Not that Mr. Thackery will go to jail—but . . . Sharon needs our help. First we'll tell your mother—"

"No!"

"Yes. We have to."

"No, not today!"

"Rosie, I'm afraid—"

"She's *to*tally depressed. She's been crying."

Rae thought this over. She hugged Rosie tightly.

"Well. Maybe we should call someone who knows about this sort of thing, a child protection agency. We'll find out what to do—we've *got* to help Sharon."

"Can we tell my mother tomorrow?"

Rae exhaled deeply. "Yeah."

"Will you be with me?"

"Yes, of course. Why don't you climb off my lap for a moment. I'm going to look in the phone book."

"But don't tell them our real names."

"Okay."

Rosie milled around the room while Rae looked through the phone book and dialed the number of the Child Abuse Hotline.

"Hey, do you want to spend the night?" she asked Rosie, as the phone rang.

"Okay!"

"Hello? Yes. I need some advice. A little girl that I know has been molested, by her best friend's father."

Rosie shuffled over to Rae, with her head down, and stood at her side, sad and confused: God, what a mess. It was the end of the world. Sharon's dad might go to jail, might want to kill her when he got out. Rosie saw him in prison stripes, gripping the bars of his cell. Sharon would hate her guts, and Mrs. Thackery would cry forever.

Oh, Mama; God, she thought. I don't know what to do.

Chapter
✿20

The next morning, Elizabeth sat on the porch swing reading *Excellent Women*. It was a brand new day, white, warm, and blustery, and she had slept well the night before. James had been trying to work since eight. At eight fifteen he had appeared in the kitchen to harp briefly on mediocrity in the publishing world. At eight thirty he had returned to the kitchen for a second cup of coffee and said, "A vale of tears, Elizabeth. A vale of tears."

Several minutes after she'd come out to the porch, he stepped outside and stood staring out into the garden, as if overseeing his fields and workers, and then abruptly went back inside to his study. After five minutes, she heard frantic typing, and then the sound of paper being ripped from a typewriter. In another minute, he came outside and sat down beside her. She put down her book.

"What's the matter?"

"My writing days are over."

"Ah."

"I'm pathetic. I sit there hunched over the typewriter, poised, as if I'm about to start conducting the *Eroica* at Carnegie Hall,

✿ 236

and then—nothing. I feel preoccupied, but I don't know what it is."

"Is there anything I can do?"

"Nah." He got up and went back inside. Elizabeth shook her head.

He re-emerged five minutes later with a platter of brittle, black french bread toast, dripping with butter, and sat beside her.

"Here. Have a piece."

"Those are burnt beyond recognition."

"Oh, no, they're perfect this way. Try one."

She shook her head.

"Suit yourself." He bit into a piece, with a thunderous crunch that became a sound suggesting automatic gunfire, or babies rolling on dry leaves. She was unpleasantly reminded of her mother eating bacon. "What are you going to do today?"

"I don't know."

Crunnnnch.

"There's Rosie," he said, pointing. "And Rae."

"Rosie actually looks cheerful, doesn't she?"

"Hey, Mama, hey, Mama, hey, James," Rosie called from across the street, in front of Mrs. Haas's house, waving wildly beside Rae, as if trying to flag them down. "Leon!" From out of nowhere, Leon tore past the porch carrying a small red rubber boot in his mouth which he dropped at the open gate. Rosie ran out into the street ahead of Rae, calling to Leon, who galloped toward her, "Here, buddy, here, buddy," and just as Rae stepped off the curb, with Rosie and Leon twelve feet apart in the middle of the street, they heard the roar of a motorcycle: the adults on the porch leaped up off the swing, and for all of them time slowed all the way down, to a single played at 33, as a two-manned Harley plowed into Leon and sped on.

Leon shot into the air like an acrobat, as Rosie and Rae screamed, and James and Elizabeth raced down the stairs to the gate. The motorcycle had disappeared. Rosie closed her eyes and shouted, Leon lay four feet away, and Rae swept Rosie up into her arms.

"Rosie," Elizabeth cried, rushing over to them. James stared at the two women holding Rosie and finally bent down to his dog, who was smiling, with shining-still eyes and blood pouring out of his mouth.

"Leon?" he said, stroking his fur. "You okay?"

Rosie ran to James, who looked up at her in terror.

"You gotta be more careful," he said slowly.

She squatted beside him and they both started crying, but bravely. She stroked Leon's head, with fingernails painted pink by Rae, then turned to James. "You think he's dead?"

James nodded, scratching behind Leon's ear.

Elizabeth's mouth was agape. Rae stood beside her.

"Rae? Am I dreaming?"

Rae shook her head.

"Are you positive?"

Rae nodded.

Elizabeth stared like a ravenous zombie at the man whose dog it was, at the girl whose life it might have been, at the dead dog. It was a dream, it had to be.

"Maybe we should take him to the vet," said Rosie.

James shook his head.

"How come?"

"Because he's definitely dead." He wiped at his eyes. Rosie wiped at hers. He watched her.

"God," he said, and closed his eyes for a minute. "We got off easy."

Rae and James carried Leon to the back yard to bury him. Elizabeth and Rosie trudged slowly behind, Elizabeth more badly shaken than ever before, too shaken even to scream at Rosie about running into traffic. Either this was a dream, or it had been a dream yesterday when she'd run over the dog.

They buried Leon in a corner of the garden, beside a bush of American beauties, each person taking a turn with the shovel. James and Elizabeth lowered Leon into the hole, while Rosie stood holding the shovel like the farmer in "American Gothic," and Rae dabbed at her red nose with a Kleenex.

"Okay. Let's cover him up."

"Wait," said Rosie, handing him the shovel, and dashed off to the front of the house. The grown-ups stood looking into the hole.

"I wonder what she's up to," said Elizabeth.

James looked wistfully at his dog and exhaled in that rare way of his, the faraway tropical wind from deep inside.

James thought it was his fault. He'd left that gate open.

Elizabeth thought it was her fault. She had killed a dog the day before and kept on going.

Rae felt guilty too, out of habit; it was as much second nature by now as her generosity.

And Rosie *knew* that it was her fault.

"I wonder where your daughter is," said James.

James made a bull horn of his hands. "I owe You one," he called to the sky.

Rosie walked purposefully toward them, with what turned out to be a balsa-wood tombstone, on which she had written, in black magic marker, *Here Lies Leon. R.I.P.*

"Good thinking," said James. "Thanks."

She jammed the bottom into the dirt at the end of the grave, where Leon's head was, and patted dirt firmly against it as if potting a sprig cutting. Dirt got underneath her pink nails and on her face when she stopped to push blue-black curls off her furrowed forehead. When she got it just right, she stood, put her hands in the pockets of the red bermuda shorts, and nodded. James threw a shovel of dirt on top of Leon. Rosie watched the body disappear, spellbound.

Elizabeth turned and walked several steps away, trying to collect her thoughts. She licked the corners of her mouth. Looking up she saw, in a windowpane, clear reflections of her family, graveside, framed in black, beside a bush of American beauties; and the image almost undid her.

Hang on, old girl. The worst must be over.

James left for the beach on foot after his dog was buried. Rosie and Rae and Elizabeth went into the kitchen. While Elizabeth made coffee and cocoa, Rosie and Rae sat at the table. Rosie whispered something to Rae, who nodded.

"Mama? We've got something to tell you."

"Well, go ahead."

"I think you better sit down," said Rae.

"No, go ahead."

"I'm serious. You really better sit down."

Elizabeth came over from the stove and sat down. "Okay. Now tell me."

Rosie and Rae looked at each other.

"Elizabeth, it's a horrible thing to have to hit you with, after what just happened, but it really can't wait."

"Okay. I can take it."

"There's no way to prepare you for this. But a couple of weeks ago, Mr. Thackery exposed himself to Rosie. In his study. He rubbed his prick on her arm."

Elizabeth's face, arrested and expectant, slowly dilated. She straightened her head, and an invisible hand on her chest seemed to push her backward in her chair, and her face contracted and she gripped the table, digging her nails into the wood.

"What?"

Rae and Rosie nodded.

She looked at Rosie, tilted her head, half squinted.

Rosie nodded.

"That goddamn son of a bitch! That fucking scumbag! Rosie! Jesus! How come you didn't tell me? Goddamn." Elizabeth scratched her head, gripped a mass of hair tightly, looked at the table, and then up at Rosie.

"I swore to God I wouldn't. To Sharon."

"He apparently shows it to Sharon routinely. He told Rosie that all fathers do it."

"He said Sharon likes to touch it, but I'm positive she doesn't."

"Tell me exactly what happened."

Rosie told her every detail she could remember.

"That bastard."

"And he said I'd be in trouble if I told anyone. But then Sharon came home and she could tell what had happened."

"Poor Sharon, goddammit. The sweetest person in the world. Poor you, baby, what a shitty thing for a man to do." She looked at Rae. "Well, I guess the thing to do is call the cops."

"No, not yet. Rosie and I called the Child Protection Agency. They said the cops don't have to be notified yet."

"Listen, any man that shows his cock to my *daughter—*"

"Wait, wait. Think about it. Do you want Rosie on the witness stand?"

"No. Of course not."

"The social worker said we should tell Mrs. Thackery—we didn't use names—and insist that she confront her husband and insist that he seek psychiatric help. There's a program available for child abusers: family counseling, rehabilatative treatment for him, therapy for Sharon and Sybil."

"Am I dreaming this?"

"That's what I thought when it was happening," said Rosie. "I wonder if Sybil knows?"

"The social worker said it's likely; or it may be that she knew only subconsciously and turned a blind eye to it."

"God! To stand by while your husband molests your child."

"The man at the agency said that more than four out of every ten girls are sexually abused by a male member of the family by the time the girls are eighteen. And that's a conservative estimate."

"It should be grounds for capital punishment."

"Yeah, but. It's a deep sickness. The man said Mr. Thackery will be relieved that it's finally out, that it's over."

"What if he doesn't agree to therapy?"

"Then we call the cops. And we tell the Thackerys that we're going to call the cops if they don't go get help."

Elizabeth tapped a fingernail against her beer glass and gave Rosie a long sideways look.

"You okay, baby?" Rosie nodded. "Jesus. What a secret. When did you tell Rae?"

"Last night."

"I'm glad you told her, sweetheart. You did the right thing. Come here."

Rosie got up and went to her mother, who pulled Rosie into her lap.

"What do *you* think we ought to do, Rosie?"

"What Rae said."

"Tell Mrs. Thackery?" Rosie nodded. "Okay."

"Today?"

"Yeah."

Rosie inhaled loudly. "Okay. He's gone on business, anyhow."

"Good. I'm so sorry this happened to you."

"Yeah. But think about Sharon."

"Yeah. Your telling us was a huge favor to her. It's going to radically, for the better, change her life. But things might be weird between you in the beginning—because she's going to have a lot of guilt for and about her dad; she'll feel all this twisted-up loyalty, and also that she was doing a sick thing all these years. But she needs, A: protection from him, and B: counseling. And he desperately needs help. He's a sick, sick man."

Elizabeth nuzzled the top of Rosie's head, and Rae watched them together. Their eyes were downcast, blue and hazel, dark lashes and brows, arched swanlike necks; they were one black-haired unit.

"It never rains, does it, Rae."

"No."

"You don't think he'll hurt Sharon or his wife, do you?"

"No," said Rosie. "He's mostly really nice."

"And we're all positive that this isn't a dream?"

"No, Mama."

"Okay, then. I guess. I should get up. And call."

"Are you going to tell her over the phone?"

"No. I'm just going to tell her I'm coming over to talk."

"I'll go with you, Mama."

"I think I should go alone."

"No, Mama. I should go with you."

"Okay. But I want to be alone with Sybil." She dialed, and Rosie came to stand miserably at her side, like her pet hunchbacked midget, burrowed against Elizabeth, staring at the floor. Now she wasn't positive it had really happened at all. Maybe it had been a dream. She bit a dirty pink fingernail, as if testing the authenticity of a gold coin. It hurt.

"No one's home."

Phew.

"Do you have any idea what their plans are today?"

"No."

"Well, let's wait around here for a while and try again."

"You're going to go crazy waiting around here. Why don't you two walk over and wait for them? You could tape a note to the door, for Sybil to call you."

Elizabeth looked at Rosie. "You want to do that? Leave a note?" Rosie shrugged.

"Okay."

Elizabeth left a note to James on his typewriter, took a sheet of paper, a pen, and some Scotch tape from his desk, put them in the pocket of her jacket.

"Ready?" she asked Rosie.

Rosie shrugged again. "Yeah."

"Call me as soon as you get home," said Rae.

"Yeah, I will. Wish us well."

Mrs. Thackery's car was not parked in front of the house when the Fergusons arrived, but on the off chance that it was in the shop, they walked up to the front door.

Rosie pushed the doorbell and stood furiously wiping the soles of her sneakers on the sisal welcome mat. Elizabeth reached down and rubbed the warm downy base of her daughter's neck. They took simultaneous deep breaths and stood waiting, turned to look at each other and then back at the closed door. Rosie knocked, but no one came.

They sat down to wait in two wrought-iron café chairs at a wrought-iron table in the garden, underneath a beige umbrella. Elizabeth savored the smell of wet, bright-green grass, studied the fruit trees in the garden, heavy with lemons, pears, figs, and apples. Sunlight made everything golden.

Rosie kicked off her shoes and went off to climb in a tree. After a minute, Elizabeth looked over at one of the world's oldest banyan trees, expecting to find Rosie in its low, thick branches, but found her, instead, three quarters of the way up the trunk of an aged pepper tree, shinnying up the dark gnarled bark like a baby gorilla. Elizabeth gasped involuntarily.

"Be *care*ful, sweetheart—there aren't many branches." Get the hell down off of that tree, you're going to fall and break your neck. She heard her mother's fearful voice, marveled again that anyone lived to adulthood. "Honest, baby. I can't take much more today. Come and sit here with me."

Half an hour later, Mrs. Thackery's station wagon appeared at the curb. The Fergusons looked at each other and stood.

The two women, virtual strangers until now, sat side by side at the kitchen table. Elizabeth had the sense that Sybil knew why she had come, just as Sharon had: the initial defiance on their faces, and fear fluttering just below the surface.

Elizabeth took a deep breath and put her elbows on the table, interweaving her fingers as in prayer, took a sudden breath and raised her brows, as if about to jump into a frigid lake, and turned to Sybil.

"I'm sick about this. It must be the hardest thing you'll ever have to hear." Black button eyes, frightened and helpless like a child's. "But: several weeks ago your husband exposed himself to Rosie. In his study."

"She *knows* she's not to come into the house when I'm not here."

"Well, Sybil, that's not the point. The point is that your husband exposed himself to my child and routinely makes Sharon touch his genitals." Elizabeth shook her head.

"My husband is a very fine man," said Sybil, beginning to cry.

"Maybe in some ways. But he's sick. He's hurting your daughter. Sharon needs to be protected from her father's abuse."

"I've tried to protect her. I'd die for her."

"Of course you have, of course you would." Sybil looked urgently, beseechingly, at her. "But it isn't enough. He's done—and will continue to do—ugly, sick things to your child, to our Sharon. And now he's done it to Rosie, and I'm not going to sit by and let it happen again—to either of them."

Sybil held her belly, as if she had cramps, and wept.

Elizabeth reached out and massaged her shoulders. "It's a nasty business, but it's not the end of the world. I've already called the Child Protection Agency. He's got to turn himself in to them."

"What if he refuses?"

"Then I'm going to notify them, and a social worker will confront him, and if he still refuses and denies it, the police will be brought in."

"He's not a criminal!"

"Yes, as a matter of fact, he is."

"He'd never hurt her."

"Sybil! How can you say that? He *is* hurting her! He's a huge, male grown-up who takes sexual advantage of his own child!"

Sybil nodded her head, and tears streamed into the lap of her dress. Elizabeth got up and found a box of Kleenex.

"There's a chance he's going to be transferred. We may be moving."

"It doesn't change things."

"Palo Alto. He's been promoted."

"Well, Sybil. What you've got to do is, get in touch with the Child Protection Agency here, get your husband involved in therapy, and then, when you move, continue treatment in Palo Alto. Because if you don't call them, I will. And if he refuses treatment, the police will be called. I don't want to see the girls on the witness stand."

"I don't either."

Sybil stopped crying.

"I tried to leave him once," she said. "Before we moved to Bayview. He said he'd kill himself. I thought that—he had stopped doing it." Elizabeth listened quietly.

"That's why Sharon needs you to step in," she said.

Sybil dabbed at her nose. "Don't tell Rosie yet—that we may be moving. Sharon doesn't know."

"Okay."

"It was good of you to—look after Sharon like this."

"Well, I love her, you know. She's one of the kindest, most gentle people I've ever known. You've done a beautiful job raising her. Sybil, do it as soon as you can. Everything is going to be all right. Starting now. Painful and hard but all right."

Rosie and Sharon were sitting outside on the bottom step of the house, hunched over, with their heads jammed between their knees, drawing in the dirt with sticks. Neither of them looked up. "Sharon?"

Sharon looked up, with her mother's black button eyes. Elizabeth sat down beside her. "I know your dad's a wonderful man, but he needs help. And so we're going to make sure he gets it. Okay? That's a girl."

"They won't arrest him, will they?"

"No. Not if he agrees to get help."

"You know what Sharon said? She said, 'Why'd you have to go and open your big mouth?' "

"What did you say?"

"I said, Because what he was doing was wrong."

"Good girl."

They were on the way home, holding hands on the sidewalk.

"God," said Rosie mournfully. "You're a great mother."

Chapter
❦21

James, the crafty ambassador, approached Elizabeth in the kitchen several days later, at the stove, where she stood navigating a garlic sausage flotilla through boiling water with a wooden fork, listening to the radio.

"I don't know," he said, pressing his face between her shoulder blades. "I for one am just getting very sick of drinking."

"Yeah?"

"I'm ready to quit." He stepped away, and she turned to look at him.

"But you don't even drink that much."

"I don't drink as much as you—but I drink too much. I think my work would be better."

Elizabeth turned back toward the stove.

"Why don't we just—you know—*quit*?"

"Right now?"

"Why not?"

"I've already had several glasses of wine."

"If you quit right now, you won't have a hangover tomorrow."

"There's no point tonight, James. Really. I mean, *maybe* tomorrow."

"I don't understand."

"Well, James, it's like when you're going to start what may be a long-term diet: you decide you're going to start tomorrow, you swear to yourself, and you spend the entire day gorging, because you'll be going without for so long. It's a tradition."

James sat down at the table, mulling this over. "Okay," he said. "Tomorrow, then."

Elizabeth stared down into the pot with unfocused eyes. After a minute, she shrugged her shoulders. "Okay."

"Great! Good!"

Elizabeth nodded, turned to him, and grinned. "Okay, yes, tomorrow." She raised her glass and toasted: "Tomorrow." Then she sat down beside him. "It'll be great to quit."

"She said dully."

She smiled at James. "No, I mean it. One day I consciously realized that I was trying to break myself down, so that I'd hit bottom and *have* to quit Because I didn't think I could do it otherwise. And I told myself that there would be a day—an inevitable, unavoidable day—when it would come to a head, and I would have to begin to recover from—this. Alcoholism."

The word drowned out the Scarlatti horns. They both held their breath.

"Whoa, *shit!*" she exclaimed, looking around, bedazzled. "I'm having a *hot* flash." She looked intently at James. "*Al*coholism."

He nodded.

She smiled at the glass of wine and took a big sip. "You know," she said fondly, to the wineglass, "alcohol has been one of my very best friends. I used to look forward to drinking in the afternoon in the same way that I looked forward to seeing you again each night. God." She set down the glass and scratched her head. "I knew there would be a *day* that was . . . conspicuous, when I'd have to quit, but it's been more like a conspicuous couple of weeks. Starting with the day Rosie stole the money, when she and Sharon found me passed out . . . and then, you know,

Thackery, and Leon," and the puppy. "I mean, Jesus. What do I need, a burning bush?"

James smiled. "Oh, Elizabeth."

She got up, with her wineglass, and went to turn off the stove. "These sausages are probably way overdone. Rosie should be home any minute—she's been at the fort with Sharon all day." She picked up a fork, opened the oven, poked a potato, and turned off the heat. "Poor Sharon, and Rosie. . . ."

The front door opened and slammed, and they turned toward the sound of heavy, hunchbacked trudging.

"Speak of the devil." They heard her climb the stairs. "Will you go tell her that dinner is almost ready?"

Five minutes later, he reported back that Sharon was moving. That Mr. Thackery had been transferred.

Elizabeth exhaled wearily and dried her hands on a dishtowel. "Well, I'm not surprised."

"I smell a rat."

"Mrs. Thackery told me that he might be getting a transfer and promotion. And I told her that even if they moved I'd be doublechecking as to whether or not they were getting intensive therapy."

"Well, Rosie's *bummed,* but good."

"I bet she is. I'll go see if she feels like eating. Or talking. I guess it's all right to leave the sausages in the water. Will you make a quick salad?"

"Sure."

She took a sip of wine and left the kitchen.

"Can I come in?" There was no response, so Elizabeth opened the door and found Rosie lying on her bed, staring at the ceiling like a recent corpse.

Oh, Rosie.

"I heard the bad news. I thought you might feel like some company."

Rosie rolled her eyes angrily, as if it was the stupidest thing she'd ever heard.

"There's not much I can say that will make you feel better. But at least they're only moving a couple of hours away."

"Chhh."

Elizabeth reached over and mussed up her soft, wild hair.

"Do you want to be alone?"

"Yeah."

The losses in her daughter's life, now and prospective, descended on Elizabeth's chest like a leaden x-ray apron.

"Okay."

"Don't go."

Elizabeth sat back down on the bed and lifted Rosie into her lap.

"How would you feel if Rae moved away?" Rosie asked.

"I'd feel like *shit.* I'd be sore at the world. And at her."

"You said everything would be fine."

"It will. But it will be sad for a while."

"Then there'll just be some other sad thing."

"Well, sure, but—sometimes you get a long stretch of good days between the sad things."

"Yeah, but who cares about *them* when you're having one of the *sad* things?"

"You've just got to remember sometimes you'll be on an upswing, everything's coming up roses, and sometimes you'll be on a downswing, a broken heart or depression, but although you never believe it at the time, you'll start an upswing again."

"But Mama, it was my fault that Sharon has to move."

"Oh, Rosie, listen. It wasn't even the tiniest bit of being your fault. It's Mr. Thackery's profession, his character, his problems—completely. Honest to God."

They heard James coming up the stairs and stopped talking.

"Hi," he said at the doorway.

"Hi," said Elizabeth. James came over to them and sat at the foot of the bed. Rosie pulled at a coil of hair, unwound it, and pulled her head sideways, as if it were on a leash.

"Listen, I know how you feel," he said. "Remember my best friend, Denny Hoods, who used to lift me up to the water faucet?" Rosie nodded but did not make eye contact. "Well, we were inseparable from the time we were five until his family moved away, when he was thirteen. I was heartbroken."

"Oh, yeah?"

He nodded.

"Did you cry?"

"Hey, man I told you, boys didn't cry. What we did was, I went over to his house the day he was leaving, and we wrestled on his lawn—not affectionately at all. We were red-faced and rough. Then for the next couple of weeks I skulked around the house, punishing my parents; laying all these creepy trips on them."

"Then what happened?"

"I made a new best friend."

Rosie scowled sadly. "Yeah, but I won't."

"I promise, on my honor, that you will."

"Oh, sure."

"Let's go eat," said Elizabeth.

"I'm not hungry."

"Then keep us company," said James.

Rosie picked at her food. James looked away every time Elizabeth poured herself another glass of wine.

"I think I'd better call Sybil," Elizabeth announced as she made a leaning, wobbling stack of dishes and silverware. "Make sure they're doing something about it."

"Don't call tonight, Mama."

"Why?"

"Because, you know: there's all this stuff happening at their house already, like getting ready to move and stuff."

The dishes clattered in Elizabeth's arms as she turned to go. "Yeah, I know, but moving doesn't get them off the hook."

"James," Rosie whispered when Elizabeth was out of the room. "I don't *want* her to call, she's *tight*."

"I know she is. But she'll pull it off."

"God, I'm so sick of this."

"Yeah, so am I. So is *she*. We're quitting tomorrow."

"Oh, yeah, give me a break."

"Honest to God, Rosie."

"*She's* quitting tomorrow too?"

James nodded. Rosie stared off into space.

"So tell me. Has your husband begun therapy yet?"

"Well, no, not exactly."

"Sybil, either he has or he hasn't." She poured an inch of burgundy into her wineglass.

"He has agreed to, Elizabeth, and we'll go, as a family, when we're settled in Palo Alto. And in the meantime, there's absolutely no chance of his doing it again."

"And what guarantee do you have?"

"I have his word."

"His word isn't good enough for me."

"Oh, Elizabeth, I know how you feel—you're right, of course—but . . . for the next two weeks, he's going to be working overtime trying to get his office ready for the move, training his replacement, and *I'll* be here supervising the packing— there's going to be very little free time."

"Sybil. His word is not assurance enough for me that it won't happen to Sharon again."

"Elizabeth, please. You have my word, we'll get counseling . . . but in the meantime—"

"In the meantime, one of us is going to contact the Child Protection Agency, explain what his pattern has been and about your moving, and ask *them* what to do. Will it be me or you?"

"Elizabeth?"

"I'm dead serious. Notify the right people up here, now, explain that you'll be moving, and give them your new address. And ask them what they suggest."

"But—"

"I mean it. Tomorrow."

"All right. *I* will."

"I'll call you tomorrow, in the evening."

"No, don't. He'll be home."

"In the late afternoon, then."
"All right."

"You were good," James said from the doorway.
"Thanks."
"Shall I give you a hand with the dishes?"
"Not tonight. Go keep Rosie company."
He nodded and went to the living room.

She poured another glass of wine and tackled the dishes; in the other room, James put on a record, Dylan, "Blood on the Tracks." Soapy dishes slipped through her hands, clusters of bubbles slithered down the side of her wineglass, and when the existential western soap opera "Lily, Rosemary and the Jack of Hearts" played, she sang along with the refrain, watching herself wash dishes as she would watch television.

She could hear James and Rosie talking, but not what they were saying. To her, they were real, authentic, flesh and blood, she did not quite have this sense about herself. Is Elizabeth the woman washing the dishes, or the mind that hovers above this woman, watching her wash the dishes?

"Listen. 'Tigers in India eating villagers—sixty-five dead to date.' *Sixty-five dead to date,* James." Rosie looked up at him with a listless terror.
"Wow."
"Oh, Rosie, don't read the paper before bed. You *know* it'll give you nightmares," said Elizabeth, coming into the room.
"But I couldn't help it. It was just sitting here."
"Come sit with us, Elizabeth."
"Oh, the window seat gets crowded. I'll sit on the couch."
Now Dylan was singing "Shelter from the Storm." James was reading the pages he'd written that day, marking them up with a pencil.
"Come here, sweetheart. It's almost time for bed."
"Noooooo," Rosie wailed.

"Yes."

"But I've been *good.* I haven't even been bugging you."

"Come here. I want to hold you." Rosie got up and walked to
her mother, head down and shuffling. Elizabeth reached out and
drew Rosie to her side, as an elephant draws a trunkful of hay to
its mouth. "I'm not making you go to bed as *pun*ishment, baby.
It's because I care about you. You're a little, growing person,
and you need sleep, like you need good food."

"I'll never be able to fall asleep."

"How come?"

"I don't know. Because I'm starving to death."

Elizabeth smiled. "Yeah?"

Rosie nodded.

"Okay, then. Do you want a bowl of ice cream?"

"Yeah."

"And then you'll go to bed?" Rosie nodded. "James?"

"None for me, thanks. I'm going to lose a few pounds."

"Oh, James. You're just right."

"I want to be lithe, and sexy, and evil."

Elizabeth smiled at him.

The Fergusons went to the kitchen. Elizabeth got Rosie two
scoops of peach ice cream, and another glass of wine for herself,
and they sat side by side at the table. Rosie took a tiny bite and
savored it. Then she mashed the ice cream against the side and
bottom of the bowl, stirred it, whisked it into a thick liquid state,
and began to eat it drop by drop.

"Come on, sweetie, don't dawdle. It's nearly ten."

"God! You don't have to rush my eating!"

Elizabeth rolled her eyes.

Rosie lay awake in the dark, staring at the ceiling. Outside, lit by
the moon, tigers milled around the rosebushes, licking their lips,
prowlers in the garden. Little Black Sambo. Nothing to worry
about; they'll be butter soon, for the pancakes her mother Black
Mumbo will make. Amber eyes, tiger stripes—suddenly one of
them leaps into a bush, emerges with Mr. Thackery, yelling and

bloody, between its teeth. The vision filled her head, and she stared, awestruck.

She dreams of tigers at an outside circus, jumping through hoops of fire. She is sitting ringside, with James and Sharon, when suddenly they hear the drone of approaching planes. "Bombers," says James calmly, and the planes get nearer and louder. Elephants trumpet over the sound of the engines, the sky is red with the flames of distant bombings, and they sit waiting quietly in their seats for the end of the world.

Elizabeth ricocheted off the wall twice when she finally went upstairs to bed. She lay down fully clothed and closed her eyes, felt her mind swirling through quickstand, felt the bed spin. She had passed out by the time James joined her and did not wake up when he rolled her over to undo the buttons on her skirt. He pulled it off, dropped it on the floor, and let her lie on top of the covers in panties and a shirt, while he stripped down to nothing and crawled between the sheets beside her.

He read Greene's *The Human Factor* for an hour or so, glancing from time to time at his softly snoring lover. He closed the book, put it on the floor beside the bed, got up, and went to the bathroom, where he filled a glass of water and got the bottle of aspirin out of the medicine chest. He carried the water and pills to Elizabeth's bedside table, put them down, and went to the window, where he stood staring for a long time at the night sky. He turned to look at Elizabeth, handsome, serene, and dead to the world. He heard an owl, crickets, cicadas, a distant siren, wind in the trees, and went to lie down, smoking in the dark with a cold glass ashtray on his chest, beside the black-haired woman who might one day be his wife.

Rosie awoke an hour later and sat up in bed, terrified of nothing in particular. The old house was settling down for the night; downstairs a floorboard groaned—was that a footstep on the stairs? She held her breath and strained to hear. He's coming upstairs to kill them all: it's Norman Bates, dressed as his mother, holding a long sharp knife; or it's a crazy laughing black man with a gun; or it's Mr. Thackery.

Crrrreak.

She scurried under the covers down to the foot of the bed, pulling her blankets and sheets into a pile on top of her, so the killer would think "Hmmm, no one to kill in *this* room." After a while, the sounds on the stairs ceased, and she came up for air, alone in the dark. God! Rosie scrambled off the bed, holding her breath, and turned on the light. She tiptoed toward the door, looking as frail and feverish and ethereal in her white flannel nightie as a pre-tubercular Dickensian orphan. She walked down the hall to her mother's room.

"Mama?" she whispered, outside the closed door. "Psssst. Mama?" No one answered. She cleared her throat and slowly opened the door. "Pssst?" Neither James nor her mother responded.

The room smelled of wine and tobacco; she was safe. She tiptoed to Elizabeth's side of the bed, lay down on the carpet, and was soon breathing peacefully.

Elizabeth whinnied at dawn.

"It's all right," James said. Rosie woke up.

"Whaaa?"

"You were dreaming. Chasing rabbits."

Elizabeth groaned.

"What were you dreaming?"

Elizabeth groaned again. "I don't remember."

"There's water and aspirin by your bed, if you need it."

Rosie watched her mother's arm reach out above her. Bug-eyed, a Little Rascal, about to start whistling, she watched the arm and a glass pass back toward the bed, listened to her mother drink water.

"Oh, I don't feel well at all, James."

"This will be your last hangover."

"God, I get to stop *drinking* today."

"Yeah."

In the lulling silence, Rosie smiled, crossed her fingers.

"What if I can't do it?"

"I know you can. Think of how good you'll feel, clear-headed, healthy. Less guilty, less sick."

"I guess that doesn't sound so bad." She laughed softly, groggily. "I quit smoking, you know."

"I know. If you can quit smoking, you can quit anything."

"Oh, James. I don't know if I can do it."

"One way to find out."

"God, I am *so* fucked up."

"Yeah, but on top of that, you're perfect."

"Don't make me laugh."

"You are, for me. I've been waiting for you all my life. I want to grow old with you. We could spend the rest of our lives getting to know each other."

"Yeah."

"I mean, we should get married."

"Oh, God, I don't know."

There was a long pause. Say yes, Mama, say yes! The pause continued.

"Elizabeth? When did you first notice that you'd lost interest in me?"

Elizabeth laughed. "I never will, I promise."

James exhaled loudly.

Rosie heard them kiss. After a long while, she could tell by their breathing that they were asleep. Rosie got up and tiptoed out the door.

Her bedroom was lit by the sunrise. She took off her nightgown and put on her shorts. Her T-shirt was so cold against her chest that for a moment she thought it was wet, and the voice within her head said, Mama's gonna quit!

Chapter
✿22

Sober for two days, Elizabeth felt that her windows had been washed: her mind and eyes were clear again. It was a miracle, to not have the drinks that she craved.

The phone rang, and she went to the hall to answer it. James, at his typewriter, looked up and listened:

"Hi. How are you doing? . . . What's the matter? . . . No. Oh, shit. What did *you* say? . . . Oh, no, Rae, you're kidding me! You gotta call him back and tell him you've reconsidered. . . . Because! The guy is a jerk and an asshole, and you've worked so hard to get over him! . . . I *know* you're lonely, but you were lonelier when you were with him; you spent all day every day swallowing golf balls. . . . Of course he misses you. You were the best thing that ever happened to him. But he didn't want you. . . . Oh, good, now he does, right. Wonderful. . . . Ohhhh, gee, was he crying? My heart bleeds for the guy. I hate that kind of man! Who makes you console him for needing you! God. Call him back, then call me. . . . Because! He makes you feel clingy and neurotic and obsessed, and lucky to get whatever little morsel of time he can give you. Because, Rae, as long as some man is making you feel that way, you know who you are; if somebody makes you feel insecure and needed and abused, you exist; otherwise, if a man made you feel loved and wanted and deserving of being loved and wanted by a great person, you'd have a massive identity attack. . . . Oh, come on, sweetheart. If *I* could find a great man who loves me and wants me, you can. There's a good one out there waiting for you. Don't settle for a selfish, boring little boy. . . . Okay. Call me back. We're going to the city tonight—me and James and Rosie. Come with us. We'll eat in North Beach and then go see a movie. Something funny. Rosie's pretty low, too. . . . Oh, she's upstairs in her room, brooding. James is working. I'm about to go work in the garden. So—call him up, all right? Then call me back. . . . Oh, Rae. It always feels that way, that you'll never fall in love again, that no one great will ever fall in love with you, but I promise. It'll happen. . . . Look, I spent my whole life looking for a friend like you. I'd given up. And then we found each other. Or rather, you found me, and weaseled your way into my heart, and now you're part of the family. And James is part of our family too, and when a good man comes along for you, he'll be part of our family too. Okay? I promise. . . . Good, okay, call me back. Be brave. I love you, Rosie loves you—"

"Tell her I love her too!"

"And James loves you too. Call me back. 'Bye."

Elizabeth stood in the doorway of the study, smiling.

"Were you eavesdropping?"

"Yes, of course. You were terrific."

"Brian—"

"I gathered. You were great. There's got to be a job out there for you, for when people are having episodes and you tell them what to do." Elizabeth shrugged. "Seriously; you have no idea what a difference it makes to have you, Elizabeth Ferguson, on your side—on my side, or Rae's side." The phone rang again.

"I'll be right back."

When she left, James picked up his clipboard and scribbled furiously on the top piece of paper.

"Good work, Rae. How do you feel? Do you want to come over and weed? . . . Yeah, that's a better idea—put on a stack of records and finish up that weaving. We'll come get you at six. But don't play all those mushy torch songs; stay away from Linda Ronstadt. . . . Okay. Call me if you have a relapse. Take it easy. 'Bye."

"So. You're going to garden? Good. I'll make lunch in a while. How are you holding up? Don't you like not drinking?"

Elizabeth shrugged. "I don't know. Yeah, I guess. It feels . . . phony now, though. I mean, I know I can go for several days, or a week, or whatever—but I *know* I can't face the rest of my life without . . . I mean . . ."

"I know what you mean."

"Yeah?"

James nodded. "We'll work it out."

"I feel . . . I—well, when Rosie was little, and everything would be going all right—she'd be playing happily or something—and then she'd fall, land on her butt or her face. And we'd watch her rev up for a great explosive cry; there'd be a few moments of silence while she was taking this huge, revving up sort of breath and she'd look all wild in the eyes. And Andrew would say, 'You're okay, you're okay.' And she'd think about it for a second, and realize that she didn't hurt, and the fit would never happen. She'd get on with playing. And that's how I'm feeling today. I have to keep saying, 'You're okay, you're okay.' "

"One day at a time, and all that."

"Yeah, but it's like one *hour* at a time."

An hour later, James poked his head into Rosie's bedroom door, thumbs in his ears, waggling his fingers. She was lying on the bed, reading *Pippi Longstocking* for the umpteenth time, and gave James the polite smile of a visitor at an insane asylum.

"Hey, Rosie. Do you want to play catch for a while?"

"No, thank you."

"How come? It's a perfectly splendid day."

"Because I'm reading."

"It's too nice to stay inside. Let's go outside and bother your mother."

"Nah."

"Come on."

"I just don't feel like playing, James."

"I'll give you a *pig*gyback ride."

"I really just don't want to."

"Will you come play with me if I give you my car?"

She scowled and smiled at the same time. "No."

"How come?"

"I'm not even old enough to drive."

"You're not?"

"Duh, James."

"Rae's going to come with us to the city."

"Good."

"Okay. I'll be in my study if you need me."

James heard her stomp down the stairs some time later and looked up from his typewriter. The front door opened and slammed shut. From where he sat, he could see Elizabeth sitting Indian-style by the lattice of sugar snap pea vines, dropping green pods into the lap of her red sundress. Then Rosie came into view and walked slowly toward her mother, head down. Black curls, white T-shirt, red bermudas, and red bobby socks with dime-sized black polkadots. He reached for his clipboard, extracted a pencil from behind his ear, and scribbled something. Then he lifted a feathery lock of hair with the pencil lead and twirled a strand around the pencil as if winding spaghetti onto a fork, daydreaming.

Elizabeth looked up from the snow peas and watched her brown and rangy child approach, trudging, really, looking almost rickety. Rosie spat through the gap in her teeth at the marigolds, wiped spittle off her chin, and trudged over to Elizabeth.

Poor old Rosie: I seen sunrise, I seen moonrise, lay dis old darkie down. Elizabeth smiled.

"Gudd-eetings in de name of his royal majesty, Emperor Haile Selassie," she called.

"Tsss."

"Ever feeeerful, ever shoor. Jah! *Ra*stafar-eye—"

"Mama, can't you just *please* take me seriously for once in your life?" Rosie's face quivered from the strain of her indignation. "God!"

"Come here, sweetheart."

"No."

Rosie whispered something toward the ground and then, in a grimly casual daze, ground out the pad and berries of a strawberry plant with the toe of her sneaker.

Elizabeth looked up into the unhappy face. "Thanks, doll. I hadn't gotten around yet to stamping out the berries."

Rosie scowled.

"Do you want to talk about it?"

Rosie exhaled noisily, still looking down.

"Do you want to sit in my lap?"

"No."

"Why not?" Elizabeth placed the snow peas on the ground.

"You have a crummy lap."

"What?"

"You're too skeeeeny."

"Darling, coming from you—"

"It's like sitting on books."

Elizabeth grabbed her by the wrist and pulled her down into her lap. "I want to hold you."

"How come?"

"Because I love you more than anything. And you're depressed."

"What about James?"

"I love James more than anything too."

"What about Rae?"

"I love Rae more than anything too. But Rosie, I love you with all my heart, and all my soul."

Rosie sat stiffly while her mother blew warm air into the curls on the back of her head. Elizabeth enclosed Rosie in her arms, rubbed her knobby shoulders, felt her daughter's shoulder blades dig into her big soft breasts. They listened to the birds.

"Are those the socks Rae gave you?"

"Yeah."

"They look terrific. Every ladybug in the garden is going to fall in love with you—"

"I don't want to talk about my goddamn socks!"

"What do you want to talk about?"

"I feel like being dead."

"Yeah?" Elizabeth exhaled loudly, nuzzled Rosie's soft downy neck.

"And I just wish that Sharon would die."

"It's a bitch, isn't it?"

"Totally."

"You won't feel so bad for much longer."

"Oh, yeah? Wull. *James* still misses his mother. And she's been dead for *years.*"

"But he doesn't ache very often. You're aching now. It's a fresh wound, losing Sharon. James still has pangs of—homesickness for her. Like you miss your daddy sometimes."

"Oh, no, sometimes I *ache.*"

"Because he was a great father. You were lucky. Look at who Sharon got for a father. But . . . my point is: that the jagged hurting part ends. Honest. Right now, your best friend in the world is leaving, and you're left holding a bag of knotholes. But after she's gone, you'll miss her less, every day."

"God."

"You'll make a new best friend, I promise. And besides, Palo Alto isn't so far away. We'll work it out so you two get to be together every so often."

"But I like to see her every day."

"I know you do."

"Do you still miss Daddy?"

Elizabeth didn't respond immediately. "It's funny. I don't miss him anymore, but I think about him all the time, every day, every time I watch you read, or run. And I'll always love him, for giving me you. But—I don't miss him, exactly."

"Wull, I do."

"Of course you do."

"I just feel like screaming, about Sharon."

"I know that feeling so well. All I can say is, it passes."

"When?"

"What can I say? A week from Tuesday? I don't know. Probably when school starts up."

"What if I start crying at school?"

Elizabeth shrugged. "Maybe you will, maybe you won't. I bet you won't. I bet on the first day of school, you find someone neat to play with."

"What if I don't?"

"Right now, you're feeling like there's a vacuum in your life—I swear to you, I know the feeling perfectly. But remember what James said?"

"Nature hates a vacuum."

"Yeah. And so all sorts of stuff rushes in to fill it."

Elizabeth leaned them both forward and picked a small fat strawberry from beneath a green pad, held it with her long fingers up to Rosie's right eye, as if to let her view a ruby, and then popped it into her child's mouth. She picked another for herself, picked another for Rosie, listened to the soft wet sucking, felt Rosie's jaw move up and down: nursed her with berries.

Rosie crossed her outstretched legs at the ankles, stared with an angry expression at her red and black socks. Elizabeth gave her another strawberry.

"I don't even feel like *see*ing her right now. I feel like wrecking all her stupid toys."

"Try to be a good sport, baby. Sharon feels as bad as you do. It's all right for you to be mad, but . . . try to be as good a sport as you can. I'll tell you. It's a run-of-the-mill shitty thing. Life is full of them. And it *always* feels better to be kind."

Rosie sighed.

"Let's go eat," said Elizabeth. "There's left over mu shu pork."

"There's no more pancakes."

"There's flour tortillas. And black bean sauce."

They gathered up the snow peas Elizabeth had picked earlier, and cut some flowers for the table: zinnias, roses, and bluebells.

The third day of Elizabeth's sobriety started off well enough, hot and blue, with patches of wispy tortoise-shell clouds high in the sky. James had been typing since eight, and Rosie had left at noon to spend the day swimming with Sharon and her mother. Elizabeth read the *Chronicle* twice, washed a cashmere sweater, went around the house picking up after James and Rosie, read a chapter of Anthony Powell, watered the ivy, made an appointment to have her teeth cleaned, defrosted the refrigerator, and sat down in the window seat with the Help Wanteds.

None of the advertised jobs caught her fancy. What did she like to do? Read, talk, walk, garden, sleep, make love, ruminate, eat, laugh, loaf, hardly marketable interests: the muted clacking of James's typewriter reminded her that her days lacked structure and invention. But staying off the bottle took all her time and energies. Would alcohol one day cease to be her automatic and primary response? Would it cease to be a craving and an obsession? What if those jungle drums—I want a drink I want a drink—never stopped?

She went to the phone and dialed Rae's number. She needed to be babysat today, needed advice and encouragement, because she needed a drink, needed some moments of peace of mind. Needed Rae. She had been there when Rae needed her, two days before when Brian had called, when Rae had been weak and depressed. Rae owed her one; but Rae wasn't home.

She went to the door of the study, listened to the furious typing, hung her head, and rubbed her eyes. She turned around and walked to the kitchen, licking at the corners of her mouth, blinking back tears.

She stood staring out the kitchen window at the garden and the trees and the birds and the sky, feeling concurrently crazy and numb. Finally, she walked back to the study and opened the door. James continued typing for several seconds, and then looked up at her.

"I'm going to go for a walk," she said.

"Okay. Is everything all right?"

"I guess so." Except that I cannot handle my feelings: boredom, resentment, guilt, panic, and oh-yes-everything's-all-right-I-guess. She gave him a weak smile and shook her head. "I'm not having a day of power," she said, quoting Rae, quoting Castaneda. "A good brisk walk on the beach—"

"Do you want to talk about it? I'll be done with this section in—I don't know, half an hour."

"No. I'm okay."

"I love you."

"I know. Thanks."

If you love me so goddamn much, why do I have to wait half an hour? Don't let me go. Can't you see that I need you now?

"See you in a while."

"Okay. 'Bye."

She headed toward the beach in a foul, shaky mood, full of resentment and undelivered accusations. She wiped sweat off her brow, licked at the corners of her mouth. The sun, hot and bright, beat down on her. Oh, to lie on the sand with a beer; God, all she wanted was one lousy beer.

No. Don't do it. There is no such thing in your world as one lousy beer. Don't do it, don't do it, stay on the path. Boom boom boom boom, beer beer beer—the drums were beating loud and clear, like "money, money, money" in *The Rocking-Horse Winner,* and, as if propelled by a force bigger than herself, she detoured into town and bought a six-pack of ale at Safeway.

Paranoid that James or Rosie or Rae would know, riddled with bad conscience and excuses (I didn't *mean* to buy a six-pack, and if any of you had been there when I needed you, and . . .), she carried the beer in a brown paper bag to the beach.

Two beers later, she felt peace of mind. She lay with her back on a sand dune and looked out to sea, at sailboats, sea gulls, and pelicans. She languidly rubbed her sun-warmed belly, ran her fingers through her hot black hair, watched a small boy at the water's edge, hand in hand with his father.

You're okay, you're okay. Today, you needed these ales. Tomorrow maybe you won't. It takes time to break an addiction. She studied the empty green bottles lying beside her on the blond sand. Might as well have another. She had already gone off the wagon; might as well have another. She untwisted a bottle cap, dropped it in the brown paper bag, and took a sip. Might as well enjoy it, might as well forgive yourself. She heard Rae saying that if she ate some cookies on a diet, she would have a full-fledged bender, to make up for all the days of deprivation, past and to come: "It's not even eating," said Rae. "It's stoking."

After drinking the third ale, Elizabeth dozed in the sun. When she awoke, she considered the three bottles left in the bag and, after a few minutes, lifted one out. One more, and then she would go home. And, she realized while opening it, she would be drunk. And Rosie would give her a rack of shit, and James would act wounded and better than she. Well, James, she imagined herself saying, you knew I was feeling weak; do you remember what you said? You said, I'll be done in half an hour. Well, I was cracking up, James, but your work came first.

See what you made me do?

She opened the last two bottles and poured the golden-red ale into the sand, put the bottles in their carton in the bag, and rose unsteadily. She was loaded.

Yeah, I had a beer, she would say. It seemed barbaric, on a hot summer's day, not to. Want to make a big deal of it? But despite the best lies and rationalizations she could muster, remorse washed through her. Goddamn you, Elizabeth, you've fucked up again. Where is your strength of character? What does it take for you to save yourself?

She walked home with a lump in her throat, weaving ever so slightly. If only James had left for a while, she could sober up, brush her teeth, and sleep it off. He wouldn't need to know, and she wouldn't drink again for the longest time.

But when she got home and his car was gone, she panicked. He knew! He had left her, without a word, like her father had left her mother. No, his things were still there, and he had left her a note in the kitchen: *Back around seven. With Lank. XO, J.* Phew.

She went upstairs to wash her face, brush her teeth, use Visine, and reapply mascara.

Back to the kitchen, she made a sandwich to sop up the alcohol, and a cup of coffee. It was quarter to five. Rosie would be home soon, and James was off with Lank. She would make enchiladas, for something to do; she turned on the classical station to keep her company. She yawned, and suddenly out of nowhere had a vision, of James with another woman, of the two times she had called his house when a woman had answered, of the second time, when someone had slammed the phone down. . . . Stop it! He loves you, wants to marry you. She dropped an open can of whole green chiles, had to rinse them off under the faucet, thought of slugs; cut her finger badly with a knife while mincing toes of garlic for the sauce; burnt herself while lifting a corn tortilla out of the hot fat with her fingers, and burst into tears.

"Goddammit, goddammit!" she shouted at the top of her lungs. The pain had chilled her blood for a second, but now her fingers were burning and red, and the top of her head was coming off. She kicked the cabinet under the sink, whipped around and surveyed the mess she had made, took in the grated cheese on the floor, the red sauce on the white stove, the bloody paper towel on the table, clenched her jaw, shut her eyes, and bellowed.

Rosie came home at six and went to the kitchen. It was a mess; something was wrong. She dropped her wet towel on the floor, went upstairs to investigate, and found her mother lying on the bed, glowering, with red-rimmed eyes and a glass of amber liquid balanced on her stomach, a bottle of booze beside her, on the night table.

They just looked at each other, defensive and mad.

"Hi," said Elizabeth.

"Chhh."

"Do you want to know what sort of day it's been?"

"No."

"It was a pile-of-shit sort of day."

"You want to know what I want to be when I grow up?"

Elizabeth nodded.

"An orphan."

After Rosie had left, slamming the door, Elizabeth rubbed her eyes with one hand, holding the glass of whiskey with the other.

At seven, true to his word, James returned. He whistled on his way upstairs. Elizabeth closed her eyes until she heard his hand on the knob.

"Hey," he said.

She took a deep, loud breath, and he walked over to the bed. They didn't take their eyes off each other. He sat down and looked at the glass of whiskey on her stomach, then back at her. She closed her eyes and tears rolled down her face. He took the glass away from her and put it on the table, wiped the tears into her cheeks, tilted his head, looked at her, and shrugged, with a look on his face of pure, empathetic love.

"I love you," he said, "but *I* can't get you to stop, drinking." He looked away for a minute. "But I don't think you have to hurt so bad. Unless: you want to. And if you don't want to, there's a way . . . but it's going to have to be an inside job."

Ten days later, Rosie, Elizabeth, James, and Rae sat on the porch waiting for Sharon's farewell appearance. Rosie, in a Stewart plaid jumper and white Mexican blouse, sat stiffly in the wooden armchair, looking hard and noble one moment, bored and aloof the next, and then her face would scroonch up with the effort of fighting back tears. James and Rae sat on the porch swing, chain smoking: Rae looked like a mother cinnamon bear with a missing cub. Elizabeth, sober nine days running, sat on the banister, looking fatherly, lean, and kind.

Rosie was all alone with this one and, to keep from crying, studiously avoided looking at the melancholy faces of the grown-ups.

"Gee, you look pretty, Rosie," said her mother.

"Thank you, Mom."

Mom?

Mrs. Thackery pulled up in their station wagon, with parcels tied to the top of the car, and Sharon got out. Mrs. Thackery did not turn off the engine or watch her sturdy girl walk through the garden to the house: she had, in her purse, a carbon of the letter Elizabeth had mailed to the Palo Alto Child Protection Agency.

The people on the porch watched Sharon approach: she looked beautiful. Rosie stood and waved, Sharon waved back. Rosie looked down at her feet, at the tiny violets embroidered on her socks, and then began to whistle, softly.

"So," said Elizabeth, standing. "You're off."

Sharon stood at the bottom of the stairs, shuffling, and Elizabeth felt great fondness for the small girl with the scalloped white teeth, the broad brown face flushed between her cheeks and jaw-bone. She would miss her.

"Hi, Rosie."

"Hi, Sharon." 'Bye, Sharon. Rosie traced letters on the porch with the toe of her patent-leather party shoes: B-Y-E.

"Hi, James, hi, Rae."

James said hello, Rae didn't. Elizabeth turned toward the porch swing and saw that Rae's head was bowed, and her hand was over her nose, and tears were streaming into her lap. James jabbed her in the side with his elbow, and Rae, still not looking up, waved with the hand that wasn't holding her nose.

Oh, Christ, Rae, Elizabeth thought, and almost burst out laughing.

Rosie and Sharon looked mortified.

Mrs. Thackery honked the horn, and Sharon jumped.

"I'll walk you down," said Elizabeth.

"Give me a kiss," said James, standing up. He walked down the stairs and kissed Sharon on the lips. Rae wept bitterly. Rosie shuffled and walked down the stairs. She and Sharon looked at each other shyly, like lovers.

"Well!" said Rosie, as Elizabeth came to join them. "So!"

Mrs. Thackery honked again, and Rosie turned to give the car a look of annoyance.

"We better walk you down now," Elizabeth said.

" 'Bye, James."

" 'Bye, Sharon. See you soon."

"Okay. 'Bye, Rae."

Rae, with her chin buried in her heaving chest, waved. Rosie looked at Sharon and rolled her eyes. James smiled and shook his head at Elizabeth. Rosie drew herself up to her full four-foot-three and appeared on the verge of saluting. Elizabeth languidly stroked Sharon's bangs away from her eyebrows, and Rosie took the opportunity to work over a scab on her elbow. James looked over and up at Rae, who was hugging herself and sniffling loudly.

Elizabeth took Rosie's right hand, Sharon's left, and led the two small girls down the path through the garden, to the car on the street.

Epilogue

In March of the following year, when the plum trees on Willow were bushy with pink and purple blossoms and the wet green fields were filled with heathery browns and mustards, with orange-magentas and birds, when creeks and streams rushed, full of rain, and cracked sprouting sidewalks held heaps of dump-bound clutter, when redwing blackbirds and wildflowers, sour-grass and white butterflies were everywhere and you couldn't help but think that spring had truly arrived, Elizabeth and James were married.

They drove to Municipal Court with their family in the back seat of James's car. Rosie, in her best white party dress, sat between Rae and Lank. Chubby, red-haired, Lank wore a rented tuxedo. Rae wore Belgian linen and lace and complained off and on about her pantyhose, which were a size too small and made her feel (she claimed) as if she had webbed thighs. The bride wore a plum knit suit that her mother had bought thirty years ago at I. Magnin's, with gardenias in her black hair, and Rae's pearls. She felt as if she were about to face major surgery, or as she had in fourth grade, about to perform in the school play, worried sick that onstage, in front of her family and friends, she would giggle hysterically or pee. She clutched at her pearls, readjusted the ivory combs in her hair, and worried that James would die shortly after the wedding, or that she would find it impossible to put up with his less endearing neuroses and would destroy the relationship. She sighed distantly and reapplied lipstick: steady, steady, old girl.

And James wore a new three-piece English suit, pencil gray with blue pinstripes—purchased with option money from Harper & Row—a green wool necktie to match his eyes, one of the half-dozen new cotton dress shirts he had bought to please Elizabeth, black wingtips—and red argyle socks, to show that he couldn't be socialized.

In the hallway of the venerable courthouse, James and Rosie sat side by side on a bench, while the other three stood. Every so often he let go, to jot something down in his notepad or to light another cigarette. Lank paced the hallway, whistling, while Elizabeth and Rae stood together against a wall. Rae, who wanted to burst with joy and jealousy, laid her head sideways on Elizabeth's shoulder, and after a moment, Elizabeth scratched her behind the ears.

The clerk appeared and asked, "Atterbury?"

"Yeah?" said James, as if, What's it to you?

"You can come in now."

James and Rosie stood, Rae pinched the bride on the bottom, and the party of five followed the clerk inside to the courtroom.

Elizabeth had left her body, was watching it all from above, was watching the thing they called Elizabeth Ferguson walk with great feigned dignity up to the magistrate.

"Elizabeth Ferguson?"

Inside her, Danny Torrance crooks his finger: Elizabeth isn't *here* right now. But if you'd care to leave a message. . . .

"Yes." Get a grip.

And so the service began. James held her gloved hand, lordly and bemused. Rosie, Rae, and Lank stood in an arc behind them, and it was soon clear to these witnesses that James and Elizabeth had stopped breathing.

"Breathe," Rae hissed, and they gasped for air.

Rosie, embarrassed by the service, blushed and squirmed. Rae watched the bride and groom with the rosy, rubbery look of a person in love, and puddles formed in her eyes. Lank was smiling proudly.

Elizabeth and James stared deep into each other's eyes, but in her mind, over the drone of the magistrate's voice, she suddenly heard the theme song to "Crusader Rabbit." She tried to block it out, but the music played and Rags the Tiger appeared clear as a bell on her mind's projector, and she heard the notes of the song move up and down like a procession of carousel animals or camels. James squeezed her hand and brought her back. But she couldn't shake the theme song, and hysterics rose inside and she had to bear down to contain them. She looked at the floor, saw her husband'a atrocious socks—and a flattened honking sound escaped from behind her nose. She pinched her nostrils shut and pretended to have stifled a sneeze, but it only amplified the proboscular jackhammering noises. Out of the corner of her eye, she saw Rosie shoot her a look that would turn her to stone, and it saved the day.

The magistrate went on monotonously. Elizabeth now seemed to hang on every word.

Husband and wife, James and Elizabeth kissed.

They all went home to the house on Willow, where they were joined by Grace and Charles Adderly, and Rosie's new best friend, Tina Greene.

The dining table had been moved to the living room and covered with a dark, creamy Irish lace tablecloth. The women and girls had made the feast the day before: dolmas with yogurt on top, prawns to dip in Dijon mayonnaise, small buns stuffed with roast beef and horseradish and mayonnaise, mushrooms in butter and garlic, and a double creme brie. There was Moet Chandon and pitchers of lemonade.

"Oh, Come Ye Sons of Art" was put on the stereo, and Charles made the toast, "To your great love, today and forever," and they all raised chalices to Elizabeth and James. Elizabeth, smiling to beat the devils, raised her glass of lemonade.

Later, Grace would say, "Oh but you weren't a *real* alcoholic," and Elizabeth would simply shrug. She and James had been going to Alcoholics Anonymous now for six months, to meetings almost every night, one hard day at a time. When, at the end of the first meeting, everyone had joined hands to say the Lord's Prayer, Elizabeth could not remember all the words. She was still resisting; the meetings were hokey and moving, and although the room reeked of miracles, she couldn't bring herself to fall for "God."

"God is just a word," said James. "It means truth, and you know, the truth shall set you free."

"Yeah?"

"To face and tell and love the truth is what they mean by 'God.' "

"What they mean," said Rae, "is love. Don't let the word get in your way. It's just a convenience. All that God means is love, God is love and love is God."

"Don't beam at me like that."

"Wull, see," said Rosie. "It's like when you're *to*tally happy, and everything seems so beautiful that you just go *"God."*

But although Elizabeth couldn't quite surrender, she kept on going to the meetings.

Long after the sun went down in an explosion of reds and tangerines, long after Rae served up bowls of raspberries, Rosie and her new best friend left their seats by the fire and went outside with a quilt. They sat under a Mars-black sky dotted with stars. While Tina chattered about the wedding gifts, Rosie stared at an unoccupied spider web that hung from the banister, gummy beads glistening on spokes which radiated out in bridges of silk. At school they were making webs of cotton threads, delicate orbs with supports and rungs; the third grade was studying spiders. Rosie had reported to James that spiders had glands called spinnerets, with which they spun silk for their webs, and for parachutes, so that the wind could take them from place to place. James had written it all down, would use it in his book. . . .

Where was the spider who'd built this web: airborne, or hiding, or taking a walk?

Tina stopped talking and looked at Rosie, saw the distant day-dreaming gaze, and sat humming beside her until Rosie returned to earth.